Samuel Osgood

Mile Stones in Our Life-journey

Samuel Osgood

Mile Stones in Our Life-journey

ISBN/EAN: 9783744799591

Printed in Europe, USA, Canada, Australia, Japan

Cover: Foto ©Andreas Hilbeck / pixelio.de

More available books at **www.hansebooks.com**

Mile Stones

IN OUR LIFE-JOURNEY.

BY

SAMUEL OSGOOD, D.D., LL. D.,

AUTHOR OF "THE HEARTH-STONE," ETC.

New and Enlarged Edition.

Why should we fear, youth's draught of joy,
 If pure would sparkle less !
Why should the cup the sooner cloy,
 Which God hath deigned to bless!

Who but a Christian, through all life
 That blessing may prolong !
Who through the world's sad day of strife
 Still chant his morning song !

KEBLE.

NEW YORK:

E. P. DUTTON AND COMPANY,

713 BROADWAY.

1877.

TO

THE CLASS OF 1832,

(HARVARD UNIVERSITY,)

IN REMEMBRANCE OF PLEASANT YEARS TOGETHER,

AND WITH EVER DEEPENING AFFECTION,

This Volume is Dedicated,

BY

THEIR CLASSMATE.

PREFACE.

THE papers that make up the substance of this volume, aim to treat the chief stages in human life, in connection with their attendant lessons and experiences. Thus the volume seeks to do for our pilgrimage what " The Hearth-Stone" sought to do for the household. It is written in a similar vein, with an equally practical and religious purpose, and the author will think himself very happy if he is allowed to attend as a companion by the way, the many kind readers who have admitted his former book to their homes.

The introductory chapter was an after thought of the writer, during the leisure of his summer vacation, and may be omitted by all readers who do not care for such personal reminiscences. Perhaps, however, to not a few, these introductory sketches may give the key note to the whole, and win to the survey of life in general an attention quickened as well as sobered by each reader's personal remembrances.

If this volume makes one young man more thoughtful, or one old man more cheerful, nay if it leads one pilgrim to go on his way more bravely and faithfully, with sober memory as the guide of his sanguine hope, the author will be repaid for a service that has cost him not a little care, however simple his work may seem. If his style seems sometimes too plain and hortatory, let readers allow him to be content with directness and usefulness, if at the expense of more stately elaboration. He is encouraged to believe that these essays will meet with some sympathy, because each of them embodies an actual experience, either personal or professional.

To the above Preface to the first edition of this book, the author needs only to add the remark, that after going through several editions, it has been for some years out of print, and that the friends who wish to see it again will find some fresh notes of the author's experience and thought in later years in the closing chapter now added.

New York, *November* 1, 1876.

CONTENTS.

8   CONTENTS.

Companions by the Way.

AN INTRODUCTORY SKETCH.

Companions by the Way.

AN INTRODUCTORY SKETCH.

" Come then, my friends, or sad or smiling,—whether
On you life's load weighs heavier day by day,
Or blessings over new like summer weather,
With flowers adorn, with fruits enrich your way,
We go to meet the coming day together.
Then live we, walk we happy while we may.
So, when our children mourn that we are past,
To cheer their souls, our faithful loves shall last."

GOETHE.

COMPANIONS BY THE WAY.

An Introductory Sketch.

A YEAR ago during the summer vacation, I prepared for the press a volume of essays upon home-life under the name of "The Hearth-Stone." The kind reception of this book has led me to think of another of somewhat kindred purpose. These "Mile-Stones" are intended to mark the leading points and passes of our pilgrimage, as "The Hearth-Stone" aimed to note the chief experiences of our abiding place. The pleasant summer time has come once more, and with it a short season of leisure that is made all the more cheerful by some occupation that is not hardship. Before approaching the graver topics to be treated, may not author and reader have a little chat together upon old scenes and friends by way of Preface, with the hope of making the circle more close and social? This is peculiarly the season of reunions, and few persons are so engrossed in business as not to find a few days' leisure for revisiting the old homestead, or running away to some country resting-place. Right heartily the summer resting time chimes in with the winter's merry-making and the genial crackling flame of the Christmas log seems to be discoursing of these happy hours in the country under the greenwood tree. This book that may not make its appearance until the winter holidays, will not be any less fitting because it brings a summer garland upon its front.

Every man is largely a debtor to his companions, and in revising these unambitious essays that undertake to give some practical views of prominent passages in human life, I see in every page some traces of the kindness and wisdom that have never in one form or another ceased their sympathy and their counsel. Take from a man all the knowledge and strength that he has received from associates, and you strip him of himself, and take his inmost life away. Before using our own eyes, we first see through the eyes of others; and however mature our vision, there will always be some subjects that we study better by hearty sympathy with others than by any proud philosophy of our own. It would be a somewhat interesting study for any man to trace his character, his habits and opinions to their source in his personal associations, and ascribe each dominant tendency to its cause. The grave-digger in Hamlet makes the groundlings in the pit shake their sides with laughter as he strips off garment after garment, and at last his rotund figure, robbed of its lendings, stands out in its own sorry dimensions. Far sorrier would be the plight of any man who could limit his experience to his own intuitions and throw off all dependence upon the fellowship of friends and the gathered wisdom of his race. A young man does not of himself know the whole of youth, nor does any old man exhaust the whole meaning of age. Young and old can be wise only by breathing the atmosphere of good society and good books, and rounding their own narrowness by such high communion. Surely were it not for such helps, even a task like the present, which seeks to treat but cursorily of very various stages and experiences of life, would have been dismissed as presumptuous. It is not presumptuous in this connection to give some desultory reminiscences of companions that may be recognised by a friendly knot of readers, and may, perhaps, start kindred retrospection in others. Our reader will be in the better mood to think of the lessons of the great pilgrimage if our chat together may jog the elbow of his own memory, and move him to illustrate the way-marks of the journey by scraps from his own unwritten journal.

I.—SCHOOL DAYS.

It is not well for a man ever to forget his childhood, and it is a sad and sterile experience that parts company with young hopes. To many of us the old play-ground that we have set aside as the haunt of folly, may teach a lesson deeper far than what our worldliness is proud to call wisdom. In a late trip to Massachusetts, I re-visited familiar scenes of boyhood and youth, and our school and college days rose as freshly to mind as if they were of yesterday, and the absentee had been a middle-aged man only in dreams. I stood upon the old battle hill whose northern slope, reaching to the river, was our play-ground thirty years ago, and it was not difficult to people the place with shapes far different from those that meet the eye. Then from the hill-top with its modest little monument to Warren and his fellow martyrs, down to the shore of the Mystic, the land was a great pasture, unbroken, except by one or two little cottages. Now it is covered with houses, and the pebbly beach of the river which was our perpetual delight, has been possessed and hidden by wharves and factories that are usually called improvements. That stately school, fitly the pride of the whole neighborhood, stands upon the bed of an old pond, and scores of urchin republicans now learn to read and spell where frogs croaked to the evening stars, and turtles basked in the noonday sun. The tall obelisk that now crowns the hill is itself far less a wonder than the great landscape which it displays from its summit. Within thirty years the whole vicinity has changed; and whether we eye the dome of the observatory at Cambridge, the score of railways that stretch their iron web in every direction from the Pilgrim city, or the steamers that ply through the harbor, the proofs are clear that the new powers have invaded those old haunts, and the nineteenth century has encamped a host more powerful than the British invaders about that old battle ground.

A river is a famous playmate, and is quite ready to join in almost any game. The Mystic, notwithstanding its utilitarian metamorphosis, seems now in the gleam of sunset to give a look of familiar recognition, as if beneath all his new cares and burdens, remembering his old play-fellow, with whom, years ago, he used to swim and row, and fish and skate, and lounge and dream. He was a versatile companion, whose resources never were exhausted. His moods were as many as a poet's, and changed with every sky, and wind, and tide. Nothing could be more cheering than our Mystic, when the full tide, flooding his green banks, gave his bright face the look of inspiration; and when the tide was out, and the dark flats were laid bare, his face seemed emptied of its glory, like poor Cowper's, when deserted by the genial muse, and left to the mud and ooze of Acheron. Yet even this gloomy aspect of the river was not without advantage. His bare shores were a mine of wealth to many a fisherman on the lookout for shell-fish, for bait, or for his table. Then, moreover, the tide never left the channels wholly bare, and two threads of deep water never failed to mark the deep bed of the river with their silver, so that this son of Neptune slept like a sea-king. Adventurous boys, the writer among the number, would sometimes swim across the channel to explore the great central bed, not without ample reward in the brave store of fish of various kinds, and sometimes of rare size, that were stranded upon the bank, or imprisoned in the little basins. In full tide our river bore noble freight upon its bosom, and harbored creatures of no mean pretensions in its waters. The hulls of huge vessels from the shipyards of Medford came floating by us on the way to their ocean home, and we surely thought that the great leviathan had come, whenever a stray seal lifted his cynical nose above the surface. There were some personages that seemed to have a peculiar relation to the river, and to be as much a part of it as the fish or the banks. There was an old man, an ancient mariner indeed, who seemed to have a secret understanding with the stream, to know every turn and eddy of the tide, the haunt and likings of every fish, and the place and use of all kinds of bait. I can see the old fisherman as plainly as the day now, although years ago he was hooked by the great fisher of men; and I can never see a perch or a flounder in the market, without thinking of S——, the fisherman of the Mystic. To children there is something weird and imposing in all kinds of special knowledge or power, and S. shared this prestige with another odd character, who made his appearance about twice a week in a skiff from the opposite bank of the river, usually well laden in summer with apples or some kind of farm produce. He was a cross man, and report said that the little keg in the bottom of his boat was not intended for water only, yet we were always glad to see him starting out from the creek on Chelsea shore, and pulling with his adroit oars for our beach. We never could make him out satisfactorily, being especially puzzled by his uncertain distribution of apples, and boys are like men in taking " *omne ignotum pro mirifico*," so that this familiar oarsman stands even to this day among the mythical personages of our annals. On the bridge which crossed the river, we used to watch the great throng of Eastern travel, and felt that we were quite in the world, as we counted their number and variety. The bridge is comparatively quiet now, and the

incessant lines of stage-coaches have yielded to other con-
veyances, that make small account of the horse's speed.
We cannot meet now in an evening walk the characters
whose step we used to mark in our rambles over that tho-
roughfare. We held our breath, with admiration, many a
time, as we looked upon a man of foreign mien and dress,
who used to distance all competition with his angling rod,
and drew huge bass from the river, as if they were min-
nows. He was said to be the Russian consul of Boston,
and I must confess to a certain involuntary respect for the
empire of the Czar, that dates from that early knowledge
of the prowess of one of his subjects. There was a memorable traveller over the bridge, whom we used to eye with
equal interest but less admiration. He was a tall man,
with long hair, and a stooping, awkward gait, yet a very
fast walker, who seemed to ignore the use of the horse,
and put himself upon his own independent footing. He
was thought to be immensely rich, and to be the solitary
lord of a whole island near the Chelsea shore. His walks
are now over, the drawbridge to his lonely domain is dis-
mantled, and through a deep cut in the high back of his
island, the locomotive thunders along with its huge burdens, and whistles democratic defiance at the dust of the
old proprietor, and at every remnant of feudal despotism.

Beyond our river the Chelsea shore rose by a graceful
slope to a considerable hill, over whose shoulders towered
the summit of another and distant hill that seemed to our
boyish eyes the very limit of the horizon. When leave
was granted one holiday week to pass a day with a play-

fellow whose father's farm was at the foot of that height, the little journey rose into the grandeur of travel, and Ledyard himself never felt more proud of his marches. To crown the whole, when our adventurous little company scaled the summit, looked out upon the vast ocean, then descended the opposite side, bathed in the sea surf, and came back laden with a goodly store of luscious berries and strange shells, never was Alexander more proud of his conquests; although, as we saw the big sails in the offing, sweeping towards foreign lands, we knew that we had not yet quite compassed the globe, and could not share his chagrin that there are no more worlds to conquer. The river and that distant hill had appeared to bound our universe, and childish as the illusion seemed, it is one that every age of life in some way repeats, and as long as we live we are crossing some last stream, or climbing some final obstacle, only to find broader waters and higher obstacles rolling and swelling before our path. Sad blow to our childish romance! our Ultima Thule has fallen into the hands of speculators, and the stately hill, with its graded house-lots, figures among the fancy-stocks of the land market.

The better philosophy that is now gaining ground is rescuing childhood from contempt, and finding traits of Providential wisdom in the play-spirit that makes so much of the poetry of our early years. Surely we can never work well when we forget to play; and I verily believe that some of the worst traits and coarsest vices of our nation come from over much worldly care and utter neglect of healthful sports that stir without inebriating the blood and nerves. In childhood, the force of nature educates us in spite of ourselves, and every genial playground is a monitorial school to teach the muscles, senses, and faculties, their offices. Our circle of playfellows has disappeared, and many of them have gone to their graves; yet mature years have but deepened our conviction of their power, and our charity for their defects. Looking back now with a keener eye for character, it is not difficult to remember traits of enterprise and daring that needed the arena only to make their possessors famous. Almost every boy was distinguished for something. The biggest dunce at books was the chief hero among horses, and with his critical eye and firm rein made the rest of us fall abashed into the background as he rode proudly by. Not a few sprightly natures that were very wizards in inventing sports for our Wednesday and Saturday afternoons, could not summon a single *spell* to their aid when called up for recitation. The great wonder is, that boys are preserved safe in limb and life in spite of their reckless pranks. What one of us now would, as of old, venture at any moment's offer to extemporize a fast gallop upon any chance steed without waiting for the saddle; and who of us, who have kept up our acquaintance with salt water, can look without a shudder now to those high wharves and buildings from which we used to jump and dive in the merriest sport? Surely there is a guardian angel over the bones as over the heart of childhood; and call the benign power " Nature," or some more winning name, we must all own

its ministry, and be thankful for its blessing. There is
something in the Catholic " Hymn to My Guardian Angel" that comes home to every school-boy's experience,
and which he need not be ashamed to repeat in mature
years :—

> " Thy beautiful and shining face
>   I see not, though so near;
> The sweetness of thy soft, low voice
>   I am too deaf to hear.
>
> " I cannot feel thee touch my hand
>   With pressure light and mild,
> To check me as my mother did
>   When I was but a child.
>
> " But I have felt thee in my thoughts
>   Fighting with sin for me;
> And when my heart loves God, I know
>   The sweetness is from thee.
>
> " Ah me! how lovely they must be
>   Whom God has glorified;
> Yet one of them, O sweetest thought!
>   Is ever at my side."

No man, indeed, who has a keen memory, will take a
wholly roseate view of boyhood and its associations, for
too many of its passions and strifes have stamped themselves upon the very threshold of his career. Yet time
never fails to bring out a meaning, deeper than we of old
knew, and it is surely no small part of manly wisdom to
buy experience with the small coin of childish humors and

follies, instead of postponing the purchase until fortune and character may be given in exchange.

From the old battle hill, I can see the site of the school house where two or three hundred boys were gathered together to be whipped and taught as their fathers were before them. A new edifice, indeed, has taken the place of our school, yet upon its statelier front I can see, as if drawn in the air by a strange pencil, the outline of that ancient building with its round belfry, whose iron tongue held such imperial command of our hours. It costs no great effort to summon back one of those famous Examination Days that absorbed the anticipation of months and made the week almost breathless with anxiety. There shines the nicely sanded floor, which the cunning sweeper had marked in waving figures, to redeem it from association with any vulgar dust. There sit the School Committee, chief among them the trim chairman, upon whose lips, when he pronounces the final opinion of the board, the very fates seem to rest their judgment. There too, is the throng of parents, kindred and friends, who have come to note the performances of the boys, to look pity upon their mistakes, and to smile sympathy upon their successes. Should the presidential chair fall to his lot, no prouder and more radiant day can come to the school-boy, than when, with new clothes and shining shoes, he stands forth to speak his well-conned piece, and wears away among the admiring crowd, the ribboned medal that marks his triumph.

Our schoolmasters were great characters in our eyes,

and the two who held successively the charge of the gram mar department, made a prominent figure in our wayside chat, and to this day we can find some trace of their influence in our very speech and manner.   They were men of very different stamp and destiny.   The first of them was a tall fair-faced man, with an almost perpetual smile.   I always felt kindly towards him, though it was not easy to decide whether his smile was the expression of his good-nature, or the mask of his severity.   He wore it very much the same when he flogged an offender, as when he praised a good recitation.   He seemed to delight in making a joke of punishment, and it was a favorite habit of his, to fasten upon the end of his rattan the pitch and gum taken from the mouths of masticating urchins, and then, coming upon their idleness unawares, he would insert the glutinous implement in their hair, not to be withdrawn without an adroit jerk and the loss of some scalp locks.   Poor fellow! his easy nature probably ruined him, and he left the school, not long to follow any industrious calling.   When, a few years afterwards, I met him in Boston, with the marks of broken health and fortune in his face and dress, the sight was shocking to all old associations, as if a dignity quite sacerdotal had fallen into the dust.   His earthly troubles have long been ended, and I take some pleasure in recording a kind and somewhat grateful feeling towards one whose name I have not heard spoken these many years. His successor was a man of different mould, a stern, resolute man, his face full of an expression that seemed to say that circumstances are but accidents, and it is the will that makes or mars the man. He was not in robust health, and it seemed to some of us, who were thoughtful of his feelings, that were it not for this he would have been likely to pursue a more ambitious career, and give to the bar the excellent gifts that he devoted to teaching. He was a most faithful teacher, and his frown, like the rain cloud, had a richer blessing for many a wayward idler, than his predecessor's perennial smile. He has borne the burden and the heat of the day for many a long year, with ample success, and when he falls at his post, it will be with the consciousness of having done a good work for his race, in a calling far more honored by Heaven than any of the more ambitious spheres that perhaps won his youthful enthusiasm. Well says the noble Jean Paul Richter: "Honor to those that labor in school-rooms! Although they may fall from notice like the spring blossoms, like the spring blossoms they fall that the fruit may be born."

There are two other personages that have much to do with every youth's education, and whose names are household words in every New England home. The doctor and the minister figure largely in every boy's meditations, and in our day, the loyalty that we felt towards their professions had not been troubled by a homœopathic doubt or a radical scruple. In our case, it needed no especial docility to appreciate these functionaries. Our doctor was a most emphatic character, a man of decided mark in the eyes alike of friends and enemies. He was very impatient of questions, and very brief yet pithy in his advice, which was of marvellous point and sagacity. He lost his brevity, however, the moment that other subjects were broached, and he could tell a good story with a dramatic power that would have made him famous upon the stage. He was renowned as a surgeon, and could guide the knife within a hair's breadth of a vital nerve or artery with his left hand quite as firmly as with his right. This ambi-dexterity extended to other faculties, and he was quite as keen at a negotiation as at an amputation. He was no paragon of conciliation, and many of the magnates of the profession appeared to have little liking for him, and sometimes called him a poor scholar, rude in learning and taste, but lucky in his mechanical tact. But he beat them out of this notion, as of many others, by giving an anniversary discourse before the State Medical Association, which won plaudits from his severest rivals, for its classical elegance, as well as its professional learning and sagacity. It was said that the wrong side of him was very wrong and very rough. But those of us who knew him as a friend, tender and true, never believed that he had any wrong side. Certain it is, that they who grew up under his practice, have been little inclined to exchange the regular school of medicine, with its scientific method and gradual progress, for any new nostrums of magical pretensions.

Our minister had the name of being the wise man of the town, and I do not remember to have heard a word in disparagement of his mind or motives, even among those who questioned the soundness of his creed. His voice has always been as no other man's to many of us, whether heard as for the first time at a father's funeral, as by me

when a child five years old, or in the pulpit from year to
year. He came to our parish when quite young, and when
theological controversy was at its full height. A polemic
style of preaching was then common, and undoubtedly in
his later years of calm study and more broad and spiritual
philosophizing, he would have read with some good-natured
shakes of the head, the more fiery discourses of his novitiate, whilst he might recognize, throughout, the same
spirit of manly independence, republican humanity, and
profound reverence that have marked his whole career.
There was always something peculiarly impressive in his
preaching. Each sermon had one or more pithy sayings
that a boy could not forget; and when the thoughts were
too profound or abstract for our comprehension, there was
an earnestness and reality in the manner which held the
attention, like a brave ship under full sail that fixes the
gaze of the spectator, though he may not know whither she
is bound or what is her cargo, sure enough that she is
loaded with something, and is going right smartly somewhere. It was evident that our minister was a faithful
student and indefatigable thinker When the best books
afterwards came in our way, we found that the guiding
lines of moral and spiritual wisdom had already been set
before us, and we had been made familiar with the well
winnowed wheat from the great fields of humanity. Every
thought, whether original or from books, bore the stamp
of the preacher's own individuality; and many will indorse
the saying, that upon topics of philosophic analysis and of
practical morals, he was without a superior, if not without

2.

a rival, in our pulpits. It is a great thing for young people to grow up under happy religious auspices, and religion itself has a new charm and power when dispensed by a man who is always named in the family with reverence and tenderness. The world would be far better, and Christian service would be much more truly valued, if there were more just and emphatic tribute paid to efficient pastoral labor.   Our well known minister has now a more conspicuous station ; but he cannot easily have deeper influence than when pastor for a score of years over a united parish, and one of the leaders of public opinion upon all topics of high importance.   It is well that the new post is in such harmony with the previous career ; for the head of a college, according to our old-fashioned ideas, should be a minister, and he should always abide in due manner by the pastoral office.

Our town, although but a suburb of the great city, was not unvisited by the noted personages of the land, and Presidents, Governors, Senators, &c., astounded our boyhood with their presence. I remember creeping into a very small place to catch a glimpse of Webster as he stood up to give his oration at the laying of the corner-stone on Bunker Hill, and the tones of his majestic voice chimed well with the massive strength of his brow. Never were our people more moved than when our own representative Everett, gave us the first specimen of his charming oratory not long after he bore his classic laurels from the Professor's chair of ease into the dusty arena of political life. He appeared first in the procession, and astonished us by

so youthful looks in a man of such name. He was not far
from thirty, and his cheek was full of color, his eye brilliant, his hair curling, and to some of us who had not then
gone far in the Classical Dictionary, he seemed like a Pericles started into life from his marble sleep to charm our
day. His oration was upon the death of Adams and Jefferson; and if school-boys had been umpires, the palm of
sovereign eloquence would have been given him by acclamation. It may be a small thing to say about so eminent
a personage, but one who was in youth a neighbor, may
testify of him that no man, probably, has ever figured in
our public affairs who has said so few unkind words, and
done so many kind deeds as he.

The Navy-yard gave our town some peculiar features,
and whilst robbing us of our wharf lots, it added something to our social privileges. There is much to like in
Navy officers; and in point of manners and intelligence,
the better part of them equal any professional class, in
spite of their frequent temptations to idleness and frivolity.
The school in which some of us were prepared for entering
College, was composed chiefly of the sons and daughters
of Navy officers, and of course there was no small infusion
of romance and chivalry in the studies and recreations.
Our master, fresh from College, was one of those who
have a charmed manner, and who seems to have won the
world's favor by the same power that carried the day with
our wayward wills. His ready sympathy and strong sense
and fine face disarmed all opposition, and a word or a look
would subdue the wildest boy or soothe the most fidgety

girl.   Two of us remained under his care after he left the school, and recited to him at the Marine Hospital across the river, where he pursued his medical studies.   It was strange place to frequent, and we learned many things besides our Latin, Greek, &c.   It was like a great ocean beach, upon which the wrecks of every clime were washed. There were gathered together in that house of mercy the sick and feeble from every race under the sun, from the chattering Italian to the phlegmatic Swede, from the Malay, whose eye seemed looking for a chance to aim a dagger under the ribs, to the amphibious Sandwich Islander, who amazed us by playing the fish on the water and under the water.   Youth leans readily to an ideal philosophy and a spiritual faith quite in contrast with the startling materialism that is apt to hover over such a haunt of bodily suffering, mental eclipse, and frequent dissolution.   It was well that our minister had schooled us in the argument for spiritual realities, and that our early years were lighted by a torch proof against the damps and darkness of such a Golgotha of disease and death.   Some classes of disease were stern moralists, then, and these poor waifs of the sea taught the laws of health and obedience more eloquently than our worthy College Professor whose lectures upon Preserving Health, strange to say, were, in our time, given to the Senior Class, when it is too late to rob vice and folly of their victims.   Those months were full of study and progress, small as was the class and busy as the teacher was with professional cares.   One of the two scholars has passed away, and under circumstances that have given him a martyr's name. The other scholar, and the master, are now near neighbors in the great city; and not long ago the doctor, who presided at the banquet of American Physicians, and the minister at his side, who was called to speak in behalf of his own profession on that occasion, bandied merry words together over those old days of pupilage, when the doctor was master, and the minister the scholar. I met the physician but a few days ago, and we came part of the way into the country together. His hair is far from keeping its coal black hue, but his eye is about as bright as ever, and the amenities still hold their place upon his tongue now so honored as oracle.

II.—COLLEGE LIFE.

It is not easy for a stranger to understand the feelings that have long prevailed among a large portion of the people of Massachusetts, towards their chief seminary of learning, Harvard University. The oldest college in our land is, of course, in some measure, a matter of pride to every liberal American; yet to the Massachusetts men of the Old School, Harvard College is one of the articles of their creed, and the fundamentals of their allegiance. Those of us who were brought up under the auspices of Conservatism in politics, and Liberalism in religion, im-bibed this sentiment with daily bread and the common air. It seemed a prodigious safeguard to have this stronghold of learning near us, and the youth who could win entrance to its privileges and have the endorsement of its name upon his professional career, was looked upon as one of the favored of earth, and the elect of heaven. Things have changed somewhat now, and the age of steam and cotton-spinning has made sad havoc with academic habits and dignities. Wealthy parents do not wait as often, as of old, to give their sons a thorough intellectual training before sending them into the world, and not a few prominent graduates cheapen their Alma Mater by sinking their literature and profession in some kind of stock-jobbing. Yet to this day, old Harvard has no small company of faithful disciples, who look upon her blessing as beyond that of pope or council. Imagine our feelings twenty-two years ago this August, when entering the charmed seat of letters that we had so long looked at from afar with such reverential eyes. We mustered seventy-two, an unusual number for a Freshman class in those days; and so great was the occasion to our juvenile eyes, that it did not seem a strange thing that signs and wonders should appear in the heavens. The brilliant Aurora that mounted to the very zenith the eve of our admission, and from East to West formed an arch of flashing light, appeared to us a not unworthy sign of the mysterious world of lore which we were entering. More than one of the seventy-two devoutly believed that all human knowledge was stored up within those walls, and that the student need only go far enough to find human knowledge open into divine wisdom within that shrine.

It must be confessed, that college life soon throws cold water upon the novice's fond enthusiasm. A boy who has studied mostly by himself, and goes to college with the idea that his fellow-students have come there for a thorough education, and that to be a good scholar is, of course the main thing, will find himself for a time strangely mistaken. Appreciating reverently the endowments there made to learning by the faith and public spirit of ages, and not a little subdued by the kindness, and, perhaps, the self-sacrifice of parents and friends in securing him his position, he is amazed to find that nothing is so unpopular among the stripling throng as faithful study, and nothing more in favor than a free and easy contempt of industry and its honors. The strangest thing of all is, that the best scholars are very likely to fall in with the idlers in crying down plodding fidelity, and to use the rich stores of learning reserved from their elaborate preparatory training, to eclipse their studious rival's recitations, and at the same time to throw contempt upon his drudging care. We must not judge, however, too harshly this wayward temper of youth. Young blood generally has some redeeming element even in its follies, and the objection to devoted study comes quite as much from love for a brave, generous spirit, as from wilfulness or indolence. The hard-worker, who was at first decried as a spiritless *dig*, soon overcomes the prejudice, if he is found to have a brave and hearty purpose back of his work, whilst the contemptuous idler sinks into insignificance as soon as his poverty of motives and ideas is discovered. A great change comes over the dispositions of students when the first illusion of their novitiate passes away. Even the doubtful code of college popularity demands that every youth shall have some positive ob-ject, and that if indifferent to the fixed routine of study, he must find a substitute in some taste, or art, or science f his own. This demand shows its working more and more as the years pass. With us the clique of idlers be-came less and less, until at last it was not easy to find any companion, of any sort of consideration, who was not making his mark upon the class at large, as well as upon his own mind, by some elect pursuit of his own. Not a few of our fellows, who stood at great discount in the scale of general scholarship, learned, in some one study, some branch of natural history, or chemistry, or belles-lettres, to surpass some of the very first names upon the rank list. In fact, the whole development of intellect and character during college life, is as rich a lesson as any taught in the manuals; and no books in the library had contents more strange and occult to our understandings, than the seventy-two volumes which we brought with us under our caps and jackets, or in the hidden man of the mind and heart, to be interpreted in the school of life.

As a theatre for the exhibition of character, our college was indeed a University, and our class in itself was no poor exponent of the mixed elements of humanity. It is a favorite amusement with some to read over the names of the old set on the catalogue, and gossip about their various characteristics. Destiny, from her mysterious urn, has assigned very different lots to our different classmates, and a third part of them are no more with us in the world. As life appears to us now, and as we have learned more of our own infirmity and of the force of circumstances, we take a more kindly view alike of the excellencies and of the foibles of our comrades, and we can smile at many traits that used to irritate us. A Theophrastus or La Bruyere need not have gone beyond our border to find subjects for a volume double the size of his own. One man (*man* is the favorite word for student), appeared to be an ingrained dandy, to whom the tailor's fashions are the sovereign ritual, whilst another, from the very same preparatory school, would be an utter sloven, not seldom accused, on especial occasions, of robbing the washerwoman of her regular spoil, and putting on a soiled shirt for a Sunday or holiday. We had devotees who did not scruple to warn the indifferent, and to exhort the believing by the most enthusiastic religious appeals, not without reliance upon supernatural conversion and authority from mystical visions; other classmates we had, who would not call it slander to reckon them among the doubting Thomases and careless Gallios of the class. We had some men who were glib speakers and poor writers, and others, who held the easy pen of an Addison, yet were seized with more than the dumbness of Zacharias when called to take part in extempore debate. We had some prosers that could never even take a joke, and some drolls who could not help looking a joke when not speaking one. A metaphysician might have puzzled himself much, by trying to analyze the varieties of wit and humor among our fellows, and perhaps some specimens of roguishness might have been found that have escaped the pen of Dickens or Thackeray

2*

Our most mischievous rogue soon finished his collegiate career, and entered a larger field of enterprise. He was a genius in his line, and his room was a complete magazine of mischief. He kept on hand a variety of fulminating powders of his own manufacture, and often a half-dozen bomb-shells, filled with water and tightly corked, would be hidden in his fire, to astound the unwitting visitor with the innocuous yet emphatic explosion of cork and steam. His room communicated with the cellar by a trap-door, which allowed the occupant free exit and ingress. If his door were watched, no sound or sight indicated the inmate's participation, and some eager proctor, bent on personal in-vestigation of the premises, would be very likely to find the perpetrator of the mischief quietly seated in his study-chair, conning his book with the puritanical gravity so habitual to his long face and straight hair. Every bold prank that startled the faculties of the vigilant Parietal Board was supposed to originate in him, whether the bell was tolled at midnight with no hand visible at the rope, or the Commons' knives and forks disappeared, or a hogshead of molasses was emptied of its sweets in the Commons' kitchen, or the College pump was blown up by a shell. Our droll rogue was of wholly another complexion, with a face capable of as many funny wrinkles as there are leaves in Punch's Almanac, and with powers of legerdemain and ventriloquism that might have made his fortune in that craft. He went through his course without censure, al-though chief source of all the milder practical jokes, and it is not easy to see in the man of science and the grave citizen now, our funny comrade of bygone years.

The contrast between the early indications and the final developments of character, is one of the marked points of student life. Not seldom the sedate and almost austere youth becomes a gay and even a dissipated man, and not seldom the frivolous, reckless boy settles down into an earnest and even severe manhood. Among our fellew-students in the various classes, how many strange metamorphoses have taken place! Among us, the prettiest boy of our Freshman year came first to mount the judge's bench; the most bashful youth took the lead in matrimony; and more than one gay sauce-box has donned the black coat with proper grace, and won high name in the pulpit. In the class before us, a famous feud broke out between the plainer and the more dashing fellows, the *plebs* and the *patricians* of our academic polity, in connection with the Hasty Pudding and the Porcellian Clubs. A vehement radical led the plebs, and a youth of aristocratic bearing and lineage headed the patricians. Strange, yet not unaccountable transformation! the radical now impresses conservative order upon a host of operatives under his rule, and the aristocrat is the Coryphæus of extreme reform, advocating the rights of black and white, male and female outcasts from the elect circles, with a splendid eloquence that might well win plaudits from the hardest-faced Toryism or Hunkerism. One remark may be fitly made in regard to the development of youthful character. It relates to the worth of mere amateur culture, in comparison with a devoted life-purpose. The most brilliant men amount in the end to very little, if they are so little bent upon some chosen work, as to think more of shining in general, than of shining with a true man's light upon some chosen path of service. In our early college years our horizon was luminous with the splendor of certain men, especially in classes before our own, who were the observed of all observers, and the predicted chiefs in literature or the professions. The air seemed charmed by their presence, and every ear was erect when they spoke. They were often engrossed too much with their own shining, to think of the prosaic task of being a useful light to others ; and with very few exceptions, these men have wholly disappointed the anticipations of friends regarding their career. Life needs an object, as well as a subject, and the more humbly and devotedly the object is chosen and pursued, the better for the strength of the intellect, as well as for the health of the affections. Many a plodding worker, with a single eye to his vocation, has won a position and evinced powers far beyond the lot of the most brilliant rhetoricians, who were in the sunshine of admiration when his name was unknown. Transformations of moral character no less signal, are to be observed, and if any one fact is more important than another, to be pointed out to young men, it is the invincible power of a faithful ruling purpose to mould and transfigure the whole character, giving to unpretending worth an energy, and in the end a high enthusiasm, that abide by a man when youthful blood has calmed its pulses, and youthful sentiment, if left merely to itself, has turned out to be the emptiest of chimeras. It was a happy circumstance for the future of our class, that the practical spirit was so dominant, and whilst our fellows had their full share of genial fellowship and literary taste, we were, most of us, led to look early to some chosen object in life. From various causes, whether from the example of a few leading companions, or from the excellent ministrations of the College Pulpit under the two Wares and Palfrey, or from the influence of the churches and ministers under whom we were educated at home, theology was the favorite profession with us, and no class on the catalogue of late, has equalled ours in the number of names italicised as ministers. Nothing in professional life has been happier with us, than this association of its cares with the hopes and affections of our youthful days. Our classmates in other professions undoubtedly share the same satisfaction, and the charm of our meetings is in the harmony of variety, which different tastes and pursuits bring to the genial circle.

I have been this summer upon a flying visit to Cambridge, and it seems almost a sacred duty, as well as a high pleasure, to make at least a yearly pilgrimage to the old shrine of faith and learning. It is pleasant to have uch assurance that in this changing world, some of the ancient landmarks remain, and to refresh our careworn minds by the sight of scenes and friends so cherished. Time has dealt very gently with our good mother, and her years are marked by progress without decay. The new arts and sciences have come to lay their trophies at her feet, in the treasures and appliances of the Scientific School and the Observatory, and the old Puritan worthies still keep their places in the buildings reared by their bounty, and the books and professorships founded by their piety and patriotism. We miss many of our familiar teachers, yet not all have gone; and it is cheering, indeed, to find our own President, who took office in our Freshman year, still vigorous as ever, and although no longer in the chair, as ready in speech and keen in thought as any man in the assembly. There is nothing under heaven more cheerful, as well as more venerable, than a ripe and genial old age; and compared with the hearty, sagacious, reverential words of the old man, the usual round of jokes seemed flat and unprofitable. College Green was greener than ever, and the saplings of our day had shot up into tall and stout trees. As we were called into the procession, our place seemed to be somewhat too near the gray heads of the elder classes; yet we took comfort in this grave feeling by walking with very elastic step, and saying, valorously, that forty is not quite the prime of life, and that we never felt younger than now. I suppose that men always think of themselves and their early companions most frequently in the form and feature of youth; and in this sense, as well as in others, early impressions are the most enduring. We are probably a somewhat careworn set of middle-aged men; yet to each other, we are very much the same as twenty-two years ago, when we sang Auld Lang Syne together in a brotherly circle, and with clasped hands wished each other a " God Speed " upon the great life-journey at hand.

A man cannot revisit the place of his education without some very wholesome impressions; and our firm, yet benign Alma Mater, never so thriving as now, puts to all her children some very searching questions as to their discipline and career, since leaving her favored halls. If some unworthy sons may be permitted to counsel their venerable mother, may they not hint to her the prevailing danger in the whole country, of sacrificing the old spiritual faith to the new science and arts, and of placing the study of physical laws above that Word which made the world, and dwelt on earth in the Man Divine? We all share, especially all theologians and preachers, in the blame of this state of things; and the age itself is prone to count all value at the cash price, and of course prize lucrative utilities above the goods that are beyond price. Must we not believe that science itself, for her own true light and life needs the consecration of faith, and that our material civilization is but a whited sepulchre when divorced from the Spirit which builds up the kingdom of God upon the earth? I know well the difficulty of combining religion with education, especially where there are so many rival sects contending for the palm; and it is a fact, that in our day, sectarian presses attacked one of the college preachers for advising some of our class upon the subject of religion, and inviting them to become communicants of the church. Yet Christianity demands a positive place in every scheme of education, and no obstacles should be allowed to shut it out. In common with not a few friends of Harvard, we hope to see an attractive chapel ere long upon College Green, and an earnest attempt to kindle a living Church spirit among the students upon a broad Christian platform.   In shunning the Pharisee's traditions, and the Essene's mysticism, we must remember that the Sadducee's worldly conservatism may be a poor exchange for either of those superstitions.   Yet the ancient faith still lives among those hallowed walls, and no new inscriptions shall blot out from our allegiance the old motto, " Christo et Ecclesiae."   In some way, not very clear to us now, the new science and the old faith shall join hands. Surely the learned scholar, and Christian sage now in the Presidential chair, is as well entitled as any man to consecrate this union, and his administration will tend, in no small degree, to bring it to its consummation at Cambridge.

III.—A VILLAGE CHURCH.

Our theological course of three years at the Divinity school in Cambridge, seemed in many respects like a continuation of the four years' collegiate course.   The greater liberty allowed us, did not by any means amount to a complete emancipation from authoritative discipline, and the summons of the bell to prayers or recitation, was about as imperious as before our emancipation from the undergraduates' restraint.   We had eminent and faithful instructors, excellent companions, and all access to the best books and the best society.   Yet after this is said, it must be allowed that something is lacking towards the best management of theological education among us. It is not well to build the school of the prophets directly within the shadow of the classic halls, where an over critical understanding is so prone to lord it over the heart of faith, nor is it always expedient to continue college associations into theological studies. But the gravest of all objections to our present method of educating ministers, lies in the absence of that church feeling and pastoral life, without which, Christianity itself is but a name, and the New Testament but a sealed book. We tried in our day to make up for the deficiency, and to guard against the cold scholastic spirit, by doing our part in the real work of life. We each tilled our own garden, and made presents of our own flowers and melons to friends. We did some missionary service, and in jails and prisons we sought out the sad and benighted. We collected the statistics of benevolence, and had reports and debates upon questions of the day. We were no strangers to elevated society in parlors as well as in students' rooms. Still a great want remained, and it is felt more or less in all theological schools. I have heard the most eminent mind in the Baptist Church, Dr. Wayland, declare himself decidedly opposed to most theological schools, on account of the want of pastoral training,. and the predominance of the critical over the devout spirit But every human institution is imperfect, and, it may be, that the defect of which we are speaking, is only a fair share of this imperfection. It is certain, however, that a wholly new meaning attached to religion, the moment that it presented itself to us in the warmth of parish sympathy and in the earnestness of practical usefulness. Our life among the churches threw a new light upon what we had read in books. Perhaps the larger number of graduates from theological schools settle down at once into the pastoral office, whilst others, like the writer, pass a year or two in travel and miscellaneous professional service These Wander-years, as the Germans would call them, are of inestimable value, alike in securing experience, health, and literary resources for the pulpit. They must end, however, at last, and regular pastoral care must begin.

No subject, except perhaps the Slave question, has been handled more' frequently of late than that of parish life, especially in respect to its trials, and at least a half dozen books have been sent out within two or three years, claiming as much sympathy for the clerical martyr and his consort, as is claimed for Uncle Tom and Aunt Chloe. These books probably do good, and will accomplish much towards correcting the faults and mistakes of that ruling ecclesiastical polity in this country, the individual church and its people. The little sketch that I shall try to pencil in these few lines, does not ask for a place in the public portfolio, but will answer its purpose if it meets the eyes of friends not indifferent, and is then forgotten.

I remember well, shortly after returning from the West at the close of my Wandering-years, receiving a visit from a most excellent friend, Henry W———, who was unable, from illness, to fulfil an engagement in the town of N———, New Hampshire, and asking me to take his place for a

Sabbath. He, poor fellow, never, I believe, stood in the pulpit again, and the parish that would otherwise probably have been his, became mine for five years. It was on Saturday, in the middle of June, 1837, that I first visited N———, and taking the cars to Lowell, glided up the Merrimac in a wheezy little steamboat, that was soon to be displaced by a railway. It was easy to see, on Sunday morning, that the people who gathered together in that little Grecian temple, under the trees of the rural cemetery, were indeed a parish, and not merely a chance assembly of individuals. There sat the venerable Squire and his portly, sagacious lady, with interest evidently almost parental, in the welfare of the church. There was the young Squire, not son but partner, and likely, it seemed, to be son-in-law to the former. There appeared the keen, sensible face of the Member of Congress, the leading politician of the neighborhood, and ere long to wear a Senator's laurels. There too was the worthy Superintendent of the Sunday School, with kindness and reverence overflowing his face and eyes, to say nothing of his excellent wife, who with himself managed to do an amount of good in the course of a year, quite sufficient to do honor to a parsonage. There was the bookseller, with his temper so sanguine whether for a new publication, or a new political move and there was the editor, with all the cares of the village paper upon his thoughtful and somewhat anxious face. There was the postmaster, with his military honors; and there the cashier of the bank, with his mild yet scrutinizing look. Other characters equally marked, and afterwards to be very important personages in our pastoral round, were in their places, and not least among them, appeared a goodly proportion of youth and children, the future hope of the flock. There was an air of self-respect, mutual kindness, and Christian reverence about the congregation, that was quite impressive. The singing was hearty, and in good taste, under the direction of a tall chorister, who evidently magnified his office, and fulfilled its duties with a right good will that extended itself to the other members of the choir.

Nothing human is perfect, and of course our parish had its faults, faults that were the theme of much perplexing thought, and vehement exhortation, on the part of the pastor. Yet, as the world goes, they were a kindly and earnest congregation, not negligent of worship, not slow in good works. Surely, so far as their conduct to their pastor was concerned, all that he can say is, that their forbearance and good-will were wholly beyond his claims or deserts. With great individual independence, and exemption from merely ritual or dogmatic rigidity, we enjoyed a very genial and hearty church life together, and social affections seemed to flourish quite in proportion to the growing love for the sanctuary and its services. The great point was to interest the young people, and they answered encouragingly to every appeal. Among them, one grea truth was exemplified, which is made of little account in our scholastic training, the truth that the power of religion in a church, depends as much upon the receptive and devotional element in the people, as in the intellectual or active element. A company of docile children, or impressible young people, or a few really devout men and women in a parish, have an effect over the pastor and the whole sphere of church life, which cannot be estimated in language. The Divine Word, like the luminary to which it corresponds, has its virtue drawn out by the lowly plant, more than by the flinty rock, and the gifts of God in nature are constantly illustrating the gospel doctrine, that divine grace is given in the measure of human need and yearning. In looking to my first parish, I must own that I feel a profound gratitude, especially towards those waiting, lowly minds, who blessed the pastor more than any courtly patronage could do, simply by allowing him to serve them, and by expecting of him that direct usefulness, which is a minister's highest duty and richest blessing. In some cases, the sick and the dying evidently exercised, directly or indirectly, a commanding influence upon the whole congregation, even as some herb almost too lowly to meet the eye, will gather from the sun, and earth, and air, a healing and diffusive grace, that is not to be found in the rose's beauty or the oak's strength.

Many a baptism and communion in that embowered church comforted the worshippers by the assurance of new zeal and sympathy among the people. A very genial, social life prevailed; and the quite frugal and republican manners of the community combined with the good example of the chief citizens to keep up a style of visiting and entertaining, quite in contrast with the usual petty ostentation and exclusiveness of small places. It was a cheering time when the parish came in a body to visit the minister. He lived in priestly isolation, a bachelor; yet his lot was not desperate. A kind neighbor lent him for the occasion a large house adjacent to his lodgings, and the young people of the parish made it a bower of flowers from the produce of their gardens, whilst the notable housekeepers loaded the tables with all manner of good cheer for young and old. The evening was auspicious; the whole congregation came with their most cheerful looks, and the occasion, in its social cordiality and Christian tone, was one that Fenelon himself would have thought worthy of his smile and his benediction. Not a few guests came from neighboring parishes in town, and this was one of the least of the indications of the good feeling that prevailed between the various congregations and their pastors. I have never seen a more neighborly state of society than that which prevailed in our village alike among pastors and people during those years. We freely co-operated together in all matters of public spirit, especially education; and one of the most welcome reminiscences of parish life in the country, is connected with the teachers and scholars of the schools, all of whom I knew quite well, from those in the brick temple of learning in the centre of the town, to those in the wooden ten-footer in the outskirts.

There is in many quarters a disposition to underrate the population of our manufacturing towns. But a fair observation must satisfy any candid man, that these towns certainly in New England have their full share of intelligence and character. I mingled very freely with the operatives of every grade, and had a considerable number of them in the parish. It is simple truth to say, that I have never known a more exemplary class of persons. The oung men were very desirous of improving alike in knowledge and principles, and no appeal to them for help in any good word or work was unanswered. I have kept especial account of a little knot of young men who used to meet together for conversation and inquiry, and it has been very cheering to note their respectability and progress. A few weeks ago I met one of this set at Springfield, Mass., and found that he had risen gradually from his subordinate place in the mill, to the charge of a manufacturing establishment of a thousand operatives. The whole retrospect of those years, in the manufacturing village, is eminently cheering in respect to the fortunes of enterprising and capable young men. Wherever situated, the American youth who croaks over the obstacles in the way of his rising, and gives himself to despair and idleness, is too chicken-hearted to use success even if forced upon him.

I do not care to say with what feelings that little Church was resigned for another charge, and how many wistful yearnings have, from time to time, been sent back to those years of comparative retirement. The neighboring city and large towns never seemed more attractive and edifying than when revisited, for a few days, after a season of hard work in the country. How delightful was the elect circle of brethren that met together every two months for professional sympathy; and each man went back with double heart from this chosen fellowship, always very sure of preaching an uncommonly living sermon the next Sunday. What a privilege it was to join occasionally a conversational club in Boston, where the choicest spirits spoke freely their best thoughts, and Channing himself was a frequent guest. He was emphatically kind and encouraging to young men, and he used to inquire as earnestly about my unpretending charge, and listen as respectfully to my poor words, as if humanity were to him the same every where, and whatever is worth doing at all, is worth doing well, whether in a small sphere or a large one. In that club the progressive spirit prevailed, and not a little of the transcendental philosophy figured in the conversation. Behind none of the most zealous reformers in his zeal, and earnest as any transcendentalist for the spiritual worth of every soul, Channing never failed to show his strict allegiance to the gospel, and on one occasion maintained, at considerable length, his conviction of the permanent ministry of Jesus Christ to the human family, and of his actual presence with believers, especially at the season of communion.

A familiar poet has told us that,

> " Lands intersected by a narrow frith,
> Abhor each other. Mountains interposed
> Make enemies of nations, who had else
> Like kindred drops been mingled into one."

and sad to say, not long after my leaving, that village was divided into two jealous towns, on account of the little stream that flowed so tranquilly through its domain, and preached peace with every ripple as it turned the millwheels that created the general wealth. In trying to locate the new town-house, the citizens quarrelled, and preferred having two town-houses to giving the prerogative to the rival side of the river. In a few years, however, the old good neighborhood, confirmed by not a few inducements from mutual interest and public pride, returned, and a city charter was the reasonable pretext for uniting the two sides of the river into one efficient community. Great indeed was the joy when this was done; and I am not ashamed to say, that when word came to me of its consummation last year, I felt much disposed to run to the door, to announce the fact to the people in the street, and was obliged to sober the enthusiasm by remembering that a policeman lived opposite, and that New York cares too little even about its own affairs to care very much about other places, great or small.

It is a great privilege to go from time to time to the old place, and hunt up the scenes and friends that cannot be forgotten. The cemetery in which our church stands has many voices to the visitor's memory, that chime well with the whisper of the winds through the trees that overshadow the graves. A large portion of the congregation that I met in the church the first Sunday there, that has been spoken of, have gone from their habitual seats, and laid down to their rest under the green sod. The good Squire and his wife, the former not long after the latter, have gone in the peace of a firm faith, and their names are pointed out to the young as household words, in every family where the husband's neighborly kindness, and the wife's careful thought, are as fresh as the day. This couple were more than legislators to the community in which they lived, since social influence is stronger than written law, and the peacemaker, and the housewife, who give the true tone to the whole neighborhood, scatter good seed that lives long after they have gone. The young lawyer, too, has gone to his rest. F—— was my most intimate friend and a constant helper, a man of keen intellect, fine taste, acute, and in some respects, morbid sensibility, an accomplished scholar, a graceful writer, a learned and able lawyer, an upright and influential politician. He overworked his powers in codifying the State laws, and sought in the air of Spain, the Mediterranean, and Egypt, the health that he was never to find. We used to hunt the first spring flower, the Epigæa Repens, together, and that fragrant and unobtrusive plant, in its fragrance, in its early bloom, and its tenacious grasp, is no inapt memento of F——'s gifts, and his fate. I shall never forget the one political idea that was most prominent in his creed. He always maintained that the first danger to this country was in the centralization of government and influence, and that just as surely as great sums of money are placed in the hands of the Cabinet or Congress, to be disbursed for pet local enterprises, just so surely will all manner of peculation be fostered, and Washington will become a nest of manœuvring jobbers. Every year of the nation is but illustrating the justice of this idea, by revealing some new depth of the knavery and covetousness of public men. Not far from the grave of this young lawyer, rests the dust of the Senator who has been already named. Just as great wealth was poured into his lap, and he was made the leader of the dominant party in the national Senate with any office in the gift of the Cabinet apparently open to his grasp, he was stricken down speechless and ere long died. He was an accomplished man, a very shrewd observer of character, far more cautious than sanguine, a cool and sagacious calculator of political probabilities, and probably, at the time of his death, the most influential public man in the State. He was a courteous and agreeable parishioner, instructive and genial in conversation, and although very little of a devotee or enthusiast, he was very ready to assert the necessity of religion to human nature, and to sustain by his presence and means its public institutions. There was somewhat of a sarcastic element in his nature, and he was the last man whose name I should have associated with the vagaries of the New Spiritualism. Yet I have heard of quite an elaborate communication to his old pastor, professing to come from him since he left the body, and without stopping to discuss the philosophy of spiritualism, it is enough to say that if my shrewd and somewhat cynical friend indeed dictated that letter from the spiritual world, he has singularly changed his tone. There is much that is very marvellous in the late letter-writing and table-tipping movements, but I should value far more such a return of my intelligent friend's spirit, as comes to me from revisiting the favorite haunts of our walks and talks, in the woods and by the river side, than any of the revelations of the new magic. It is probably true that the alleged communications from the spiritual world which are now so prominent, will be found to illustrate the power of the mind in acting upon itself, and in mistaking its subjective impressions for objective realities. A volume might be written upon the Pythian element in our nature, which would throw light upon many other oracles than that of Delphi. We will not turn from our musing in the cemetery, however, to follow these speculations. The thought uppermost in mind, is, of course, the great instability of human life, for in less than twenty years, a large company of persons well known to me, have gone here to their rest, and the names upon the grave stones win an easier recognition, than many names that now mark the living worshippers in the church. Yet the world does not stop its motion, however many or conspicuous are her sons and daughters who cease to be. The little river runs in front of the cemetery as merrily as ever, and turns thousands of spindles, quite as eager as ever in the whirl for gold. There too, in the distance, Old Monadnock lifts his bald head to the heavens, indifferent as fate itself to the beauty of the ever-returning stars, and to the sighing of the restless winds, and to the toil and trouble among the pigmies who worry themselves to death in his valleys. Along new roads of iron, fresh crowds hurry to and fro upon their round of pleasure or business, and a new generation of children come to church to learn their catechism under the guidance of grave elders who were children or youth twenty years ago. Under such impressions a man feels himself within the grasp of an inexorable destiny, that seems hurrying him away in its fated march, utterly indifferent to the joy or sorrow, life or death, of the individual, and careful only that laws and races shall be preserved. What is life, and what is death, without a Comforter beyond the world, beyond nature and man—a Comforter who can lead us to Him, who cares for each soul with a parent's love, and through the wreck of matter and the fall of nations, will preserve unto life eternal the soul that trusts in His love? Such a Comforter speaks from the Word in that sanctuary, to that dust in the cemetery.

IV.—CITY EXPERIENCES.

Each community, like each individual, has a character of its own that cannot be measured by size or figures, and it is very obvious, that if the Apostle Paul should make the circuit of American cities, he would have a word for each of them, quite as characteristic as any that he addressed to the Galatians or the Romans, to the people of Corinth or Ephesus. Surely he would find occasion for all his insight and sagacity, in dealing with our two chief Northern cities, Boston and New York, and perhaps in some respects the intermediate thriving little metropolis of Rhode Island, might task his acuteness and tact quite as much as any place ever visited by him in his mission through the empire of the Cæsars. If most communities are proud of certain distinguishing traits in their manners

and institutions, the Rhode Islander carries the individuality a step farther, and believes in every man's being a manner, institution, and character to himself. Bostonians and
New Yorkers, of the genuine stamp, are not very difficult
to be defined, and their dress and furniture indicate their
distinctive characteristics tolerably well. But gather together fifty regular Rhode Islanders, select them if you
please, any day, out of Westminster, or Benefit, or Water
street, in Providence, from the men over forty years old,
and you will have about as many original characters as
you have individual specimens. The idiosyncrasy is not
confined to the ruder sex, but walks in silk quite as emphatically as in broadcloth. Enter a choice coterie of
knowing women, generally having a large and valuable
proportion of those who have never consented to narrow
the largeness of their sympathies and ideas by any domestic fetters, and you will find that Roger Williams has
daughters as well as sons who scorn all subjection to
priestly prescription or social tradition. More than one
affable matron will broach, with full confidence, her own
theory for the reorganization of society, no matter what
Plato or the Pope may say to the contrary; and more than
one eloquent maiden will set forth a system of metaphysics
emanating from her own intuitions, no matter what Emer-
son may whisper with his honeyed persuasion, or Carlyle
may growl with his savage humanity. No extreme of political conservatism appears to take away the least of a
genuine Rhode Islander's individuality of thinking and
acting. The solid Chief Justice, who was called by the

thorough-going radicals, the very Jeffries of judicial conservatism and rigor, no sooner quits the bench and enters his study, than lo! the severe magistrate has become the most adventurous of metaphysicians. He is ready to show how time and space exist, and the universe is made, ever anew by man the microcosm. The Pan-Idea of the Rhode Island Chief Justice, exhibits speculative daring enough, to make a regiment of the common order of political radicals scamper with affright, if they do not first fall down dizzy with the vain attempt at comprehension.

A stubborn individualism has been, in some respects, the strength, and in other respects, the weakness, of Rhode Island. It has raised up many remarkable characters, and given a peculiar life to private enterprise; but it has stood much in the way of proper public spirit, and of efficient associate effort, until of late. Of late, a new day has come over the State, and apparently from the very tendency that has so long worked in the old direction. The want of due conciliation led to the recent sad feud, and this very feud led to a kind of combination and sense of citizenship that have widened into a broader and better public spirit, than before was known, and which has in fact taken at last some of the bitterest political antagonists within its larg embrace. Probably none of the old States of the Union ha improved so much as Rhode Island within ten or fifteen years. Schools, Libraries, Academies, Art, Industry, Collegiate education, all have taken a new start, and there is apparently no place in the whole country that secures to a right-minded citizen a larger average of social, literary and religious privilege, than the city of Providence   I can say from pretty thorough experience and observation, that no man who has taken root there among books and friends, pleasant scenery and good institutions, willingly seeks another home.

Perhaps the last thing expected to come from the threatened civil war was such a result as actually came. There was a fearful state of feeling for about a year of my residence there.   It was a strange and startling transition from the peaceful village of N—— to the rule of martial law.   We indeed had our soldiers in the country, and I had there taken my turn as chaplain in asking Heaven's blessing on the brigades before their attack upon the collation, or the summons to the sham fight.   The commander of our crack company in N——, an artillery corps a hundred strong, had heard real bullets whistle during the war of 1812; yet in spite of his frequent desires to bleed for his country, he was a most pacific Christian man, and his voice had been trained to its sonorous pitch more by the exhortations of the Conference Meeting than by the passions of the camp.   It was very evident that playing soldier is a very different thing from being soldier, and that during that crisis in Rhode Island, so far as the feeling was concerned, men were now quite ready to meet a bloody crisis.   The scenes in the streets, the troops, bayonets, cannon, munitions, were not the worst of the evil.   The greatest sufferers were those, who from their homes, waited the fearful tidings that were anticipated. The alarm bells that made the night more than dismal, struck more panic into the wife and daughter in the house than into the armed man in the street or field. But a trifle was needed, a chance discharge of a musket, or a spark of fire upon a field-piece, to have kindled at once a civil war, whose extent and horrors no man could calculate. But no such mishap occurred. The revolutionary passion cooled and died out without the convulsion of a fatal crisis. "Nothing," says a keen Frenchman, "succeeds so well as success;" and notwithstanding all the rhodomontade to the contrary, Rhode Island has been uniting and consolidating her resources since that time, under laws that appear to have the countenance of leading men from both the old belligerent parties. Probably the old Charter of King Charles never did the State more good than in the convulsions of its final gasp.

Merciful Heaven sent to some of us a blessed anodyne to the war fever, in the arrival of the librarian of Brown University with a great collection of choice books from Europe. Professor Jewett, with his ten thousand tomes, did more to calm some troubled spirits, than the Paixhan guns and the Horse Guards. The College Library became a charmed place of resort, and supplied in the classics and modern languages all the deficiencies left by the admirable English Library of the citizens' Athenæum. The President's emphatic figure was no unusual sight among the books. It needed few words only to prove the weight of his mind. He is the Cromwell among our College dignitaries—a sturdy Independent, in religion utterly opposed to every form of priestcraft in America, and touching with no

3*

feeble hand the springs of anti-prelatical Protestantism among the Missions of India. He is an academic radical, yet a firm disciplinarian, and leads off the collegiate revolution, now going on in the land, by bringing into the field to cope with those old cavaliers of letters, the Classics, those pugnacious Roundheads, the gases, metals, mechanic powers, and the whole rank and file of physical science and art, determined, as he is, to educate boys to do the head work of the manufacturer, engineer, merchant and mechanic, as well as the learned professions.

It is sometimes as hard to regulate a parish as a State, and more than one minister has found the dogged independence of Williams too strong in his descendants to move parishioners to that cohesive zeal which does as much for the edifying of the church, as for the comfort of the pastor. With one minister whom we well knew, the great question was, how to mould the stanch individualities at the heads of the pews into a homogeneous active body. The men were indeed faithful to whatever they undertook, always true to their word, abounding in the business virtues, not wanting in liberality of purse, yet strikingly wanting in what Bushnell calls churchly life, especially in regard to the Christian ordinances. Their creed was, in some respects more from Zeno, with his stout will, than from St. Paul, with his devout faith; and it became a pressing question how to win them to warmer church feeling, to kindle the sentiment of Christian communion, and to nurture that evangelical tenderness, which is as essential to the welfare of a congregation, as to the peace of the soul. Kind Heaven helped him out of the difficulty, by raising up a new parish from the teachers and scholars of the Sunday School. He tried to do what he could for the men, and certainly he had for them great respect and affection; but his hope for the devotional life of the church was in great part from the young, and the comfort and aid which he found from them alike in social and religious relations, gave new strength to his own labors, and in due time wrought a change in the whole sphere of the parish. As much was accomplished in the Sunday School room as in the church, and no scenes of pastoral life are more gratefully remembered, than the cheerful and earnest reunions of scores of young people at the parsonage for social fellowship and religious instruction. Thus, what he could not do of himself, he tried to do by new recruits; and in some cases, they who were proof against the minister's appeals, surrendered their indifference before the little host of their own children that were brought into the field. It was reserved, however, for the next minister, an admirable scholar—an exquisite writer—to do a work far more remarkable, and not attempted before. Surely he must have great powers of persuasion, who could induce those units of manly independence to coalesce into something of ritual unity, and say litanies, psalms, and collects together quite after the old church method. Our good old deacon, whose love for this church and its people was a part of his very life, was opposed to having the Commandments set up in the sanctuary, as the pastor desired, because it looked, he said, so much like Episcopacy. What would he say, could he see the reading desk and prayer-book that are now fixtures of the altar ?   But whatever the outward fixtures are, we may be sure that there are other fixtures of a deeper kind that abide through all administrations.   I can never think or speak of the city of Roger Williams and of the people there best known, without remembrances that make the changing years more blessed as they pass.   Here, in this rural nook, from among the trees, the waters of Long Island Sound are full in sight, and many of the white sails that flit by in the distance will not cease their course until they are furled in front of familiar counting-rooms, and watched by the passers by on the Weybosset Bridge, so often trodden by our own and our friends' feet.   Nearer to the writer's shady arbor, now some more lively mementoes of that city are to be found.   Two sprightly girls are gamboling upon the lawn, with a greyhound for a play-fellow, who remember Providence with a birthright affection, and who cannot be induced by any of the wonders of the new home in the greater city to renounce their first love.

The greater city—our huge, tumultuous, impassioned New York—the home of all faiths and practices, creeds and characters—what shall we say of it, who have tried to scrutinize its ways carefully, and who, in spite of our many misgivings at too prevalent faults, must in truth confess our great attachment to the place and people so hospitable to us as strangers, and so friendly to us, now strangers no more.   Probably few thoughtful men ever came to New

York, or to any like enormous city, of their own accord, from a more tranquil and stable home. There is something at first desolate in the aspect of a great city to a visitor who has been used to live in a community where most of the people are acquaintances, and no small portion of them are his friends. The open ocean or the unbroken forest, hardly gives a greater sense of loneliness than the presence of a vast crowd of strangers, to whom we are so utterly unknown, that if we dropped down in the street, the incident would be of no especial interest to any body, except, perhaps, to some newspaper reporter on the lookout for items for his chapter of accidents. It is usually some prevailing train of circumstances not of his own devising, that brings the quiet provincial to the great city in the current which draws such vast and heterogeneous numbers into the remorseless whirlpool. Yet ere long the novice begins to be reconciled to the throng. He is no longer made dizzy by the swaying crowd, and the hum of the busy streets seems to him little more than the swell of the sea to the sailor, or the murmur of the forest to the backwoodsman. He forms a kind of general acquaintance with the city and people, whilst he has friends enough at home and abroad to assure him that he is a man among kindy men, and not a solitary unit in the general mass. Many of our satisfactions depend upon contrasts, and the contrast between the view of the great crowd of strangers and the recognition of our own acquaintances, gives us a mingled pleasure quite peculiar from its union of novelty with familiarity, very much as when friends journey together in foreign lands, constantly enjoying new scenes with old affections.

Our better sensibilities are more in danger in the great city than we can well define. The amount of misery in the general crowd, and in cases making an especial appeal, creates a draught upon the sympathies that threatens either to craze a man with solicitude, or to harden him into desperation and indifference. I have lived years in a community where the sum total of poverty and suffering could be easily measured, and quite effective relief could be given at once to every needy family. In our neighborhood there was one town so thriving, that charity had to go begging for objects of its bounty; and after a public festival, the managers were unable to think of a single family in the place who would not feel themselves insulted by the bestowal of the dainties remaining from the feast. In New York, such a fact seems the most monstrous of absurdities; for there every stray rag or bone has a claimant, and misery has legions that no man has numbered, and no man can fully relieve. The necessity of discriminating between honest want and knavish pretension, where begging is a trade, and imposture is a profession, lays a perilous snare for the conscience, by affording selfishness the easy excuse of deceit. But do our part as well as we may to relieve suffering, we cannot do every thing; and there is a constant array of sufferers before our eyes, that must harrow the sensibilities, if they do not harden the heart. In fact, the problem is still unsettled as to the fate of the heart in a great city. Not the least of its perils is the frequency of dramatic and romantic appeals to the feelings by the theatre and the opera, the newspaper and the novel, that tend to make real want repulsive in comparison with the more fascinating victims of the plot or the story. Yet God is every where, and the man who tries to keep within his love, and to do good to his neighbor according to opportunity, will find that Divine Providence rules over city as over village, and the dews of heavenly grace are ready to descend upon both.

One experience has struck me since living in the great city, which has not been remarked upon with sufficient emphasis. It is the sense of the absolute need of religion, not merely as a source of spiritual life and hope, but as a safeguard against the craving excitement and perpetual unrest of the current world of business and pleasure. A man needs here the rest of a divine faith, as much as he needs the cooling water or the soothing pillow. It is very clear to me that all thoughtful people are conscious of this want, and that their decided attachment to church worship, especially to its directly devotional elements, is proof of a craving for the peace that is not of this world. It is not uncommon to hear New York spoken of as a very irreligious city; but a fair inspection will reveal among the regular, and especially the American, residents, as large a proportion of devotional sentiment and practical benevolence, as any large community in the land can show. It would be a dismal confession of shallowness and conceit, for a man to call any great city truly Christian; but truth and candor forbid our joining in the poor disposition of many critics, to purchase self-complacency by the whole-sale condemnation of neighbors.

Without God and Christ, and the Divine Spirit, wha are we in the great tumult, the fearful play of fortune, character, life, death ? The heavenly mercy never deserts us, and always offers some blessing suited to the peculiar trials of our position. He who sent Jesus Christ to Jeru-salem and Capernaum, and Paul to Antioch, Corinth, Athens and Rome, has not deserted his people, nor shut up his grace within any village walls. A man of devout disposition will feel his heart drawn more tenderly to the mercy-seat, and more into harmony with the great masters of the devout life, from the very tumult and unrest around him. Every sorrow has its providential remedy; and to those who live in cities there is balm in Gilead, and a Divine Physician there. Surely, he who wishes to appre-ciate the majestic Quietists like à Kempis, Fenelon, and other peers who have learned so profoundly the peace that is in Jesus, will find himself quite as much quickened and subdued into a congenial temper, by seeking that rest divine near to the mighty heart of the great city, as when within the calmest rural retreat under shady arbors that offer tranquillity, yet tempt indolence.

The season of respite from the usual round of labor now closes, and the writer puts by his errant pen for toil less a pastime, and, perhaps, more a utility. Let not the reader call him an idler or egotist, for passing some of these leisure days in reminiscences of scenes and friends that seemed to present themselves of their own accord, to be sketched. If his own mood shall seize others with a kindred fit of retrospection, they will be in better frame to survey for themselves the landmarks of their career. Is it out of place for him to wish his friends and readers a happy life-journey, whose Mile Stones draw ever nearer the Eternal Home?

FAIRFIELD, CONN., *August* 30, 1854.

I.

God's Blessing on the Journey.

God's Blessing on the Journey.

Now that the sun is beaming bright,
  Implore we, bending low,
That He, the Uncreated Light,
  May guide us as we go.

No sinful word, nor deed of wrong,
  Nor thoughts that idly rove,
But simple truth be on our tongue,
  And in our hearts be love.

And grant that to thine honor, Lord,
  Our daily toil may tend;
That we begin it at thy word,
  And in thy favor end.

St. Ambrose.

GOD'S BLESSING ON THE JOURNEY.

IT is well for a man to keep sacredly his own birth-day,
and to give serious thought to the tenor of the momentous
life, whose beginning he celebrates.   There is a place for
festivity, the most genial festivity in the occasion, and in
a thoughtful, affectionate family, the least child will learn
to welcome the little round of anniversaries, that bring
the greetings in due turn to each member of the home circle.   But the festivity is vain, and worse than vain, if it
does not spring from a cheerful sense of the solemn meaning of existence, and the gift of life is not held in reverent
trust from Him who is the Father of our spirits.   We begin
these thoughts upon the life-journey by asking his blessing
upon our career.   What better topic can we have than
that of prayer, not a separate prayer for some single blessing, but the prayer that cares for all our needs, and lays
them all before the mercy-seat.

Human life is a constant want, and ought to be a constant prayer.

It is a constant want, certainly. Who is not always wanting something? They that have no money, want some; they that have much, want more. The beggar begs bread at the prince's kitchen; the prince hunts the world through in search of a new pleasure. The captive weeps for the free air, and his own home; the conqueror, whose chattel he has become, weeps that there are no more worlds to conquer. Life is surely a constant want.

Nor does any superiority of culture or character, take from life this attendant. In fact, the best mind has the most wants, and in place of every foolish whim or base appetite renounced, many refined tastes and aspirations are sure to come. The Christian, by the very fact of his faith and purpose, wants more and better things than any worldling possibly can. He is content with a frugal table and limited purse, yet he claims an ever increasing interest in all true goods; with an undying yearning he wants whatever is pure and lovely under God's providence; nay, he wants God himself, the Infinite and Eternal Good, for his Friend and Comforter.

So Christ came, not to do the Stoic's work for man by blunting the sensibilities, but to carry out the Creator's work by quickening every sense and faculty, to make life a constant prayer for a blessing ever enlarging. The word of the Messiah calls man to receive, in the whole compass of his being, the good that God's love provides. The word is: "Ask, and it shall be given; seek, and ye shall find; knock, and it shall be opened unto you." Remember this saying as we continue our meditation.

What does this teach, but a prayer as comprehensive as life itself—a prayer in word, indeed, but more than that—one in thought and action also. Let us think of it in its chief points of duty and privilege.

It begins with *asking*. "Ask, and ye shall receive." Then the method of discipline which the earthly parent adopts, the Heavenly Father has ordained. The child of man learns by asking, and it is so also with the child of God, in that discipline that does not end with childhood or youth. The prayer of asking is commended to us then by the most obvious of analogies. Whatever good we want from God we are to ask for, especially that good which is peculiar to his own being and action, the good that is moral and spiritual—the light for our guidance, the strength for our path, the peace for our trial.

But does any one say that the analogy breaks down just in the most essential point? The parent does not know what a child wants, and therefore needs often to be asked, but God knows all our wants, and therefore needs no asking. The objection is plausible, but not sound. It is not merely the parent's ignorance of a child's wants that requires the expression of the want, but it is the parent's desire for an obedient, respectful temper in the child. Right asking is of itself an action having a moral quality, and entitling the asker to benefits not otherwise appropriate. It acts at once upon the disposition of him who asks, and upon the administration of him who gives.

So, then, we claim for the prayer of asking, an effect

twofold—or, in the language once metaphysical but now popular, an effect both subjective and objective—acting upon man and upon God. It acts upon man. Intellectually speaking, what habit strengthens and invigorates the faculty more than the habit of reducing our vague thoughts and feelings to distinct forms? By words, in fact, we learn to think; and he who does not speak or write his mind, becomes a vain dreamer. It is not, of course, merely audible language that we insist upon, but distinct, clearly conscious prayer, spoken or unspoken. It collects the thoughts, and quickens the attention, to bring a definite prayer before the mercy-seat. They who slight this fact, and substitute meditation for prayer, will soon substitute reverie for meditation, and let reverie run wild at the mercy of every idle fancy.

Morally, it acts upon man. It makes him feel the benignant and solemn presence of God, thus to review his own wants before him, and implore the Almighty to grant him the good he needs. To speak to a fellow-creature brings him near to us, and of itself is an act so expressive, as often to call for no little conflict with our timidity. To bring our petition before the Infinite and Eternal One with any kind of seriousness and reverence—how can it but subdue the will and rebuke the passions, and confirm the faith and exalt the affections?

But is this all? Is man helped by prayer, solely by the effect of it, as an exercise of his thought and feeling? The Bible does not read so—nor the best experience teach so—nor a judicious philosophy intimate so. Nay, prayer loses its power as an intellectual and moral exercise, if pursued merely as such, and the devotees of a cold rationalism soon weary of the spiritual gymnastics that aim only to stir their own faculties. The gospel teaches the power of prayer to win good from God, and the experience of all ages and lives illustrates the truth of the doctrine. But look to the very nature of things—the nature of the soul, and the attributes of God. Are not all the best gifts of Heaven contingent upon some act of man? The earth is the Lord's, and the fulness thereof; but must not man sow and reap and garner, in order to enjoy the harvest? Nay the simplest and most essential gifts, light, water, air, man truly enjoys, only when he truly uses. Shall any earth-born philosophy presume to say, in the face of revelation and experience, that in the mysterious region in which God moves, this law of conditionality so entirely ceases, that no thought nor effort of the soul can win any peculiar blessing from the Father of our spirits? Absurd idea! Far better the philosophy of the Bible, which says, draw nigh unto God, and God will draw nigh unto you. Then lift to God the asking prayer. Let our word breathe our want and win his blessing. Our word to man bears something from us, and brings something from him. Our word to God—it shall not be in vain, and may win the kindest return, when unanswered to the ear or to the impatient sense. Let the word of prayer begin with our first conscious want, rise with our growth, and deepen with our experience. So we understand the life-prayer in its first and most obvious form—asking.

4

This first leads to the second, and implies it. Asking is, in fact, a form of seeking, and suggests all forms. Depending upon God, craving his blessing, not in the pride of our own self-will, we are to search out the true way of life. Seeking it of God, we find. The living prayer of the true seeker, has a twofold virtue, acting upon his own mind and upon the paths of Providence. It acts upon the mind of the man. He who seeks for any good, real or imagined, is successful very much according to the spirit in which he seeks, whether pure and wise or the reverse. The common proverb says, that necessity is the mother of invention. Say rather, that desire is the mother of invention, and the vision is always keen in the direction of the ruling love. See the gold-hunter — what perils of man and nature he braves to win the shining dust, and what trifles to a common eye, are, to his sharp sight, signs of the precious ore. See the angler with his line, the hunter with his gun, the naturalist in search of bird, insect, or mineral, how sagaciously each finds the path to what he seeks. Nay, the very inventive genius that has changed the face of the earth, and marked lands and oceans with its triumphs, what is it but the result of the desire of material goods, so characteristic of modern times? The inventor is a seeker, and the useful arts all are his findings. These are well, but not the best. A man may have them all and be wretched. The great discovery, is that which opens the path of divine peace and strength. He finds it, who seeks it by studying devoutly the mind of its Maker, and has his way in God as he walks the highways and byways of life. No man has exhausted this discovery, or learned to see the paths of usefulness and enjoyment which every day brings near. The sense for them is keen, as our sense of God's love is tender. We understand a fine estate, by knowing the mind of the proprietor, and all is clear as we walk through the grounds and halls in his company. Who shall presume, without devout communion with God, grateful sense of his wisdom and love, to learn the true uses of his wonderful domain? Who can seek wisely the ways of life without the Divine Guide?

Nor does the good stop here, with the effect on the seeker's own powers. Providence helps him with peculiar aids. We are not among those who are fond of dogmatizing upon particular Providences, or presuming to know all of God's meaning in any of the events of life. Much less are we in favor of interpreting our times as if our own community or fortune were the chief thing in view of the Most High. But, certainly, without such presumption, we may acknowledge a providential hand in shaping the ways of life, in some measure, according to the seeker's aims. This is certainly Christian doctrine, and a faith which every trusting mind craves for its best peace and power. Who shall gainsay it? What philosopher of history presumes to shut God out from the lead of events? What observer of life in all its varied opportunities, dares to assert any fatality so rigid, as to exclude the working of the Infinite Spirit? Nay, let a man study his own life, and remember how peculiarly events have been ordered for him, how he has been led to the most important measures of his experience, how strangely strength has come from disappointment, and good from trial, how many times great results have depended upon influences from nature from human feeling, from some word or impression that might be wholly providential. Experience will then be ready to answer to the gospel doctrine, and, whilst not disparaging human effort in choosing the way, will say after all, that our way is to be sought in God, and to be found of him. God is in history, or history is the Bible of Atheism. God is in the paths of life, or life is without God in the world. No business nor profession is well, without this trust to guide its work and to dispose its gains. The business and profession common to all—our calling of God as the creatures of his power and the subjects of his kingdom—falls at once, if we lose hold of his guiding hand.

So we interpret the promise to the seeker, that his mind is readier for the true way, and the true way is readier to his mind, by the living prayer of devout seeking.

Nor is this all. Our Lord's words have a cumulative force, and each previous word blooms out in its successor. He that asks, receives light to begin his seeking; he that seeks, finds the path leading to some gate of heaven; he that knocks, shall see the gate opening to him.

How often we meet with some barrier that crosses our path and baffles our progress. Every study and enterprise is full of such obstacles, and he that has pursued any far-reaching plan, has been stopped by some closed gate-way. The path of the Christian, that noblest study and enterprise, meets such a barrier in every great stage of his journey. He finds intellectual difficulties that he cannot solve, trials that he cannot clear up, aspirations that are marked by reality. He needs not merely to go onward, but to go inward, and learn for himself the truth and peace within the kingdom. What shall open the door? We will not condemn reading, or study, or meditation, as means of clearing up the great mysteries of our being; we will not jest at the pretensions of the powerful priesthood that has claimed to hold the mystical keys, and promise the light of heaven to those who seek it in obedience. But above all there rises the office of a life, true, earnest, trusting, in word, in thought, and work, relying upon God, and craving his blessing. Such life is a constant prayer, and knocks not vainly at heaven's gate, even while on earth.

Its power is twofold—upon man and upon God. It acts upon man, by opening within his soul the faculties that make him most receptive of heavenly influence — upon the reason whose eye yearns for the eternal light, upon the conscience and affections which crave the infinite rectitude and love. What, in fact, is the noblest intellectual act, but an opening of the mind to divine things? Intuition, what is it but seeing into the divine verity, and what nurtures the power so well as devout faith and striving? He of the disciples had most of it, who had most love, for he who leaned upon the Master's bosom, spake most rapturously of the heavenly glory in Him revealed.

Opening thus the soul of man to the divine kingdom, the devout life, as it stands striving at the gate, opens the divine kingdom also to the soul. The two influences combine in one, even as in the expanding lily, the bursting bud and the descending sunshine work together in opening the flower to heaven, and heaven to the flower. It is certainly true that we are surrounded by an unseen realm of spiritual reality, and that it is opened to us only as we grow into it. There are discrete degrees, or degrees of quality, and concrete degrees, or degrees of quantity, said one of the greatest of spiritual philosophers. We open concrete degrees, simply by advancing—we open discrete degrees by rising, and can enter a new quality of being, only by living up to it. This is the law of the opening of heaven to man. When we stand at the gate, yearning for a clearer sense of God's love, craving clearer light on prevailing evil, yearning for a solution of the dark problem that most perplexes mind and heart, desolate under some bereavement, crazed by some doubt; let there be no despair if the gate seems closed upon us, and we knock in vain. It shall not be always in vain. If seeking and asking prevail not, let lowly persevering obedience, that prayer without ceasing, strive at the gate, and some good angel will appear, and he door will be opened, and light will break through. Every enigma will not, indeed, at once be solved, and door beyond door may appear unopened before us. Yet enough of the heavenly kingdom will be opened to cheer away despondency, and to confirm faith and hope

We end our meditation as we begun. Life is a constant want, and should be a constant prayer. Continuing in every word and way and work, lifting man to God, and winning God to man.

Thus let the great journey begin, and thus let it go on. Thus beginning, it will give youth noble aim and needed power, without chilling its generous fervor or taking away a single pure joy. Thus continuing, it will lead manhood to an experience better than the much knowledge with much sorrow which constitutes worldly wisdom, and will secure to age a peace deepening as futurity draws near.

Raise, then, the great life-prayer. With all our asking, above the vast host of eager desires and clamorous passions, let the heart ask God for the best gift, that consecrates every other — even the wisdom from above. With all our seeking, above and within the numberless paths that life reveals, seek the way that does not deceive. Through all startling changes and dazzling opportunities, gates of knowledge and power, look most earnestly to the gate that opens heavenly influence, and let progress be a growing revelation. Life itself then becomes prayer. Rooted and grounded in love, the deeper its humility, the higher its joy. The asking, thirsty roots of its being, send up vigor to the branches that wave in the light of heaven. Each birthday will then be more peaceful than the previous, and however encompassed with clouds and darkness, the eye of faith cannot be cheerless.

" Lead, Kindly Light, amid the encircling gloom,
  Lead Thou me on !
The night is dark, and I am far from home —
  Lead Thou me on !
Keep Thou my feet; I do not ask to see
The distant scene,—one step enough for me.

" So long Thy power hath blest me, sure it still
  Will lead me on
O'er moor and fen, o'er crag and torrent, till
  The night is gone :
And with the morn those angel faces smile
Which I have loved long since and lost awhile."

II.

Childhood.

" A child is man in a small letter, yet the best copy of Adam, before he tasted of Eve, or the Apple; and he is happy whose small practice in the world can only write his character. His soul is as yet a white paper unscribbled with observations of the world, wherewith, at length, it becomes a blurred note-book. He is purely happy because he knows no evil, nor hath made means by sin to be acquainted with misery. He arrives not at the mischief of being wise, nor endures evils to come by foreseeing them. He kisses and loves all, and when the smart of the rod is past, smiles on the beater. The older he grows he is a stair lower from God. He is the Christian's example and the old man's relapse; the one imitates his pureness and the other falls into his simplicity. Could he put off his body with his little coat, he had got eternity without a burden, and exchanged but one heaven for another.

BISHOP EARLE.

CHILDHOOD.

Our childhood, instead of being a passing stage, is a
permanent experience of our life, and gains interest with
years.   Before we know it, we flit by this first Mile Stone
of our journey; yet we are always looking back to it, and
never without seeing fresh flowers blooming among the
mosses of its time-worn surface.   Because St. Paul said,
" When I was a child, I spake as a child, I understood as
a child, I thought as a child : but when I became a man,
I put away childish things; " he is generally regarded as
disparaging the mind of childhood, in order to honor the
superior wisdom of manhood.   But a single glance at the
connection will show the error of this view.   St. Paul, in
the maturity of his powers and the fulness of his experience, is declaring the peerless worth of love as the light
of the earth and the foretaste of heaven.   Looking forward to the glories of that blessed state where this spirit
shall have full life, and see God no longer through a mirror darkly, but face to face ; he speaks of his present power
of mind as preliminary to that full vision, even as child-

hood in its simplicity is preliminary to manhood in its experience. Childhood, therefore, in its way, is just as honorable as manhood in its way, and each has a worth not only in itself, but also as a step to something higher. In this spirit, let us now look upon childhood and consider what it is, how it should be treated whilst it lasts, and how prepared for the time when it ceases and graver cares come. This paper will be one of a series, running at intervals through the volume, on the Circle of Human Life, or the Ages of Man interpreted by the Gospel.

The *Nature* of childhood, what is it? It is simply itself, and not any thing else. The child is not an angel, as sentimentalists dream; not a fiend, as dogmatists have declared; but a mingled and undeveloped creature, a man ungrown, with all the powers and passions of humanity existing, but not brought into consciousness with the natural and the spiritual forces in the bud, yet with the natural more forward than the spiritual, and needing guidance far wiser than its own.

Whether good or bad, whether well or ill trained, a child will be a child, and not man or woman; for God and nature have ordained a law over the mind quite as imperious as that over the body, and they who try to defy that law, find it easier to spoil the child into a foolish precocity than to ripen him into premature wisdom. Let the child be a child,—speak, think, and judge as such, in all simplicity. We have no doubt that such was the case with St. Paul himself in his early years, so genial and earnest his whole development seems to have been; and it is generally the case, that all truly healthy culture starts from a true beginning.

Regarding the first ten years of life as the period of childhood, we remark that the child's traits are chiefly these three; sensuousness, imitation, unconsciousness, or impulsiveness. He is sensuous; we do not say sensual, for this word is a libel even upon the earliest years, since however much the infant lives in the world of the senses, the senses themselves start elevating thoughts, and stir beautiful affections in the little creature so dependent upon sight and touch for impressions.

Compare for example the appetite of a child for food with the appetite of a gluttonous man. Give a branch of red cherries, or a ripe downy peach to that playful, curly-headed boy, and the feast is to him a lyric poem in which the merriest fancy waits on the revel of his lips. Compare him, then, with some bloated *gourmand* over his loaded table, and you see all the difference between healthy senses, and the low sensuality that makes a god of the belly.

The child is imitative, and very prone to do as others do around him. He is unconscious—unconscious of his own powers and affections, speaking and acting as the impulse moves him, without the trouble of comparing various thoughts or reconciling inconsistencies of conduct. Ideas, feelings, and purposes come and go like visitations from some involuntary source; so that his mind is as much the play-ground of its own emotions and associations, as the sky is the play-ground of the clouds.

> " Gay hope is theirs, by fancy fed,
> Less pleasing, when possest;
> The tear forgot as soon as shed,
> The sunshine of the breast."

For the first five years, this unconsciousness generally continues, and it is the office of the second five years of childhood to bring the impulses under some self-command, and educate the mind to habits of reflection and coherence without breaking down its naturalness.

Such is childhood in its most conspicuous traits; but why try to analyze and define them, when we see the original so clearly before us, and we all know so well the young life so busy with the senses, so dependent and imitative, so impulsive and spontaneous?

The practical question comes, how is this period to be treated, or what is the *religious nurture* of childhood? Our reply is exactly in accordance with its own nature, and the nature of religion. Is the child a sensuous, imitative, impulsive creature? then bring religion in such a way that he can see and feel it, without ceasing to be a child, or being spoiled into a little mope or bigot. Does he live very much under the influence of his senses, and little in the power of abstract ideas? then make religion a plain fact to his senses; let God's mind be shown in his works; let Christ's mission, character, and deeds, be set forth simply and plainly to the perceptions in simple narrative and expressive illustrations; let morality be made a specific discipline; and above all, let the elders of the family show clearly in their own temper and manners, that religion is something sacred and beautiful, something as much a matter of fact as the pleasant sunshine or the daily bread.

Again, is the child imitative, and proving thus by this very instinct that he was not made to lead, but to follow, and seeming to be looking around him for some standard of conduct, as much as to say, "I am not sufficient for myself; I cannot go alone; show me what I shall do, and I will do it?" What is plainer than that right habits should be clearly set before him, so that imitation may lead him in the true paths, and doing as others do, he may do what is right. Think of this wisely, and it may put a check upon our petulance or worldliness, yet it should not interfere with our proper ease or naturalness to know what open eyes are watching us. Artificial solemnity, a put-on sweetness, or make-believe devotion, will not do, and our children will soon find us out in such tricks. Let us have a true, reasonable, cheerful reverence and good will, and act accordingly in a sensible, consistent way, and they will know it, and their ready instinct of imitation will win from our heart and manner the grace that they need. There is a great deal too much baby-talk and baby-acting among elders; and some people try to make a child's toy of religion itself. Away with such folly. In all simplicity, but with full heart and wisdom, present Christianity before our children as it lives in our own experience; and while we teach them to say their prayers in certain words, teach them also by our own example, by making devotion a family habit, in which each child who can read a sentence shall take an active part, and so be one of God's children with us. The main point at issue is not the imitating a certain manner, but the catching a certain spirit, and be assured that there is no conviction so deep, no aspiration so tender, that something of its power may not reach and nurture the unreflective and impulsive creature so susceptible of every magnetic impression.

Is there not also a way of presenting religion to the child, as being an impulsive as well as a sensuous and imitative creature? A being so subject to moods of wilfulness, may be won to visitations of a gentle spirit, and the expulsive power of a new affection may put away the evil impulse that for the time has mastered the heart. Think of this fact seriously; remember how often we ourselves, with all our reflection and self-control, are possessed, apparently, without our own will, by some dismal fancy or petulant humor, and we fight against it in vain, until something occurs to change the scene and the mood; and then make charitable allowance for the wayward impulses of childhood. Instead of fighting against the evil spirit in something of its own obstinacy, try to touch another chord, to overcome evil with good, and charm away the dark visitant, as David's harp charmed away the gloom of the moody Saul. Great is the power of a genial, dignified religious temper, in working thus upon the impulsive nature of the child, and winning a wayward humor to reason and good will.

To reason—can a child be expected to be reasonable ? Yes, eminently so, but not to enter into abstract reasoning. He is reasonable who has a sense of what is right or proper, whether he can define or explain it or not; whilst he is a reasoner, who can state the grounds of his conviction in connected, logical propositions. According to this definition, the child can be reasonable without being a reasoner, nay, from the very dormancy of the logical faculty, he seems gifted often with a singular insight into character and conduct. Put a case of action clearly before an unsophisticated child, and you will find yourself frequently amazed by the sense of right, the keen intuitive judgment of the little umpire. You will find your own motives seen into in the same way by young critics who have never taken lessons of Lavater or Spurzheim. Let this faculty of insight be sacredly cherished ; and instead of perplexing the brain with abstract propositions or dry deductions, let the facts of life, whether religion, history, or nature, be brought before the child, and the reason will strengthen its intuition long before the time for reasoning has come. Our Saviour understood this well ; and when he called young children to him and blessed them, he left with them an impression of himself stronger than any argument,—an impression upon their reason in its quick insight long before they could reason upon his words. Let us all do likewise, and present the facts of life before the abstractions of philosophy to the young mind, and so we train it to the best philosophy at last.

Thus we believe in making a religion a fact to childhood, alike in view of its being sensuous, imitative, and spontaneous.

But the Future, the training for the cares to come, what shall we say of this? Who can help thinking of this, when we look thoughtfully upon children at their play, in the mood of the poet, as he returned to the old school-house, about which a new generation was gamboling :—

> Alas, regardless of their doom,
>   The little victims play!
> No sense have they of ills to come,
>   Nor care beyond to-day.
> Yet see how all around them wait
> The ministers of human fate,
> And black misfortune's baleful train.

Shall we sadden them with constant homilies, on care, and pain, and disappointment, and vice, and crime, and sin, and death, and hell? No, not so; but deal with the soul as God would have us deal with the body—preoccupy it with what is good and true, and useful, so shall it best contend against the world's trials, when they come. Begin from the first with recognizing the child as a religious being, a subject of the divine government, and to be brought up in its truths and affections. Take this stand, and your whole course of nurture is a preparation of the child for maturity. You will preoccupy the mind with a genial, pure and reverent, liberal Christianity, just as you try to preoccupy the veins with wholesome blood, and the lungs with wholesome air. The same method will enable you to meet speculative questions which are sometimes started by children, and which cannot be answered by any reasoning simple enough for their apprehension. Preoccupy them with a just faith in God, in Christ and immortality, and their reason will have a due sense of those august truths long before they can reason them out. That judicious writer on Home Education, Isaac Taylor, remarks that each season of life is preceded by a period of thoughtfulness, when the mind, in spite of its follies and passions, " tries its strength upon those insoluble problems which sages have so often professed to have disposed of, but which still continue to torment human reason, even from its earliest dawn. There are indications sometimes of a crisis of this sort in the fifth year; still more decisively in the tenth or eleventh; and again in the eighteenth. It is at these moments that the soul comes to a stand, for an instant, and asks, whither am I going? "

Let such states of perplexity be met by whatever arguments or illustrations may serve; but in childhood, surely the best answer is the positive truth set forth in the life or in words that carry life with them, the life of faith and love. The verses or hymns that breathe the spirit of filial trust, Christian affection, persevering obedience, heavenly hope, will carry the perplexed soul through such a time of misgiving better far than Paley's Evidences or Butler's Analogy, or all the abstract metaphysics ever written, and admirable enough in their way. We believe much in this power of verse to preoccupy the mind with truth; and in doing it, we follow the hint of Providence and fall in with the child's ready instinct for rhythm. The spring-time of life, like that of nature, may fitly begin in song, and musical words with a loving spirit fitly ushers the child into a sense of the meaning of that moral kingdom, which the graver seasons of life are to develop by so many labors and trials.

With all due sense of the infirmity and exposures of our nature, nurture the child within the divine kingdom, and preoccupy his mind with right impressions. Then childhood shall be happy and reasonable, cheerful and reverent. If the future on earth is denied, kind heaven will continue the discipline in another world, and the memory left here below will of itself be a blessed hope. Full is this blooming earth of the graves of children; and as it rolls through the blue ether, with the din of its passions and the hum of its business, and the song of its joy, there rises to the ear of Heaven the plaintive cry of bereaved parents more constant than the drum-beat of martial empire. Let that plaintive cry lose its anguish and not lose its depth by the comfort of a heavenly faith, and let us write on the sod where you plant the violets of remembrance, words like these :—

> Here rests one of few years and few sorrows.
> Living he did God's work, and dying does it still!
> Living, he opened new springs of love on earth,
> Dying, he wins new hearts to Christ and heaven.

The dust is not the saddest grave of childhood, but its saddest grave is the heart that outlives its own early days only to renounce their childlike spirit, and bury their innocence in a living sepulchre. O beware of this! and by a true, progressive life, let the child's heart still beat on in the bosom of the man. Forsake nothing that has· been simple, confiding, loving. Take one of the ruddy apples which the exuberant harvest gives, divide it, and see in its core the very mark of the blossom in which, last spring, it began. Think of this, and in the core of your mature being, cherish the blossom of your own spring-time, and enter the kingdom of heaven like a little child. This was in the apostle's thought, when looking forward from his present reasoning, believing, yet somewhat darkling estate, he contemplated the great transformation that should complete his progressive being, and bring out his early intuitions and mature questionings into the fulness of the heavenly vision, where, no longer seeing through a mirror darkly, he should see face to face in the spirit and the presence of that love which is the end of all faith and hope.

Into that presence, Father in Heaven, lead us with joy and with trembling. More and more, as earthly guardians fall and earthly homes are broken, we need the love that is eternal, and the mansions that do not decay.

III.

The Song that never Tires.

O human heart! thou hast a song
For all that to the earth belong,
Whene'er the golden chain of love
Hath linked thee to the heaven above.

O human heart! what deed of thine
Could gain a kingdom so divine?
O human heart! that singest still
Through chastening good, misreckoned ill.

S. F. ADAMS.

THE SONG THAT NEVER TIRES.

We are all of us at some time singers, and however dull our ear or poor our voice, we cannot help singing forth, in some way, the feeling that is in us. Perhaps one of the best proofs that the instinct of song lies in our very nature, is in the fact, that many who have no music for others, have enough of it for themselves, and the sweet voice within the heart itself disguises to them the discord of their lips. Most of the chief Mile Stones of our life-journey are passed with a song. We go through our infancy to the sound of nursery rhymes, and as we enter the grave, faith sings her requiem over our dust. The workman cheers his task with some stirring strain, and the marriage feast is not complete until some song or hymn consecrates the union by the harmony of voices.

This season at which we are now writing, has surely been a time of singing with us, in our great city; and in more ways than one, our people have kept up the festive tone which the old Church in some manner sanctions, wil-

5

ling to prolong the carols of Christmas into the very threshold of the Lenten Fast, and make her children the more ready to go into the shade, from satiety of the world's garish light. The glee of the Carnival, in some measure, reaches through the earth, and few persons are there so sad or so secluded, as to have no cheerful notes ringing in their ears. I would carry out the remarks upon childhood by illustrating the Christian element in song, not as a passing sound, but as a permanent force. In other words, I would speak of true life as a continuous song, alike in its spirit, form, and object.

O sing unto the Lord a new song, said the Psalmist. We repeat the words, and trace them up to the true spirit of the divine kingdom. The lyric sentiment that breathes itself out in music, is but one of the forms of that universal fact of inspiration that pervades all nature, and culminates in the human soul. We are not speaking now of that supernatural inspiration peculiar to the great prophets of the human race, but of the gift within the usual order of Providence. Every creature, in the measure of its faculties, was made to be moved by a spirit greater than itself. The insect of a day, flutters out its brief span in a glow f animal spirits passing its own power; bird and beast, in their larger care and forethought, obey an instinct higher than their knowledge; and man, made in his Maker's image, is called to keep his soul ever open to the heavenly breath that created him. Man in all ages, and under all manners, customs, and creeds, is the most inspired of beings, and feels most deeply the movings of a force within him, but not of him. This force makes him rejoice in lyrical sounds and actions, in songs and hymns, festive dances, warlike marches, and every form of music and eloquence. The Old Dispensation is full of it, and the stern lawgiver himself, more than once poured forth his devotion in a solemn song, and strung first the mighty harp which the Psalmist so perfected. What shall we do with this element under the Christian dispensation? Shut it up, as some try to do, within its ancient channels, and allow it to move only in the words of the old Hebrew Psalms? Or shall we put it under ban altogether, as others try to do, and aim to reduce man to a calculating machine, or a logic mill, without enthusiasm, without poetry or song?

Not so; but we will do with the lyrical element in our nature, with the faculty most open to inspiration, just what the Psalmist indicates and God himself decrees. Cherish it most sacredly, and make it animate the whole domain of life, instead of inditing a few hymns or framing choral dances. The new song was to show forth salvation from day to day, and thus be a daily spirit instead of an evanescent word. In the Gospel, the same idea is constantly recognized. Jesus came to incarnate the Word that breathed into nature all its harmonies, and the New Testament ends with the new song of the redeemed around the eternal throne. The gospel begins with the song of the angels at the birth of Christ, and calls on all men to live lives in harmony with that heavenly strain. It opens to us at once

the heights of the divine kingdom, and bids us open the
deeps of our own being to its promised spirit. It concerned
itself less with nicely chosen words, and balanced verse,
and cunning instruments, because it worked in a mightier
material, and subdued men themselves into its mouthpieces
and instruments, until life itself began to move to the
hymn of heavenly love. It is an essential fact of Christianity, that it calls upon men to receive the divine spirit,
as breathed from the Father through the life of the Messiah, and regards them as truly living, or fully born, only
when they are possessed by this spirit, and are thus not
their own, but God's.

This idea is, indeed, capable of being perverted into
the wildest fanaticism, and of making people rave like
madmen in the name of religion. But to deny it, is worse
than to pervert it, and the soberest practical obedience is
its most consistent declaration. What does it mean but
simply this, that, under the Christian dispensation, we are
to start with a filial spirit that shall run freely and faithfully through the whole of life, and breathe a cheerful
loyalty through all its thoughts, desires, and labors. Look
to every word of our Saviour's, look to the words and deeds
of every follower true to his kingdom, and we are at littl
loss to understand how the Gospel interpreted the Psalm,
and the new song declared the true salvation from day to
day. A true life is the new song, for from beginning
to end it is moved by the Spirit, and so follows a divine
inspiration.

Starting from such a source, the new song must take its appropriate form, and through all its changes of tones and times, it must not lose sight of its inspiring theme. In all variety, it must keep its essential unity, and in cheerful faith and good will move onward still in the march of life. The exact form of our experience, we cannot control, any more than we can control our stature, our talents or our skies. Every man has an air of his own, and must expect to keep its characteristic in whatever he does, however good or bad in his purposes, well or ill disciplined in his habits. It is in his own way that he is called to serve God, and in his own way take his part in the psalm of life. True principle and true discipline, instead of crushing his individuality, will bring it out, and so make him more truly himself, in reconciling him with God.

We cannot expect to change our temperament or our circumstances at will, but we may rule our tempers, and use our circumstances, so as to conform our lives to the right spirit, and bear a true purpose to the end. We cannot say to what heights or depths of experience we shall be called by the allotments of Providence, but we may in good measure say how we shall receive what comes to us, may never be giddy when on the high places of joy, and never despair when down in the deeps of sorrow. The new song, which the Divine Comforter inspires, keeps the same essential spirit throughout all these variations. From the same inspiration comes the Jubilate and the De Profundis, keeping humility in gladness, and trust in affliction :

O come, let us sing unto the Lord,
Let us make a joyful noise to the rock of our salvation,

as in that other strain:

Out of the depths have I cried unto Thee, O Lord!
Lord, hear my voice; let thine ear be attentive to the voice of
my supplications.

Marvellously the life of Jesus keeps the essential unity, and the same love that said, "Now is the Son of Man glorified, and God is glorified in him," also said, "if it be possible, let this cup pass from me," and "Father, into thy hands I commend my spirit." Such perfect consistency we may not expect, but surely we gain in peace and wisdom as we approach it, and through all the changes of our many-toned life, whether festive or mournful, keep the same theme, and rule our spirits in the same heart of faith and love.

What times we shall fall upon, it is not for us to decide; but it depends upon us in a great measure how we shall time our plans and steps to events as they come. Without such timing, feeble and broken is the psalm of life—far indeed from the new song that declares salvatio from day to day. Too hurried sometimes in our fever of impatience, too sluggish sometimes in our easy indolence, we go from one extreme to another, and, exhausted by foolish haste, we sink into imbecile torpor. Wiser and happier is he who keeps a healthy pulse through all vicissitudes, and has a time for every thing, and every thing in its time. Then a true method regulates the countless cares and labors of our lot. Then a round of habits, orderly, but not slavish, free, yet not capricious, wins life into its cycles, and hours, days, months, years, move on recurrent yet progressive, like the verses of a hymn which keep their appointed measure, yet swell as they continue, and concentrate force as they advance. Happy the man whose life, thus timed and toned, chants from day to day the new song of faith and love.

He draws ever nearer the true object of life, and harmonizes all his powers and opportunities into conformity with his master purpose. This is the crown of all, the hardest and noblest task, to subdue into practical harmony the various and conflicting elements of our condition. Most thoughtful men have the idea, and all earnest men have the aspiration, but only the thoroughly devoted make the realization of a true spiritual order in the whole method of life. In youth certainly we often dream of maintaining a noble ideal above jarring passions and base expedients. But the world is apt to be too strong for our aspiration, and finds in our own hearts too ready allies of its devices. Then we give in to the prevailing follies, renew our ideal only in romances or reverie, and allow life to be as vulgar and prosaic as our visions are proved to be impracticable. But no man can substantiate any claim to true culture, much less to Christian fidelity, who is willing thus to give up his fairest hope and blind himself to his bright star, because so many bewildering meteors flash along his path. The true man walks still by its brightness, until the illusions disappear;—he keeps up the just tone of his spirit, and gradually subdues all discords into peace.

Is the discord in himself or in his circumstances, he does not despair of abating it. Is it in himself? What man, who has ever aspired to wisdom and self-command, has not found himself challenged by some rebel within the camp, who says, " I defy you, O imperious conscience or master will, and if all others agree, I will not? " What man, who has ever won wisdom and self-command, has not met the challenge bravely, and made of the very rebel a submissive servant—yes, made anger the spur of justice, pride the ally of self-respect, and even indolence the helper of just tranquillity. Let each man have a keen eye on the rebel passion or habit in himself, that makes the rudest jar against the harmony of his life, and not be content until the rebel is trained into the general order and swells the general strain.

They that may triumph tolerably well in such self-discipline, may complain of the sad discord between their mind and their circumstances, and live in a continual warfare of the desire against the deed, the wish against the opportunity. Here is the grief of the noblest souls, an ideal which no reality equals, and which common life insults. Each heart shares the bitterness in its own way—complains of stinted fortune, or uncongenial society, or ill requited kindness, or limited education—complains of

some special disappointment that leaves a dark mark upon
the memory, or of some abiding grief that clouds and mars
the whole course of years. Let every man look well to the
chief point of incongruity between his lot and his wishes,
and strive to bring it into harmony with his master purpose ; he will find himself surprised at the triumph in store
for him, if he persoveres. Let him try to subdue the re-
fractory circumstance to his own mind, and the effort cannot be utterly vain ; let him, in respect to whatever incongruity is inevitable between his wish and his lot, try to
subdue his mind to his circumstance, and a deeper peace,
a diviner harmony may spring from the victory. The common people whom he befriends may school him into better
feelings than any fellowship of wits ;—the drudging labors
that he performs cheerfully may develope nobler energies
than any dainty leisure ;—the sacrifices that he bears patiently may nurture within him purer affections than the
rarest ministry of the beautiful arts ;—a brave purpose
amidst the difficulties of his position, may do more to con-
solidate his character than a library of ethical abstractions ;—fidelity constant and judicious in the trials of his
business, or the griefs of his family, may reveal more moral
beauty than Italy can unfold, and tell him more of the
divine kingdom than any oratory can convey. Not at
once, but at last, a true heart will subdue all things to
itself, bring all jarring elements into the general harmony,
and make every faculty and every circumstance join its
voice in chanting the new song to the Lord.

5*

Thus we meditate upon the new song or a life inspired by God's love, expressing itself in melodious form, and harmonizing all powers and opportunities into conformity with its aim. Is this too much to ask of us in this perplexed, working-day world, where we are beset with so many cares and temptations that threaten our temper, and break our time, and divide our thought? No man surely will be willing to state the opposite, and say that there is nothing lyrical in life, and the new song is for angels, and not at all for this world. The most practical men best exemplify our meaning, for they start with the most cheerful purpose, and bring all their faculties and chances into harmony with their aim. By all work that is earnest, and all prayer that is fervent, the end is sought, and every genuine life passes into deeper concord as it advances.

When you work, O man, sing the new song of heavenly love, and make your work lighter and stronger for the strain. Take labor as the allotment of divine mercy, and use its discipline in such a way as to work out your powers into just play, and your opportunities into just order. It is God's method of our discipline, and every man is a crude discordant creature, until he sets himself to a worthy task, and works himself into true shape and temper. Toil on cheerfully, and the cares that once threatened to make you slave shall make you master, and they shall sing to you of your triumphs, instead of groaning to you of their exactions. Your work shall open to you God's purpose in your being, and help you in your prayers.

Life has its crowning joy, when most pervaded by the sense of God's presence and grace—when daily experience chimes best with hymn and prayer. We sing the new song most blessedly when we yield up our wills to the Divine will, and the Infinite Mind guides us, the Eternal Word moves us. O how poor all our definitions are, when compared with the least personal experience of the Divine life within. What is the rhythmic joy of all nature, but the varied expression of the Creator Spirit, the uncreated Word that is ever speaking from God and of God. There is rhythm or song throughout the universe—in the recurrent order of the seasons—the cycles of the stars—the beat of the pulse—the step of the feet—the surging of the seas—the undulation of light and sound, as well as in the music of measured verse and song. Man can do nothing without touching upon this great law of creation; and the recurrent roll or dash of the most utilitarian machinery, the march of the most prosaic procession, combines with epic and psalm to illustrate the recurrent and progressive order which God has sanctioned throughout his universe. If the lowest creatures so feel the impress of this harmony, what must that mind be from whom it comes, and of whose infinite peace and blessed order, our holiest experience, our most rapturous joy, gives but a faint reflection. If God's words spoken in his works, spoken in the Scriptures of revelation, and in a measure in every writing of true wisdom and eloquence, have such inspiration, beauty, harmony—what must the *Word* itself be, the original of all that is loveliest in sound, or feeling, or thought. Glory in the

Highest, that the Word has been so clothed in humanity and dwelt among us. Behold and reflect its glory, and with heart and life sing the new song:

Worthy is the lamb that was slain to receive power, and riches, and wisdom, and strength, and honor, and glory, and blessing.

Blessing, and honor, and glory, and power be unto Him that sitteth upon the throne, and unto the Lamb for ever and ever.

Let the hymns that are taught to happy childhood be imbued with this strain; and let youth, manhood, and age, swell its volume by their greater compass, whilst they must deepen its tone by their deeper and sometimes darker experience.

IV.

Youth.

O Life! how pleasant is thy morning,
Young Fancy's rays the hills adorning!
Cold-pausing Caution's lesson scorning,
        We frisk away,
Like school-boys at th' expected warning,
        To joy and play.
We wander here, we wander there,
We eye the Rose upon the brier,
Unmindful that the Thorn is near,
        Among the leaves.
                                BURNS.

    Straight forward goes
The lightning's path, and straight the fearful path
Of the cannon ball.   Direct it flies and rapid,
Shattering that it may reach and shattering what it reaches
My son! the road the human being travels,
That on which BLESSING comes and goes, doth follow
The river's course, the valley's playful windings,
Curves round the cornfield and the hill of vines,
Honoring the holy bounds of property!
And thus secure, though late, leads to its end.
                                SCHILLER.

THE philosophy that has come from thrones is a sad one, and savors far more of the school of Heraclitus the weeper than of Democritus the laugher. They who have every luxury to satiety, and every honor to weariness, to whom fortune can add little happiness, and to whom disappointment seems very treason, have not generally had very cheerful lives, and the ascetic confessors of crowned heads, have not found much reason to call the story whispered by royal lips, any happier, to say the least, than that which has been said with more trembling by the untitled or the poor. Ecclesiastes, the preacher, in order to give point to his book on the vanity of the world, takes his stand in the palace, builds his pulpit upon the throne, and in the name of Solomon, the most magnificent of kings, discourses of the follies of mankind. Yet, in every point, he redeems satire from skepticism, and uses folly as a foil to show better the worth of heavenly wisdom. In the closing chapter, as he thinks of the happiness of youth, he quits the vein of satire altogether, the cynic becomes not a little of an enthusiast, and he bids the young enjoy themselves to the full, only remembering to temper their joy with devout judgment, as in their Creator's presence.

Here, then, is our subject, so cheerful, yet from the saddest book in the Bible. Youth:—

Its rejoicing in privileges.

Its remembering of responsibilities.

Its rejoicing. Rejoice, O young man, in thy youth. Why? For many reasons that can be specified, as well as for the reason that need not be specified, the reason, that youth cannot well help rejoicing, and the young man's heart cheers him because it is young—full of fresh life and overflowing spirits. It was said by Rousseau, that the period between the twelfth and the seventeenth year is the only time when man is absolutely happy; inasmuch as it is then only, that his forces of body and mind much exceed his desires. Surely, at this season, or perhaps during the whole time from ten to twenty, there is more power on hand, in proportion to the demands made upon it, than at any other time.

But even this exuberant strength must have a serious meaning, and its spontaneous joy is intended to be the germinating time of great purposes. Rejoice, then, O young man, in the days of thy youth, and let thy heart, in its glad fulness, cheer thee, yet remember that all power brings responsibility, and even for this joy, God will call thee to judgment.

Without dividing these remarks into two separate sections, I will follow the two lines of thought through the chief spheres of youthful experience, and show how it is, that responsibility walks hand in hand with privilege.

Among the foremost pleasures of youth, stands the growing consciousness of personal liberty. Each year, after the dependence of childhood ceases, some new drops are poured into the thrilling cup of conscious freedom. The feeling with which the man throws his first vote or first signs his name to an agreement in his own right, is as nothing compared with the feeling with which the boy first roams the street unattended, or ranges the country with his horse, or gun, or fishing-rod. This sense of liberty brings out a great and noble instinct, which God has put into the soul. Rejoice in it, O young man, and let thy heart cheer thee with the high sentiment of freedom, which has made nations great, and genius noble. But remember that fearful danger lurks in thy very joy, and that God holds thee responsible for the use of thy liberty. You are no longer to be led by the hand of your parents, and are therefore called to take hold of the hand of God. You no longer depend implicitly upon the will of men, and are therefore prepared to lean upon that will, subjection to which, is the only freedom. Your liberty will become miserable wilfulness, unless it follows law, even the true law of life, as declared in nature and by the Gospel.

Learn this truth early, the earlier the better. When you are tempted by your own impulses, or unprincipled companions, to mistake self-indulgence for dignity, or wilfulness for manhood, remember that you enslave yourself in the very delusion of your boasted liberty, like the poor sot who is dreaming of grasping a sceptre, while he drains the cup that is to drag him down to the dust. Yes, it is true —all emancipation from outward restraint becomes new servitude, unless it is made the occasion of higher allegiance. The body, emancipated from leading-strings, is lost, unless its freed limbs move in harmony with its own laws, and the laws of the universe. The mind, too, is lost unless it finds a higher authority than that which it puts off with the dress of childhood, and learns self-government with its independence.

Youth is the time to think seriously, religiously, of this great truth, and exalt and strengthen its conscious liberty, into the confidence of faith, and the steadfastness of law. Sadly it forgets this, and homes without number are made wretched, because young men mistake license for freedom, and make utter shipwreck of themselves by launching wildly upon the great sea of life, without compass or pilot, at the very time when God and conscience call them to choose the sufficient guide. Happy—happy the youth who makes so little of this mistake, that he can correct it, and taught wisdom by a sip of folly, learns that the best liberty, is the truest obedience and the most reverent conscientiousness. Rejoice, then, in thy conscious freedom, O young man, and let thy heart cheer thee, and walk in the ways of thine heart, and the sight of thine eyes, but remember that God will bring thee to judgment for this, and his sentence will not fail to arrest you, if you make liberty license instead of law.

Another of the peculiar pleasures of youth lies in the sense of growing power. Childhood is hardly conscious of its own energies, and the mind works with a certain spontaneousness that takes as little thought of itself, as the healthy blood takes thought of its own tides. But gleams of consciousness ere long come, and at the age of eleven or twelve, certainly as early as fourteen, there is something like a distinct conviction of the youth's characteristic powers. The leading tastes, and talents, and dispositions, begin to show themselves with some definiteness, and the youth takes vast delight in the consciousness of his resources. He perceives, compares, judges, fancies, schemes, and has the feeling, that within his mind, as within a tent, lie great forces encamped, and from time to time, they are putting on their armor, and each going out into the field. This experience is occasion for rejoicing, since God has attached to every faculty a peculiar happiness in its own activity, and as the insects of a day spread with joy their gossamer wings to the sunshine, so the soul, the immortal Psyche, takes vast delight in pluming and trying her pinions for her unending flight. Rejoice, O young man, then, in the sense of growing power, but remember, O sacredly, religiously remember, that for this very privilege God will hold thee to judgment. Regard those powers, not with pride or conceit, but with humility and fidelity. Yes, let each faculty, as it rises in the morning of its day into distinct consciousness, bow down before its Maker and its God, and consecrate itself to a true life-service. Without this, power is weakness, and talent is vanity. Remember that every gift brings an obligation, and as the gift first opens into consciousness, let it open into true service.

Remember this, young man, or you are nothing. You are to be weighed by God and man in the measure of your usefulness. No matter who or what you are, or who your father is, or who your connections are, or what your wealth or poverty may be, whatever your talents or position, the main point in your destiny turns upon this question, " Do you mean to be useful or do you not — do you mean to serve God and your time faithfully, and do a good work in the world, or do you mean to cumber the ground by a life of conceit, selfishness and folly ? " He who begins otherwise than with a purpose to be faithful, begins wrong, and strays worse the farther he goes in that wrong path. Shun it, and take the right way. The lives of the strong and the great of this world urge upon us this truth. Look to the graves of late greenest among the dust of the great in both hemispheres. Think of the great captain of our mother country, with all his prejudices, so faithful in peace and war to his sworn allegiance. Think of him, our own great statesman, but a little while ago laid in the grave in presence of thousands who thronged that village home, and read in the oak and the flowers on his coffin, fit ciphers of the strength and beauty of his mind. With all his frailties, and it would be strange if a man made on so large a scale should not have some, he began life with the idea of service, and his youthful aspirations and his maturest thoughts, are all stamped with that idea. He grew up with the idea that his mind was to be a working force, and the very same feeling which beat in his heart when he heard with tears his father's promise that he should go to college, came out in all the great acts of his life, and gave tone to his dying words. If in any acts of his life, he fell from this great allegiance, his own conscience became his severest judge, and his weakness, as well as his power, teaches the majesty of true service. Higher, deeper, than any standard of worldly greatness, is the rule of the gospel. The Master bids us all measure obligation by privilege, and calls on the young to give all their powers to the service of the divine kingdom. Rejoice in your power, O young man, be it much or little. Remember to use it well—to choose religiously and to follow faithfully your worldly business or profession, and above and within all other vocations, keep in mind that we are all called of God in Jesus Christ.

Once more, and to sum up all, it is one of the pleasures of youth to possess a certain indefinable enthusiasm, which gives the character a peculiar charm, and which throws over life an unspeakable freshness and delight. Rejoice in this—feel the beatings of a young heart, and do not for worlds surrender that generous ardor, for a chilling worldly prudence, which is bad enough in an old man, but more monstrous than decrepitude itself, in youth. Have your enthusiasm, have hearty hopes and warm friendships, and be willing to dream some overfond dreams. But remember that God holds thee to judgment for this—remember that this very exuberance of feeling is the substance from which your best affections and principles should be formed, the exuberant sap which should shape and mature the trunk, and leaf, and fruit of a manly character. To let it go out in youthful lusts and unhallowed passions, would be like draining the young plant of its juices, to distil them into draughts of madness, instead of leaving them in their own appointed channels. Be pure, be true, be faithful, and your very enthusiasm will harden into strength and grow into virtue, and bloom into lasting nobleness. Yes, follow God's bidding, and you will find, that as years gather over you, and your emotions are less susceptible, they lose their impulsiveness without losing their power, and the enthusiasm of the youth is consolidated into the honor, fidelity, and good-will of the man.

And this leads us to the main point of our thought, the need of making youth a season of direct religious obligation. Sad it is, when this susceptible time passes, and the affections are not led to God, and the acquiescence of childhood in what is taught as religion, is not confirmed, by the youth, on his own personal responsibility. It is never too late, indeed, to repent and believe, but it is none the less certain, that a man cannot by subsequent amendment, ever make up for the loss of early religion, for the loss of that early fidelity to God, which breathes the fresh fervor of young enthusiasm into faith, and twines all the pleasant associations of the morning of our days with the truths and hopes of Christianity. Think of this, O youth, think of this, O parents, and do not pursue your too frequent error, of consigning the most formative of all periods of our moral life, to the giddiness of the passions and the dissipations of the world. The Christian church needs the young within its fold, to give it freshness and beauty; the young need the church, to subdue their wilfulness, and to nurture their enthusiasm into a heavenly faith and hope. Think of this, youth whose eye rests upon this page, and deem your education all incomplete, until you have learned enough and schooled your feelings enough, to take your stand among intelligent believers, and sit in token of your settled faith and your avowed need, at the table of communion to which the gospel calls you. Think of this, parents, and by your example and counsel, establish your children in healthful, reasonable, quickening religious convictions, and lead the way to the fold of the good shepherd. This course is the prevention of all skepticism, by a spirit above the power of every denying argument; it is the cure for all disappointment, by the peace and love that cannot disappoint.

Seriously, now, and without any straining or pretension — what good on earth is so great, as a cheerful, large, steadfast Christian faith and purpose in youth, establishing every blessing by a duty, and exalting every worthy sentiment into a principle? What better security against the chances and changes of the world — what better safe-guard of just influence and abiding welfare — what better preservative of that which makes youth so fresh and hopeful?

There is something in youth, that of itself leads us to adore the ineffable goodness of that majestic Being, who knows no declining years, and whose bliss ever rejuvenates itself in blessedness unspeakable. The nearer we approach to God, we perpetuate our early joy and breathe the youth immortal. Do not the truest men partake somewhat of this privilege — the men who, by purity of life, and heartiness of affection, and fidelity in well-doing, have confirmed into principles the best enthusiasm of their early days, who have led liberty up to law, and power to allegiance, and impulse into conviction? Have they not about them, to their latest years, a freshness and charm that the world cannot give? Do they not carry into the winter of their days, the sweet balms of summer flowers? have they not struck *in* the fairy tints of early fancy? have they not opened, within the breaking cistern of earthly feeling, a channel into that living spring whence gush the fountains of immortal youth?

At best we are a frail generation, yet how much good, the good God offers us. The youths shall faint and be weary, the young men shall utterly fail, but they that wait upon the Lord shall renew their strength, they shall mount up with wings as eagles, they shall run and not be weary, they shall walk and not faint. The best philosophy, most confirms this blessed faith.

V.

The True Fire.

What is this that stirs within,
Loving goodness, hating sin,
Always craving to be blest,
Finding here below no rest?

What is it? and whither? whence?
This unsleeping, secret sense,
Longing for its rest and food
In some hidden untried good?

'Tis the soul!   Mysterious Name!
Him it seeks from whom it came;
It would, Mighty God, like Thee,
Holy, holy holy, be!

FURNESS.

THE TRUE FIRE.

The events that decide a man's destiny are not often those which figure most largely in his external experience, and are most frequently spoken of by his friends. We all have our own secret history, whose honor or shame can be fully known only to ourselves. At some point in the great journey, whether sooner or later, we meet some one of God's messengers who reveals himself to us alone, and our character takes its turn for good or evil, according to our reception of his message. The fire still burns that of old shone upon Moses in Horeb, and the voice still speaks that called to the child Samuel in the temple.

It was at the most momentous point of his life tha this visitation came to the great Jewish lawgiver, as h was tending the flock of Jethro in the solitudes of Horeb. The Divine presence appeared to him in a bush which burned without being consumed, and at once compelled him to listen to the voice that spoke, and became to him of itself a most expressive symbol of the light of the God speaking. "Yes," this heroic man could say to himself as he gazed, "yes, there is a fire that can burn without burning out; my hopes for my name and race are not to die away with the youthful heats that mature years have now cooled; my aspirations for some nearer presence of God are not always to waver with the lights and shades of nature and fortune; there is a glory uncreated which is to be made known; here it shines upon my poor vision, and by this bush, now bright with the heavenly shekinah, my faith is fixed, that God will be a burning, abiding light to his people, and they are called to be burning, abiding lights of his kingdom."

The passage presents two subjects intimately connected and illustrating each other. It affords an emblem of God's revelation to man through that Word of nature and Scripture, which never fails; it affords, too, an emblem of man's revelation of God through the light of a true life which never dies out. Intimately connected the two subjects are, for we cannot speak wisely of what God has revealed without looking for its marks into the experience of men, and we cannot speak wisely of the experience of man without considering God's work within his soul. We take a branch of the second subject, the light in man's own life, and treat the first, the light of revelation, only as it may be connected with it. We would meditate now upon a true life-purpose, or the fire that a man should carry within him ever, that he may do his work well, serve his neighbor, save his soul, and show forth the glory of his Creator. This true fire burns, but does not burn out; it lights and warms every sphere of life, whilst it is fed from a d.vine and unfailing source—unfailing as the immortality of which it is the pledge.

The true fire that burns without wasting away is lighted within the soul, when the will of man is brought into just contact with the love and truth of God. It is lighted whenever a man feels that there is a spirit within him, and that this spirit is bound by its own being as well as by heaven's law, to live in the divine presence and be faithful to the divine kingdom. Then the true life-purpose is kindled, and needs no change but progress to give healthful glow to every faculty and work of existence. This is the proper central fire of a man, having its seat in that power of will which gives him his personality, fed by all the affections that ally him with his neighbor and his God, spreading in all the lines of influence which heavenly wisdom decrees. Without something of this fire in him, man ceases to be man, and is baser than the grossest savage who gropes so dimly after God as to bow down to an idol in the name of religion, and so misinterprets the law of rectitude as to sacrifice his own life to revenge a wrong to his brother or kinsman; for such a savage, after his rude fashion, tries to be faithful, and is above the utter infidel's degradation. With much of this fire in him, man draws near the Father, and more approaches that perfect Son, who said, "My Father worketh hitherto, and I work," and in every thought and feeling served the living God.

Is this rightly called the true fire, and will it burn

without burning out? That surely is the true fire which best warms and lights the life. What does this better than an earnest, faithful purpose, rooted in good will and branching into true uses? Some leading passion may seem to give out more heat, and probably superficial observers might ascribe to passionate men more fervor than to faithful men. But it is by confounding .smoke and blaze with vital warmth, like the simple child that sees more power in the crackling thorns that his play-fellows kindle upon the beach, than in the calm, clear light that shines out from the ocean rock, true emblem of a good man's deeds, as the former is in Solomon's view fit similitude of the laughter of a fool. If there be any leading passion not governed by a faithful purpose, it consumes the man, and makes a victim of its votary. If the leading passion be guided by fidelity, then it becomes the *intense* fidelity that so marks the greatest heroes of history, and the truest servants of God. In either case, then, the faithful spirit is the true fire.

Do any persons have misgivings as to all fervor of character, and in their regard for sober, practical judgment, speak as if all zeal must needs have an element of folly destined ere long to burn out if it burns at all? How great the mistake, for nothing can be more sober and practical than an earnest purpose; nothing surely so favors healthy life as the active force that gives mind and body its vital glow. It is better far for a man to live the full life of his nature, with every faculty awake to its own office in its own time, than to doze existence away in the sluggard's torpor, or the worldling's coldness of heart. The natural life needs glow for its own vigor and permanence. The spiritual life follows the same law, and its vigor is as abiding as its fire is bright and full. Errors there may be, indeed, on each side; and if some men are so sluggish as not to kindle their light, others may be so vehement as to allow their light to burn out. There is moderation in all things, and true moderation helps the very point that we would urge, by securing the deepest and most abiding fervor of which man is capable. What is moderation but such a measuring of times, forces, and intensity, as to secure the most efficient power on the whole. The truly moderate man is the most fervent of all men, for he best measures his resources, and instead of wasting his fire, keeps it for its true uses. For want of moderation, many a man who thinks that he has too much fire, is actually content with too little. Many a man who thinks himself a martyr to a noble cause, because he has exhausted himself upon a single idea or in a single extravagant heat, has actually lived too coldly, instead of too fervently, and has neglected the affections and duties that would check his extravagance and revive his spirits. Many a man thinks himself a marvel of studious 'zeal, because his brain is in a fever one day or night in the week, and therefore worn out from exhaustion all other days. Many a sepulchral devotee who has worn himself to mere skin and bone by his zeal in fasting and prayer, has burned his light down to the socket by too little fire, instead of too much; for he has lighted but a single lamp of sacrifice, instead of kindling the whole constellation. Had the fire been broader it would have been abiding, and the wasted devotee would have been the affectionate, active, cheerful Christian, burning the lamp of love and joy, as well as of penitence and self-denial.

The worldling makes the same mistake, only in a different way. Many a man in this great city, who thinks that he lives too fervently for his health of body and mind, and who really seems to lose strength with years, needs more fire instead of less, to give him true life. His zeal is too narrow, and the fire burns out, because it does not touch the best resources of his being. He lives for the world and its business, not for God or his neighbor, too little for the best welfare and enjoyment even of his own family. Let him live a broader life, and it will be a healthier one. If worn by worldly care, let him find solace not in torpor or sensuality, but in the tastes that refine and elevate the intellect, and in the affections that soothe and edify the soul. Yes, there is many a man who systematically makes of our sacred Sabbaths, days of stupid indolence, because of his over-exhaustion during the week, who would awake on the morrow far more refreshed after a day of social kindness, worthy conversation, and rational worship. Follow the method of Providence in the order of nature, and we shall find in due alternation of action a refreshment far better than torpor. When daylight fades, other lights burn on high for us, and the world without is but an image of the world within. Follow the method of Providence, and we may show a broader and more lasting light, instead of finding only ashes after a narrow and wasting flame from mad intensity in some single quarter. The danger, I repeat it, is not of too much fire, but of too little, and the most self-controlled man is in the depth of his being the most fervent, and his nature, so full orbed, warms his great resolves and his quiet charities from the same vital source, like the globe itself, which tempers its salubrious springs and its volcanic torrents from the same central heat.

This fire acts upon every sphere of life, upon all just powers and all worthy actions.

Our powers, both of body and mind, feel its influence. The body needs a master, and its forces and appetites are very much what the central purpose makes it. Let the will be earnestly and wisely faithful, every nerve and limb and sense feels its spirit, and is informed with something of its fire. The lusts that burn out the bodily life, and the sloth that would not have it burn at all, are both rebuked; and this marvellous structure, this mystical tree, which physiologists have regarded as living only by the slow fire in its red arteries, glows with its true fervor and shines with its true light—active, not fevered—calm, not dull, repeating in its branching nerves and vessels the miracle of Horeb, and obliging the beholder to pause as before the work of God.

Every faculty of mind feels the influence, and truly lives only as it is animated by the central purpose that beats and glows at its heart. The intellect is wise and

6*

wakeful by learning to look at all things in nature and Providence with an earnest, faithful eye, and a man of ordinary powers animated by this spirit, becomes a far wiser man than the brightest genius bewildered by vanity, or driven to and fro by passion. The affections are inspired and fixed by the same spirit, and they give their steady, healthful glow to every element which they control. Even the imagination, that daring power that is thought to mock at all control, is invigorated and enlightened by the master purpose, and is loftier and happy in its creations from its solemn recognition of the work of life and the great life-giver's glory. Yes—*Faithful* is the word that can be written on the forehead of all the great creative minds. The visions of Milton, Dante, and their peers, were all based upon the ground of truth and virtue. They did not presume to frame new worlds before owning at heart the primal law which God, from the beginning, laid beneath the foundations of this globe. The faithful man, whatever his sphere, may find fellowship and encouragement in their pages, and their great thoughts may soothe him as he goes to his pillow as benignly with their light as the stars that look from heaven into his window. Wherever the imagination ceases to feel the true inspiration of fidelity, its fire. is a consuming curse, and Lucifer, the Fallen—that is the name of this recreant son of the morning.

Thus the powers in all their compass are animated by the true-life-purpose ; and must it not follow, that all the work of our sphere has heart from its heart ? We all have many things to do, some in themselves agreeable, some disagreeable, some likely to be done with alacrity, others in the most reluctant if not drudging spirit. Bear to our chief calling the fire of our earnest purpose, and all our labors will have something of its cheerful motive, if all are not at once animated with its radiant glow, and a man becomes efficient in detail even as he is resolute and fervent at heart. He need not wait until the globe is fashioned anew to make industry attractive to him by adapting it to his passions, for his master purpose subdues his passions to his work, and all the branches of his calling repeat in no mean way the miracle of Horeb, flaming, but not consumed.

Is it presumptuous to speak so strongly of man's power to carry fire in his heart, and to infuse it into every branch of life? Is it ascribing to man's will, the work that belongs only to God's Infinity? Not so, for all true force is from God, and man wins true fire only as he finds his way to its Infinite fountain. The fervent purpose, central in the character, is what it is, by trusting in a power beyond itself, and by being nurtured from a divine and unfailing source. God it is who has given us our will, with its mysterious power of volition according to the image of his own creative fiat; God it is who has benignly added helps to our natural power, opened the truths and graces of his kingdom all around us, and bade us work out our destiny in a faith that makes his Providence work with us. The fire within burns not merely of itself, but is fed by every word from the mouth of God, and in Jesus, the Incarnate

Word, it finds its true and abiding life. In Christ, and the whole train of Divine Providences of which he is the consummation, the love of the Father draws near to us, encourages us, revives our failing fervor by its heavenly breath, and reanimates our fainting spirit by its sacred warmth. The whole gospel system is enlivening, regenerating. As a man strives to obey its law, and breathe its spirit, he works his own nature into truer life, and brings near to his soul the heavenly fire. The humblest disciple who tries to use his lowly gifts in faith and obedience, proves this truth by his abiding power, and has deepening peace. The illustrious heroes of faith have proved it in the most noted chapters of history, and their souls pervaded by the calm, unfailing fire that came and comes from heaven through Christ and the Spirit, have acknowledged the miracle of Horeb as a fit type of the divine manifestation, and have repeated it in their own experience. Hence to the great and the lowly has proceeded the most enduring energy in this world, and hence has sprung the living witness of Life Eternal. A faithful purpose rooted in the love of God, and branching out into blessed uses, sending up its lambent flame into the nurturing airs of heaven, this is of itself promise of immortality; for this fixes the heart on God and Christ, and surely it is life Eternal to know Thee the only true God and Jesus Christ whom Thou hast sent.

Let not the topic rest in any generality, however exalted or subduing. Let each man examine himself and his ways by the principles illustrated. Is it true that the chief test of character is in the central purpose that acts upon all the faculties and works; that the true fire burns without burning out, that it pervades every branch of life when this purpose is not wilful, but faithful, and is kept in constant allegiance to the Divine kingdom—is this true? Then what are we? Much we are that we ought not to be; too little we are that we ought to be. Feeble as the true fire may have been, who of us will say that he knows nothing of it? Who of us will say that he has not been strong and peaceful as he has tended it well? Who of us will not say that he judges all men according to the evidence of its presence, and thus sanctions like judgment upon himself?

Early in life—yes, as soon as the mind knows any thing of its powers, nay, before personal responsibility begins, and as soon as a child is consecrated in baptism, or made the subject of a thought or prayer, be this the pressing wish, that a faithful purpose should be lighted within his soul, and kept under a living nurture.

And as the years roll on, and scenes, friends, plans and feelings change with time, when maturity brings its grave cares, and threatens to chill all enthusiasm into cold worldliness or drudging habit, let the fire be kept ever burning, that age may renew and brighten the best promise of youth. Let it be ever kept burning in such fulness and measure as to kindle every faculty, and shine unto perfect day. Turn ever like the lawgiver towards the symbol of the present God. Wisely one of our modern sages speaks to each of us the lesson of his own faithful life :—

> "Before thy sacred altar, heavenly truth!
> I bow in age as erst I bowed in youth.
> Still let me bow, till this weak frame decay,
> And my last hour be lighted by thy ray."

VI.

Manhood and its Business.

"But who on earth can long abide in state ?
Or who can him assure of happy day ?
Sith morning fair may bring foul evening late,
And least mishap the most bliss alter may ?
For thousand perils lie in close await
About us daily, to work our decay.
That none, except a god, or God him guide,
May them avoid or remedy provide."

SPENSER.

"The greatest man is he who chooses the right with invincible Resolution; who resists the sorest temptations from within and without; who bears the heaviest burdens cheerfully; who is the calmest in storms, and whose reliance on Truth, on Virtue, on God, is the most unfaltering."

CHANNING.

MANHOOD AND ITS BUSINESS.

WE treat now of manhood, the third stage in the circle of life under survey. If childhood is the time of unconscious development, and youth the time for conscious preparation, manhood is the time for responsible, efficient action — action amid the realities of this busy, aggressive world. At present, we treat so much of the subject as relates to its early years, especially to the third decade, or the period between twenty and thirty, reserving middle age and old age, each for separate consideration. Our topic, then, in this paper, is Early Manhood, or Beginning Life for Ourselves.

The gospel has surely been the strength of true manhood, and from the pen of one who was every whit a man judicious, patient, courageous, unflinching, we take a sentence wholly to our purpose. Hear it, as if from the apostle Paul's own lips, and from the Spirit which gave him his fire. "Watch ye, stand fast in the faith, quit you like men, be strong."

Let the first application of the words, be to the most obvious fact that meets us at the threshold of active life. I mean, our own chosen work, our business. Whatever our position or means, we all have a work to do in life, and that work must embody itself in some ·special vocation. The youth feels this fact, and his whole training, when judicious, will have an eye to it. But the man, just taking hold of his business on his own account, and he only, can see it in its vast responsibility, and feel the great difference between acting under guardianship, and acting for himself. Probably, to most men, the transition, notwithstanding all its attendant hopes and plans, has peculiar trials and perplexities. The first approach of the great world, is a rude shock to delicate sensibilities and unaccustomed faculties. Before, you had your tasks planned for you by others, and these bore the responsibility of the result, and stood between you and the world. Now, you must plan for yourselves, bear the brunt of success or failure, and stand on your own feet amidst the crowd. Before, you were learning how to manage a boat in a calm bay, with ready retreat from the storm. Now, you must out to sea, with your own hand upon the helm, your own eye upon the sails, and you must take tempest or calm as it may chance to come. Trying period for most young men, rudely jarring all the cherished dreams of their years of study or apprenticeship, and waking them from rosy fancies, into the cold clear light of this working-day world.

Shrink not, but be brave, and you will win something

better than those golden dreams. You will grapple with stern reality, and not let it go, until it yields you more than ideal blessing. Quit you like men, be strong in your purpose and your work, and your business shall bless you. You need all your judgment, your patience, your courage, your energy, to begin your work well. I need not undertake, in addressing a circle of well-informed readers, to lay down minute rules for the successful transaction of business; but as to the main principle, I can have no doubt, and I rely upon your experience, to confirm my doctrine. In this world, every man must work his way to true success, and faithful efficient work is the great, the main chance of welfare. Take hold of your business, then, meaning to work manfully, and do the best in your power, to meet your responsibilities and bring out your resources. Do you start with capital? work, or you will lose it by your folly, or disgrace it by your inefficiency. Have you no capital to start with? why be disheartened, for is not a fair character, with intelligence and energy, capital enough for you—nay, in this country of boundless opportunities, is not poverty itself an excellent tonic for a young man's stomach, and one too, that has braced our strongest men in the outset of their career?

This rule only, will I lay down for the conduct of a man beginning his business or profession for himself. Take the best opportunity within your reach, and use it so faithfully and efficiently, as to make a good mark on your own character, and the men with whom you deal. Then that present opportunity will not fail to open into something more, and your growing usefulness will give you growing influence and welfare. Woe to the man who takes the opposite course, and treats the world of business as if it were all sham, and as if men were to stumble or to belie themselves into success. With all its pretences and chicanery, business is a tremendous reality, for it is the great daily work of the world, and not even the Quixotism of the sentimentalist who expects fortune to come to him by friendship, is greater than that of the shiftless adventurer, or tricky schemer, who thinks that luck, not labor, makes the man, and that character is no element of capital. The great law of gravitation pervades all worlds, and in the long run things tend to their just level. The great law of practical life is, that he who would win and keep an honorable position, must balance himself there by efficient action, actual influence, and positive usefulness. This is the doctrine for merchants, and all artisans and artists—the doctrine for all professional men, all statesmen and rulers. Do your work well, whatever it is, and even the world's sober judgment will justify God's own truth, and measure your dignity by your usefulness. Be strong, by choosing wisely what to do, be strong, by doing well what you have chosen, and the step from youth to manhood shall be a rise not a fall.

But the business of life is not to be measured by what we call our vocation. It covers the whole ground of action, and reaches into all the springs of emotion. Our work must have an object, and the object is poor and unsatisfactory, unless it takes hold of our affections. Here is the second point of consideration for manhood. Quit you like men, and be strong in your affections, and you will be stronger in your work.

In youth, the affections fill a large place, and boyish friendships, affinities, intimacies, do much to shape and color our early years. He surely is a most unfortunate or selfish man, whose subsequent life is not happier, because of friends made in the days of school, or college, or counting-house preparation. But in manhood, the affections pass out of the airy region of sentiment, and connect themselves with the gravest reality. One great affection, which in its dawning, flushes the whole horizon with its golden light, and makes of every generous youth a hero in his dreams, and gives the hue of romance to every gentle companion, shows in manhood its serious providential purpose; and that golden light, heaven-born as it is, however colored and refracted by earthly exhalations, ere long forms itself into an aureola around some elect countenance, and guides man to the choice which creates for him a home, and gives him new and powerful objects to strive for, and live for. Let this aspect of manhood be sacredly considered, and let the thought of God, who founded marriage, and of Him who, at Cana of Galilee, renewed its consecration, save the subject from trifling caprices, and from mercenary calculation. Seriously, and with the whole compass of his nature, with his mind, heart, and conscience, as well as with his taste and temperament, let man choose upon whom to set his affections, and there rest them, with all loyalty and truth.

There is judgment in this relation, as in every other matter of feeling, and he who plays the fool, by mistaking caprice for conviction, or prudence for wisdom, may just as
well, nay far better, play the fool upon any other ground.
Woe to the man who sells himself for money, and plays
Judas to his own soul, for pieces of silver. Woe to the
man who slaves himself to a trifler, or who befools himself to a pretty toy, or who sells himself to a virago or a
dolt, and wastes his affections upon heartlessness. Home
rests upon a basis of reality, and that reality may be ac-
cursed, for the very reason that it should be blessed. It
is not for me to go into the particulars of a subject of
such peculiar delicacy, full as the Bible, and the ancient
pulpit, may be of instructions in reference to it. Let a
man, however, clearly understand from the outset, that his
character and destiny are very closely in his wife's keeping, and that it is not easy for him to live wisely with a
fool, or devoutly with a flirt — that it is hard for him to seek
the substance, when her idol is show; it is hard for him to
aspire, when the prevalent mediocrity is her only standard.
Strong indeed, let me say it in all plainness, strong is the
man who has a good wife — not an angel, for we are not
talking sentimentalism, but

> "A Creature not too bright or good
> For human nature's daily food;"

a sensible, affectionate, refined, practical woman, who
makes a man's nature all the stronger, by making it more

tender, who puts new heart into all his worthy striving, gives dignity to his prosperity, and comfort to his adversity. He who is content with any thing less than the elements of sterling character in the guardian of his home, makes the saddest of mistakes, and commits his welfare to the most fickle of chances. Life must, perhaps, have some illusions, but among them this choice cannot be, for a sham-home is no illusion, but the most sad and tremendous of realities. Let a true home, alike in its foundation and superstructure, make man strong, by giving true rest and spring to his affections.

We believe that society is sadly out of joint in this matter of marriage, and that the follies of women in respect to it, are pretty nearly equal to the vices of men. As long as our daughters are brought up to such languid health and inordinate expectations, such impersonations of exaction without equivalent usefulness, we must expect marriages to become less in proportionate number, and congeniality of age. The majority of young men will be unable to marry to their mind, and the nuisances of hotel and boarding-house life will be continued, with its attendant discomforts and vices. A race of sensible, hearty, practical young women, can correct the evil, and establish a new era of genuine homes. Many a good fellow who now pines in the attic of a seven-story hotel, or in the closet of some monster boarding-house, would rejoice in the good time coming, and make a true man of himself, in finding a true wife and a true home.

This is God's own school of energy, and it is so efficient, that its weakest inmate wields a world of power, and as a man takes his own child into his arms, and feels the soft touch of that infant cheek, he is ten times the braver for his toil and endurance, than when he had only himself to care for. Wise, indeed, is he who works the power of such great affections into the leading purposes of life, and within all his business and his ambition, cherishes the motive force of an earnest heart, loyal to the great objects for which life is providentially ordained.

It is said that one of the followers of Bruce, after that patriot king's death, had his heart embalmed in a golden casket, and carried by the standard-bearer always in the thickest of the battle. When the conflict was most desperate, the standard-bearer was ordered to throw the casket into the very midst of the hostile ranks, and the Scotch soldiery were called to the rescue of the heart of their great king from hostile hands. Their charge was then invincible. Every true life wields a still greater power, for it feels a living heart drawing it with irresistible force into every position of duty, and is strong for its work by the might of its affections.

This cannot be, man cannot be truly strong in his affections, or in his work, unless he is strong in his faith for faith deals with the only ultimate and enduring facts and gives the foothold that lasts when others fail. Manhood's contact with reality may be a sore trial to faith, and the world asks us to surrender all higher allegiance to its own claims, and sacrifice our faith to its sight. Many seem to do this, but the truly strong, instead of doing this, do the very contrary, and instead of allowing the world to subdue their faith, they make their faith subdue the world. Above all local and temporal interests, they place the divine Government and Providence. They never allow labor or anxiety to crowd out the thought that God is, that he is love, and the soul is dark and dead when false to his spirit, and away from his presence. Let us not regard this position as an ascetic or Quixotic one. Nay, it is the most practical course that can be taken, resting upon the fact of all facts, and looking to the good of all goods.

Does the world press upon you with its hard realities? then be all the more earnest to make religion a reality, and the first of realities. How sad it is to see a harsh and chilling materialism closing in all round us, and the spiritual faith and generous hope of our childhood and youth, all shut out. Let it not be so. Keep a place for faith in the central plan of life, and show the perfection of your business efficiency, by making a serious business of religion. In your own soul, say humbly yet confidently:— "Indeed I must strive and scheme in this hard and aggressive world; but it is not my master, not my God. I will labor for objects which Providence itself has made sacred, and by principles which justice, honor, nay, humanity and faith, do not forbid. Day by day, I will turn myself towards the Eternal Father, who ordained all toil, and even in the hard pressure of competition, I will not forget Him who promised mercy to the merciful." This spirit has been shown in a true manhood, and faith has then gained,

7

instead of losing power, by wrestling manfully with the cares and temptations of the world. The first spontaneous trust of childhood, confirmed by the fervor of youthful feeling, has consolidated itself by the strength of manhood, and so the character becomes trusting as it becomes resolute, mingling the two elements into the heroism that makes the true man.

We make a sad mistake, if we do not learn in season to rest life upon a basis of devout trust, as well as of resolute labor. God has given the soul, as well as the body, two feet for the walks of her pilgrimage, and true progress is made as they duly interchange their work and their rest together. We cannot know our own being, or God's love, until we use well these gifts, and by mutual faith and action, with cheerful and alternate step press on to the work of our divine calling. The world may say that pleasure is the cure for care, and that self-indulgence refreshes the fatigue of self-exertion. God knows us better, and whilst not frowning upon any innocent joy, he holds the cup of refreshing to every act of true service, as he interchanges the grace of devout faith with the striving of loyal labor. The pilgrim under his guidance, goes indeed from grace to grace, and from strength to strength.

More of this union, instead of less, we should see, as faith is more rationally settled, and life is more generously and substantially built upon it. As a matter of culture, merely, faith should go with enterprise in maturing the true character. Strength is hard, dry, and brittle, unless it is rooted and grounded in love, and stretches upward in faith. Apart from such nurture, strength loses its best vitality, and does not draw to itself the living waters, the genial dew and sunshine needed for its higher life. We must trust in something above ourselves, if we would be strong, and the stoutest forces of the soul, as of the body, come from the mildest influences. Heroism springs from filial faith and affections, even as bone and sinew are formed from warm blood in the arteries. The manhood of our time needs this influence, for it too often mistakes hardness for strength, and self-sufficiency for dignity — sets up its own right arm as the great reliance, and makes of the world its God. Sad the result, even when the most splendid success is granted; sad is the life that gains the world and loses the soul, that puts the golden cup to the lip, and finds no living water there. Sad indeed, when reverses come, and the poor man, bereft of his idols, cries, like Micah: "Ye have taken away my gods, which I made, and what have I more."

Then keep a place for faith, in the midst of worldly cares, and make it clear to yourself, and to those around you, that you do recognize a power and a good above this world. Form your plans upon this basis, order your business and your home upon this idea. Take your place in the Christian Church according to your own honest convictions, and with a stout hand help bear the ark of a generous and holy faith along your pilgrimage. You will give religion itself, a more cheerful and vigorous expression, and your own deepened peace and power, will more than return the blessing you give. Faith shall bear her witness of things unseen, in the midst of your turmoil and temptation. When in the fever of hot strifes and competitions, she will point out to you the only steadfast good. When weary with toil and care, you go to your pillow, and the din of the world still rings into your ear, and your brain itself is crowded with eager anxieties, as your busy streets are crowded with people, and sleep refuses to refresh you, then faith will come to you, and put under your head the pillow of heavenly mercy, and smooth your furrowed brow with her gentle hand, and lull you to rest with peaceful visions of the Father in heaven, and the Saviour whom he sent to call you to himself. Your childhood and youth shall be more than a bright vision; they will live and beat anew in the heart of a manly faith and affection.

VII.

Losses and Anxieties.

PASTOR ANIMARUM.

Crme, wandering sheep, O come!
  I'll bind thee to my breast,
I'll bear thee to thy home,
  And lay thee down to rest.

I saw thee stray forlorn,
  And heard thee faintly cry,
And on the tree of scorn
  For thee I deigned to die—
  What greater proof could I
Give, than to seek the tomb?
Come, wandering sheep, O come!

FROM THE SPANISH.

LOSSES AND ANXIETIES.

Manhood must needs have its anxious times, and there is no man of mature years who cannot remember some emergencies that have driven him almost mad with anxiety. Such seasons stamp themselves upon his memory, and not seldom come back to him in all their original vividness in his dreams. I propose to treat of this experience of our life in the present paper.

In simple language, taken directly from the common business of a rural people, our Saviour, in the parable of the Lost Sheep, illustrates one of the great facts in life, and its effect upon man. The fact is the existence of risks, and the effect is anxiety. We cannot but feel anxious at the prospect of losing any thing precious to our interests or affections, and no small portion of our time and thought is occupied with such anxiety. The habits of society have signally changed, since the words of the parable were spoken, and few persons live so simply that their fortunes depend upon the safety of a single flock, or the care of a few pieces of silver. Yet amid the complex affairs in which men are now engaged, the laws of life remain essentially the same. Risks surely have not ceased, nor has anxiety abated. It is important that a topic so much discussed in the street and felt in the house, should have its place with the moralist, and be considered from a Christian point of view. Many a furrowed face and troubled heart prove the need of such consideration. Many a wasted life and ruined name bear witness to the danger of false risks and morbid anxiety.

Remark first of all the fact, that there must, of necessity, be a large element of risk in the lot of men. By our nature and position we are obliged to form most of our plans, and do most of our work subject to contingencies upon which we cannot calculate with positive certainty. There are truths which are so certain as to admit of no rational question ; and on the other hand, there are notions so false or so absurd, as to rank at once among impossibilities. But the practical affairs of men belong mostly to neither of these extremes, but to the broad region of probabilities between absolute certainty and absolute impossibility. There we make our calculations and conduct our enterprises, studying probabilities as wisely as we can, and hoping by a due balance of contingencies to secure a fair return.

Yet what practical man does not every day make some allowance for risks from casual circumstance, knowing that he is not wise enough to foresee all that will happen tc him, nor strong enough to carry to the end every thing that he has begun precisely according to his plans. The whole domain in which we live is full of contingencies. Nature—man—the times, are to our limited vision full of uncertainties. Who can tell what a single day may bring forth ? Every day we watch the sky, and read the signs of health and prosperity, or the reverse in its changes. Many a life and many a fortune depends upon heat or cold, storm or calm. If the face of nature to us is so fitful, who shall estimate the fickleness of man, or calculate with entire accuracy his opinions, passions, vices, virtues ? Society, business, religion, are constantly exhibiting unexpected developments of character, and nothing but a supernatural gift of discerning of spirits can prevent constant risks from this source of contingency. When we consider the complex tide of affairs which are called the times, whether political, commercial, or moral, who can presume to calculate with certainty its changes ? Who does not feel that we are always afloat upon a changing sea, and good or ill is constantly appearing from unexpected quarters ? Let any man judge by his own experience; consider how much his own mind and fortune have been effected by contingencies, and how much he is now engrossed by the risks of his position; and we all see at once how large is the casual element in human affairs.

The question comes to us, what shall we do in this state of things, or what is the proper conduct for men as

7*

subject to contingencies. It is very obvious that God has placed us where we are, and it is in vain to ask to have the laws of existence repealed to suit our wishes. To be free from risks, we must ask to be all wise and almighty, or else to be reduced to utter nothingness, alike unable to gain or lose, to enjoy or suffer. Some men there are, who seem to aspire to these conditions, and to escape from the common lot on the one hand by rash adventure, and on the other hand by cowardly shrinking. Some men dare risks as if they could never lose; others shun them as if they could never gain; as if the shepherd should leave his sheep in the fields or mountains, confident that none of them can possibly be lost; or, on the other hand, fretted by losses, should say, " I will keep no sheep at all; I will give up my flocks, and so be rid of this annoying anxiety.

The two classes of men may be seen in every community and profession, the rash and the timid, the fast and the slow. At different stages of life, the same man may illustrate both dispositions, and he who at twenty-five was a dashing schemer, at fifty may settle down into a pattern of timid prudence. Both classes are in error, and false to the true law of life. He who encounters risks as if he could not lose, intent only on the prizes of fortune, spoils his mind, and is likely to ruin his position : spoils his mind by blinding his eyes and fevering his heart with the gambler's madness; and is likely to ruin his position by bringing down upon him some of those contingencies which he overlooks, and which sooner or later end every gamester's career. He, on the other hand, who will have nothing at all to do with the risks of life in fear of loss, must ask to give up life itself; for life cannot be held without constant risks. It is obvious that he cannot enter into any business—cannot do any work for the body or the soul; for what is there that a man can undertake without exposing himself to more or less disappointment? To shun risk is plainly impossible, and many who seek to do it only multiply the evils which they would avoid. He who says, "I will keep no sheep, for I may lose some of them," loses the pleasure and profit of his flock, and is very sure of finding or borrowing some trouble far greater than anxious and kindly search for the lost one.

The sluggard who does nothing, because he is afraid of doing wrong,—the gambler who discourages every enterprise, because men are fallible,—the egotist, who thinks to be secure by being wrapped up in himself, afraid of the world, and shy even of family and friends—these classes of men show no enviable exemption from the risks of life. Assured of drawing none of the prizes in what they call the lottery of life, they are very likely to prove that a man may have a sad blank without drawing at all; nay, that he must have a blank in himself and his whole being, if he does not commit himself to the proper labors, sympathies and enterprise of his lot. He who hid his talent in a napkin was of this class, forgetting that somebody might steal it even there—forgetting that every talent not used is virtually lost, and he always multiplies dangers who will brave none.

We most certainly believe that there is some providential adaptation between the powers of man and his position. Not content with tracing out the fitness between the eye and the light—the ear and sound—the elastic motion of the body, and the element upon which it moves—we may reasonably look for some harmony between our intellectual and moral faculties, and the contingencies amid which we live. Every being under the providence of God is adapted to its peculiar element; and the light of nature and revelation teaches us to regard man as amply endowed for his larger sphere of exposures. In this light we would interpret the risks of our lot, and the anxiety which they produce. Such interpretation will show that the very lot which fevers so many into madness, and frightens so many into sluggishness, is intended to be the school of a benignant discipline, the means of calling out our best powers, and securing the deepest peace.

What so well trains the judgment, and schools the affections, and stirs the energies, as a due sense of the exposures amidst which we live? The leading faculty of mind needed for practical life is sound judgment. God has placed us in circumstances that imperiously demand the discipline of this faculty. The world is indeed full of good books that move thought, and of fair scenes that move the fancy. But more powerful than these is the appeal of life in its constant exposures—its never-ceasing hopes and fears. It says to us all, " Your lot is cast upon an eventful tide; study its movings for yourselves; see if there is not some law to its changings; look for some rule of probabilities that shall on the whole be a safe guide through contingencies." Let a man follow this appeal, and he will not only keep his eyes open to the fair prospects of success or warnings of danger, but, in view of his own talents, disposition, and opportunities, he will form some method of action, which shall embody and carry out his principles into an habitual policy, and which shall save him from being for ever at the mercy of accidents. By a sound judgment he will regulate the risks of his lot; and, like a good pilot, if he cannot control winds and waves, he will have a ready way of meeting them and using them. He will keep out of many hazards into which others recklessly run, and will face many dangers at which others stand aghast. He will guide his affairs with a careful wisdom, that shall save him from extreme courses. He will, as far as he may, choose the sphere of action in which contingencies and certainties are so mingled as best to stir enterprise and promise returns—always insisting upon certainty enough to warrant the attempt—always expecting some contingencies to stand in the path of success. To find this sphere is the part of practical wisdom, whatever the business or profession. The practical merchant is he who thus wisely interprets the laws of risk in business;—the practical Christian, whatever his calling, is he who is willing to see life as it is, and never be weary in well-doing, whilst trying to apply Christian truth and love to the various circumstances and wants of souls,—neither a desponding drone, nor a flighty dreamer, but modestly sure of some fair success in his application of Christianity in view of the probabilities of life.

Thus a sound judgment regulates risks, not merely by meeting those that come, but by fixing the true method of planning and of living. It will teach the shepherd how to keep his sheep, as well as how to seek the one who has strayed from the flock. It will powerfully affect the fact of risks, and always the feeling which they produce. Anxiety depends in a great measure upon our habits of thought or attention. He who thinks wisely of the exposures of his position, and trains himself always to see the main point at stake, will be rid at once of a legion of borrowed fears, and will accept a just anxiety as a benignant warning of danger and stimulus to effort; just as we are to regard the pain of a wound or disease, as proof that the sentinels are true to their post, and the nerves, vigilant watchers, cry " Qui vive " to the intruder, and warn the lord in the citadel that peril is near. What a vast amount of morbid anxiety would be cured at once by sounder habits of thought. How many hearts and homes, instead of being filled with sighs and groans, at what cannot be helped, and had better be left alone, would be scenes of cheerful content under essential humiliation, and cheerful activity under encouraging duties.

Add to sound judgment fortitude, and we are still nearer the true solution of the risks of life: fortitude, when in rest, patient; when in action, courageous; bearing well what must be borne, daring well what must be done. No-

life is so quiet as to be able to dispense with this old car-
dinal virtue. Its patience we need under a thousand
annoyances that can be helped only by being borne;—its
courage we need under countless trials that will conquer
us unless we conquer them. Who will repine that Providence aims to temper us in each trial by so various experiences? One of our wise and good men has said, that a
man ought to be mortified once a fortnight to keep him
properly down; and we need quote no authority to prove
the need of a constant discipline to call out our courage
and fit us for emergencies.

To judgment and fortitude, add persevering fidelity,
or constancy, to our great life-work, and, so far as this
earth can solve it, the problem of contingencies is solved,
and man is wiser, and better, and stronger for the risks to
which he is exposed. Always at work at his post, judiciously, patiently, courageously, he will not be put down
by every casual disappointment. He will learn something
from every contingency, and win something from every
loss. Never rash, never cowardly, he will learn prudence
from other men's folly, and enterprise from other men's
timidity. Many opportunities in which he trusted may
and will disappoint him, but in his case the old proverb
will prove true, and one door will not be shut unless another door opens. He must expect to be exposed to hazards, and to feel anxiety whilst life lasts; but hazards will
more and more reveal an eternal trust beneath them all

and his anxiety will be a healthy vigilance instead of a restless fever.

Has not God been teaching us this doctrine all our lives by all our experience, reading, and observation— teaching us the need of judgment, fortitude, labor, from true power and peace? We want all the discipline that we have, and all we can get, alike for ourselves and for those whom we guide. Well may we be anxious for those whom we guide. Is our anxiety wise? Something of it undoubtedly is not well placed, and often in our laudable desire to provide well for children, we pamper wants that are misfortunes, and many a lamb is lost by being unwisely petted. The great point of anxiety should be that life may be true, and the mind may be best prepared for its duties. More of this anxiety would abate the fever of gain, and give motives strong against loss. The child in danger is always, on that account, the most cherished, and the little invalid is the centre of all thoughts. The whole family watch the sufferer's pulse and breath; and the hardy man, as he comes from his day's toil, weeps for joy, when he finds his boy or girl smiling upon him, and for the first time after sickness, taking gifts playfully from his hand. Blessed anxiety—more blessed when it is concerned for the entire well-being of the child, and forgets not that there is a loss worse than sickness and death!

Let us accept the risks of our lot, and not shrink from its true anxiety. Let God be the interpreter of the one and the comforter of the other. A faithful self-examination in these respects will give ground for very pungent thoughts. The main risk is in not meeting the main duty of our being; and the chief anxiety should be, lest we are false to our post, under the kingdom of God. A true solicitude for ourselves is the best guide to true regard for others; and as a man is a lover of the true fold, he will be anxious to win others to its peace. So the whole topic of social responsibility opens. Who shall comprehend—or who deny it. Every day we own it, as we think of peril or loss to others. We think less of the ninety and nine fleets upon the ocean, than of the one lost navigator so nobly sought for in the frozen ocean—less of the thousand ships, those white-fleeced flocks of a commercial people, that are safe on their course, than the one missing vessel so eagerly waited for now. This is well, and such solicitude is not selfish, and we are ready to make sacrifices for it, if necessary. But for society all around us—for our nation—for the world—for ourselves, there are worse exposures than these. Remember Him who came to save the lost. Remember Him to learn compassion to the erring. Remember Him to know that from all things mutable and contingent, a true life educes good eternal. He who came to be to us the Resurrection and the Life, came also to be the Good Shepherd of souls.

VIII.

The True Rest.

Rest is not quitting
   The busy career
Rest is the fitting
   Of self to its sphere.

'Tis the brook's motion
   Clear without strife,
Fleeing to ocean
   After its life.

'Tis loving and serving
   The Highest, and Best!
'Tis onwards! unswerving,
   And that is true rest.
                GOETHE.

I love my God, but with no love of mine,
   For I have none to give;
I love thee, Lord; but all the love is thine,
   For by thy life, I live.
I am as nothing, and rejoice to be
Emptied and lost and swallowed up in thee.
              MADAME GUYON.

THE TRUE REST.

AFTER anxiety, we yearn for a season of peace, and gladly we turn from the wilderness of danger, to the shrine of
true rest, with thanks to God that so many such shrines
have stood along our pathway, and that we may, if we will,
bear one with us in the ark of our Exodus.

We are a restless and egotistical people, impatient of
delay, and quite prone to glorify our own will, as if nothing
could be impossible to a force that has already done so
much. Perhaps it is precisely for this cause, that the
words of great devotees sometimes have for us such soothing power, and, weary of all this proud trust in ourselves
we sigh for a rest better than the world and our own
strength can give, and say from our own hearts in response
to the great devotee's psalm : " My soul, wait thou only
upon God ; for my expectation is from him."

We consider now somewhat particularly the subject of
mental quietude, as a practical blessing and power. We

may have time to speak somewhat of its nature, its influ ence, and its direct claims upon our attention.

Christian Quietude — the word recalls at once, to a scholar's mind, the noted controversies, in former times, between rival schools of theologians, who made the term Quietism, itself, the rallying cry of the most impassioned strifes. We will not try to revive that question, or show how Bossuet and Fenelon, with their illustrious followers, differed as to the precise degree of efficacy belonging respectively to the active and the passive states of the soul. The heart is essentially the same in all ages, and we may as well interpret it through our own experience, as by borrowing the costume of a former age. There is a yearning for rest within us, that often seizes us in the midst of our most engrossing cares, and when our busy men say, as they often do, that they are looking to some calm rural home as a final retreat from care, they express a want which no change of abode can satisfy, and which cannot be fully satisfied, until the sonl finds her rest in a peace not of this world.

What is Christian quietude? It is not a mere negation, surely? a mere cessation of care and effort? for this is indolence — one of the tempers most foreign from the Christian mind. The Psalmist speaks as if there were need, not of less, but of more earnestness, when he calls the noblest and deepest power of his being, his soul, to wait upon the Lord. The soul, that power which is in us, but which we little comprehend, and too little use, is thus summoned to her high office, as servitor before the throne of God, as if there were a blessing which she only can win, and her service were none the less earnest, because with bowed head, and veiled face, she waits the will of her Lord.

Such waiting is at once a check upon egotism and upon impatience, by showing that our will is not supreme, and even when suppliant before the supreme throne, it must be content to wait its appointed time. What rebuke there is in the language of true devotion, upon our too habitual egotism. We are apt to begin life, and allow our children to begin it, as if self were the centre and sovereign of the universe, and we had a right to complain, if we are disappointed by not having our own way. The better wisdom bids us take at once the waiting attitude, as if it were, from the beginning, a matter of course that our will is secondary, and God's will is to be awaited. Taking this ground, the soul has the quietude of reverence, and her fitful fever is soothed by obedience to the eternal law, and trust in the infinite love.

So rebuking the spirit of egotism, the true quietude also rebukes the spirit of impatience. It bids man bide his time, as a creature in whose discipline delay is an essential element, and for whom God has decreed that the harvest of success shall not come at once with the blossom of desire. More than any other being, man must wait for what he wishes, for while the insect of a day tastes all the bliss of its little life whilst one sun is shining, man is doomed, as well as blessed, to an infinite domain, and whatever his successes, his three-score and ten years find him waiting still for a good inexhaustible. Does his ambition take merely a horizontal range, and measure success by the surface of lands or goods possessed, he must wait on time to enlarge the quantity of his possessions, for time is the great power in the market-place, and they are the wisest in their own generation, who await its developments most judiciously. Has he the nobler desire which measures success, not by quantity, but by quality, and yearns for a higher and deeper mental and moral life, still he must wait, for wisdom comes not in a day, nor does the peace of God, without alloy or misgiving, reward a single work or prayer. This willingness to wait upon God's own time for the desirable measure of worldly success, and especially for growth in the moral and spiritual life, is a great source of quietude.

Such, in brief, is the nature of Christian quietude — not indolent, but calling the soul to an earnest service, and subduing egotism into reverence, and soothing impatience into calm waiting.

Mark now the practical power of this frame of mind, and we shall see that it is needed quite as much in our own every-day life, as in any devotee's seclusion — that, in fact, it is more imperatively necessary for a busy man, likely to fail of its control, than for a recluse, so ready to sink into its stillness.

What power there is in the very act of waiting, or in the patient mind — power in controlling the faculties themselves, and in securing external results. When impatient, we are not our own master, and in our very eagerness for power, we fret away the most efficient of all forces. Note the effect of a single fit of impatience upon the thoughts, when at some unexpected delay, or brief disappointment, we worry ourselves into a temporary fever, and for the time are beside ourselves. Carry out the same infirmity into the temper of a life, and how its health is broken, and its force languishes. For some spasmodic effort, there may be a convulsive struggle, that looks like energy without limit, but the result soon shows that the force is evanescent as convulsive, and it is not thus that the great work of our being is to be done. Nor is it thus that the best external results are to be secured. Our field of action is broad and long, and unless we can wait for some fruits to ripen, and the true hour to mature, we can neither have our best resources nor do our best work. As a dweller in time, man is called to be a patient waiter, and so his quietude is a power of mind and of achievement.

Not merely in waiting, but in waiting upon God, there is power. The temper which subdues the petty pride of egotism, fixes surely the lowly strength of faith, which is mighty in the measure of its confidence, and says, " because I am weak I am strong, and my strength is perfected in weakness." We feel its force whether we contemplate God as a sovereign ruling by laws, or as a spirit asking our love and offering us his own. Are there laws over nature and over life, laws over the earth and over the body, laws over the unseen spheres and over our souls,

8

how can we hope to win true power over the realms without us, or the kingdom within us, except by learning these laws, and waiting for their forces to guide and crown our work ? In every step we wait the aid of the gravitation that holds the globe together, and in every book that we read, we wait on the laws of vision and memory to guide us to knowledge. The highest of all laws is the law of the spirit of life, which presents God to us as the infinite and eternal Mind calling us to personal communion with himself. How know God at all thus, and secure aught of the power that comes from such knowledge, except by waiting reverently upon his will ? It is high ; we cannot attain unto it, any more than scale the skies, or bring down the drops that sparkle in the rainbow, or catch the sun's glory in the clouds. Wait, reverently wait, and the heavenly grace will come to you. Your sharp, critical understanding, your self-sufficient will, your impulsive passions will not lift you to the mercy-seat, nor bring the heavenly mercy down. Wait with all the faculties of our being, reverent and recipient, and God will not leave us without a witness of himself. When we are hardest at work, let the will be still waiting for a power beyond its own ; when we are studying or meditating, let though crave a wisdom higher than itself; when our affections ar earnest, and those dearest to us move our hearts most tenderly, let human love wait upon the love that is divine, and so fill its vase of alabaster with a divine sweetness, that shall shed fragrance through all the house. Let work, and thought, and love, all thus breathe the spirit of prayer, and the prayer which they favor shall return the favor with large increase, and hours of devotion shall be rich in influences over all the life. So my soul wait thou upon God, and let thy expectation be from him.

Shall not the crowning blessing be a growing consciousness of communion with God, through the opening of all the faculties into the divine kingdom, and the union of our life-plan with the method of his Providence ? Do all that we can to discipline our minds wisely and arrange our affairs efficiently, we need after our method has been well fixed, to pervade the whole with a devout seeking spirit, just as if the whole were but the path in which we look for God's blessing to come, the Jacob's ladder on which good angels come and go. How far a perfect plan of life would bring a man's soul into direct communion with God, bringing to his mind a heavenly wisdom, to his affections a holy joy, and even transfiguring his body and his senses by a divine light and health, we will not presume to say. But this we know that the best work and the best lives that the earth has seen, give us cheering glimpses of such communion, and prove that in his highest energy, man appears more as the recipient of a grace from on high, than as his own master and the sole arbiter of his own mind and deed. Even the most vulgar form of heroism, that of the battle field, proves that we need to be possessed by something beyond ourself to put forth our best energies ; and the soldier, as he goes into the fight, on fire with the martial enthusiasm, inspired by waving banners, and sounding trumpets, and beating drums,

gives some illustration of the higher and calmer enthusiasm of the true soldier of the cross, who fights to the last
the good fight of faith, looking to a cloud of heavenly
witnesses, and moved by the living witness within his own
heart.   The orator never speaks well until he is possessed
by his subject, and his very tones show that the truth by
which he would master the audience, has first mastered
him.   When earnestly pleading a worthy cause, what majestic repose sometimes comes over him, as if he less
poured forth the volume of words, than were borne along
upon its swelling tide ; and some aged patriot's face which
when unmoved seemed rough, and furrowed, and dim, is
all lighted up with meaning, as when the seamed and pebbly bed of a river is flooded by the rising waters, and the
dark earth itself appears to flash into crystalline light.   A
true life is of itself the most sacred of words, and he
who speaks it in deeds must needs be possessed by what
he utters, and wait reverently on God for the spirit of
truth.   Hence the truest men, whether their sphere has
been conspicuous or obscure, have always had a large
leaven of quietude in their composition, and have trusted
most even when they have dared the most.   The most finished culture herein meets the most unsophisticated piety,
and the illustrious Fenelon, the very paragon of refinement and taste, consecrating an intellect of Grecian beauty by a faith of Christian tenderness, at once poet, statesman, moralist, theologian, orator, spoke of the light of
God within the soul, very much like George Fox, the
English farmer ; and the Archbishop of Cambray, in his

purple, reasoned of holy quietude very much like the grazier of Leicestershire, in his suit of leather. The reason is obvious, for all who would find God's kingdom, must be like little children, and whatever their gifts, they must be willing for the crowning blessing to wait upon the Father of light and love.

If these things are so, and Christian quietude thus gives the strength of patience, the peace of faith, and the joy of conscious communion with God, is it not well to make more account of it in our plans of discipline and life ? Say for ourselves—" O my soul, wait thou only upon God, for my expectation is from him."

Let us be careful to silence all repining, to put down the fret and worry of mind that so often disturb our peace, and let us turn the soul thus freed from annoyance, in calm and earnest waiting upon the blessing of God. Even when we are sorely beset, even so perplexed with cares as hardly to know which way to turn, then still all complaining, and in the clear exercise of our reason wait serenely upon God to give us the light we need. He will not desert us, for he will not forsake the lowly, and to the upright light shall arise in the midst of darkness.

Let our general method of living partake of the same disposition, and aim to unite quietude with efficiency in every sphere. Let the household prove the worth of its union, and the ornament of a meek and quiet spirit crown its economy, and soothe its trials, and dignify its cares. Let children learn to be still in due season, and let parents be their worthy teachers, by subduing their own temper, as well as dealing in just precepts of obedience. Then the house shall be quiet without being dull, and a peace not of this world shall calm its labors, and deepen its affections, and interpret its destiny. Let the place of business, as far as it can, be regulated on the same principles, in a true order, at once noiseless and efficient, like the mechanism that works all the better for the oil that stops its creaking. A man is surely more fitted for a post of great care by the most peaceful and self-controlled temper, and by it he saves a world of needless excitement, and concentrates all his forces upon his work in due method. Nothing is gained by fretting and scolding in the house—nothing is gained by cursing and swearing under the irritations of business. In both spheres the true man or the true woman will yearn for a Christian quietude, and say—" O my soul, wait thou only upon the Lord, for my expectation is from him." Well indeed is it in the midst of our cares, to wait upon him who holds all things under his care, and whose spirit is peace ineffable, keeping the worlds in motion without haste and without jar.

Week by week God's own voice calls us to our rest from his church on our way. Should we not insist especially upon the need of quiet waiting upon God, when we enter his sanctuary for meditation and prayer? We go to church to listen to accustomed words from human lips indeed, but these words are naught to us, unless we interpret them reverently, and make them means of self-examination and worship. Common-place as this remark may be, how sadly we slight its truth, and rob the sanctuary of its due honor, by degrading it into a theatre of flippant criticism, or a resort of indolent formalism. Some of us probably are not only indifferent to the true spirit of worship for ourselves, but are willing to intrude upon the just privileges of others, by disturbing the just quiet of the place after worship has commenced. We surely call it a mark of bad breeding to go to a dinner party some time after the appointed hour, and disturb the guests seated in their places, by the necessity of finding accommodations for us. Is it any less a discourtesy to come late to church, and interrupt the order of service, by the noise of our feet, and the bustle of our movements? Nay, is it not adding irreverence to discourtesy, and breaking in upon the due quietude of the sanctuary, by negligence or indolence? We ought to think of this seriously, and if each of us will look to our own ways properly, a great annoyance will cease, and new incentives to peaceful devotion will here be given. In the sanctuary let us be willing to bring our common remembrances, and needs, and aspirations, and differ as we may in our experience, let us wait on God for the blessing that we all alike do need—more of his light and peace, for more of the wisdom that can guide us through this perplexing world—more of the faith that can keep us true to heaven, in spite of all enticing pleasures and perplexing cares. The best mark of a Christian congregation is a certain serene earnestness, a certain aspect of the ministrations and the demeanor, which says beyond mistaking, that they who come together

thus, seek a blessing above themselves or any human power, and while they accept all available privileges of man's
devising, they look beyond them to the giver of all good
the Father of Spirits, for grace and peace. More of this
spirit let us cherish, and new power as well as comfort
will come from its holy quietude. An attraction deeper
and stronger than we can well explain, will draw us to the
house of prayer, and a still small voice will speak to us
more nearly and benignly, as the years go on, and never
desert us, though the earth quakes and the thunder rolls.

With sacred constancy as the Sabbaths advance, let us
reverently meditate upon the changes of human life, which
must come even without our bidding, and which are well
met only when calmly awaited. The greatest of these
changes is of God's appointing, and if we wait on him
truly here, we can without fear resign ourselves to his holy
will. Then, my soul, wait thou upon God, for in life and
death, and worlds to come, my expectation is from him.
In drawing nearer him thou shalt better know thyself, and
find thine own true life in finding his presence.

Sitting thus devoutly at the foot of the cross, in the
holy quietude of the sanctuary, we bear the blessing with
us in our journey, and each bird of passage that we meet
will tell us of the ark of rest, as well as of the wilds of
our wandering.

IX.

Middle-Age.

"My Crown is in my Heart, not on my Head,
    Not decked with diamonds and Indian stones,
    Nor to be seen: my cr w 1 is called Content;
    A Crown it is that seldom kings enjoy."

SHAKESPEARE.

"It is not perhaps much thou&al of, bnt it 1o certainly a very important lesson, to learn how to enjoy ordinary life, and to be able to relish your being without the transport of some Passion, or gratification of some Appetite. For want
of this capacity, the world is filled with whetters, tipplers, cutters, sippers, and
all the numerous train of those who, for want of thinking, are forced to be ever
exercising their feeling or tasting."

STEELE.

MIDDLE-AGE.

Midway upon our journey, at high noon we now stand, with morning and evening looking at us from either side, and tempering with their cheerful retrospect and tranquil prospect the toil and heat of the day. The middle age of life is now our topic. It is a season too little spoken of either by the moralist or the preacher, each of whom apparently, in order to preserve the parallel between life and the year, notes only four seasons, and passes from childhood, youth, and manhood, at once to treat of Age. Strange, indeed, that the time more marked than any other by fulness of privilege and weight of duties and not without the gravest of perils, too, should be com paratively neglected; as if life, instead of being a continued and progressive history, were but an idle romance whose interest ceases as soon as the hero is married and established. After that, the burden and the heat of the day are to come, for surely the fourth and fifth decades are the very prime of our earthly being, and between thirty and fifty, our best work is likely to be done or neglected. If childhood is for unconscious development, and youth for conscious preparation, and manhood for beginning the world for oneself, middle-age or maturity is for preserving fidelity, and it must test the sanguine plan by efficient performance. Putting on the armor is one thing, but wearing it well is another thing, and it is the noonday of life that shows whether we wear it bravely or not. In view of the great work thus to be done, how natural the prayer of the Psalmist—" O my God, take me not away in the midst of my days." The prayer has its deepest significance, when we implore God not only to take us not away from life itself, but also to take us not away from the usefulness without which life is worse than death.

Let us then, with all earnestness, consider Middle Age, its Experience, its true Temper, and just Progress.

Maturity is especially to be marked as the season of experience, when the world must show most of its colors, and we must look at them with an eye somewhat disenchanted of early illusions. Our doctrine on this point is simply thus : " Let us win experience without paying the sad price of worldliness, and let us learn to see things as they are, that we may do our part the better among the realities of our sphere."

The whole of life, indeed, is experience, and we are always learning something from the cradle to the grave. Yet that knowledge is more worthy of the name which comes when the passions have calmed their first fever, when the reflective powers have been awakened, and the main facts of the world have come upon us in all their reality. How eventful even in the most ordinary lot must this experience be! Not without many cheering lessons and privileges indeed, yet always in the case of generous minds, with a large alloy of disappointment and chagrin! So many large expectations baffled, so many promises falsified, so much empty profession, so much utter deceit, such vice in the garb of refinement, such hypocrisy under the cloak of religion—what man, who has reached the noontide of life, as he thinks of these things, does not smile bitterly as he compares the reality with the ideal of his early dreams? Our experience of ourselves, too, is not all bright, for it shows us the difference between our aspirations and our deeds, and not unfrequently mocks very noble plans by very poor achievements ; nay, confounds very generous sentiments by very feeble conduct.

All too ready we are to call such experience of itself wisdom, instead of the stepping-stone of wisdom. Too ready we are to glide into the ways of the world, and give up what was best in our aspirations as the illusions of an untutored fancy. Here is one of the pressing dangers of mature years—the danger of utter worldliness at the very time when the world should be most effectually overcome. How many yield to it, who of us will presume to say? Mark the altered tone of the man of the world at forty, as he makes light of what he calls his dreams at twenty. Note the change in the very expression of his countenance

so vacated of light from above, and shining only with
earthly prudence and desire. He may call his knowledge
wisdom, but Heaven calls it folly. What folly so great as
to doubt of virtue and to deny God, and treat life as a
monstrous lie from beginning to end, or a mean expedient
from first to last.

Far otherwise the true man uses the experience of mature years. The more he detects the world's cheats, the
more he seeks the reality which it vainly counterfeits.
The more he sees of heartlessness and deceit, the greater
is his respect for the rectitude and kindness which are
thrown by the contrast into such bold relief. The more
clearly the saddest realities of life dawn upon him, the
more determined is his purpose, and the more efficient his
measures to guard against them, just as the brave pilot
watches tide and wind, not to yield his vessel to them, but
to guide it safely upon his own chosen course. Blessed is
experience when so used ! when the knowledge of vice and
misery gives strength to conscience and tenderness to compassion, when acquaintance with the mighty energies en-
listed in the world's cunning crafts lends enterprise and
vigor to virtue,—when smooth-faced worldliness in its best
success wakens the sense of a welfare beyond its gift.
Blessed this experience more than all, when God's own
hand is seen in the affairs of men, when his own grace is
felt in the heart, and the fatal taste of the tree of knowledge is cured by the immortal fruit of the tree of life.
Such experience makes one a man of God, not a man of
the world. Sad is the noon of life without its coming—

happy, happier far even than the rosy morning, when noon is cheered by such trust, and the heart of faith beats more firmly than ever beneath all the realities of the world.

Such experience cannot but act upon the temper, and we now speak of the temper most congenial with middle age. When in the midst of life, so balanced between extremes, a certain equilibrium of character would seem appropriate. By his providential discipline, God calls us then peculiarly to an evenness of temper without monotony, or in other words, to equanimity without indifference. In early life, something of impulsiveness and mutability may be expected, and the first enterprise and struggle of a noble manhood cannot reasonably be expected without some alternate chills and fevers of the blood. But in the midst of our days, God's providence calls us to a more equable frame of mind. He seeks to temper our wills to a just medium by experience of success and disappointment, as the smith tempers iron by fire and water. He educates the judgment to some due sense of the average aspect of things, so that we are not to be cast down by a reverse, as if a passing cloud were a permanent eclipse, or made giddy by some new pleasure, as if a gleam of sunshine were promise that darkness should be no more. He interprets to us the varied play of our own emotions, our glees and glooms, our elasticity and oppression, and so touches the many tones of this harp of a thousand strings that we may know pretty well its compass, and the tune and time of its notes. All this discipline should give us Christian equanimity, and keep us far from worldly indifference.

Mark the distinction between Christian equanimity and worldly indifference. The man of the world, nay, the positively unprincipled man, may win by experience a certain composure, and may look on the chances of life as calmly as the practical gamester watches the play of cards or dice. He may cater to his vilest passions on system, and follow the basest lusts with a deliberate method. Fearful, indeed, are the vices of mature years in their very deliberation. A profligate of forty or fifty is a far more wretched and contemptible creature than a wild scapegrace of twenty, since he has used the very experience and discipline which should bring wisdom and sobriety, to minister to folly and shame. With all his keenness and composure, he will not escape retribution. He is playing with an awful power that is serious when it seems to jest, and he who makes of himself a whited sepulchre, cannot stop the work of moral corruption and death, by the fair outside. When his course is smoothest, it may, like the river on the very verge of the cataract, be nearest the fall. Surely he who reasons most keenly on false premises, must one day come to the end of his reckoning, and figure himself out a deliberate lie and sin. The composure of deliberate vice is not equanimity, nor can we speak more favorably of the mercenary coldness that freezes the whole current of our being, and calls the icy death philosophic calmness.

No. Christian equanimity is the balance of all powers, thoughts, affections, upon their true centre, which is God, and the fidelity which God approves. It is the harmony of our whole being in its healthy action. Folly may mistake it for dulness, but wisdom sees in it the fulness of life. Its love is no wasting fever of the blood, but the healthy beating of a heart true to all worthy affections and duties—a love more deep, more true, yes, before God more lovely than any of the fitful impulses that set youthful passions on fire. In the calm, loyal, considerate affection of a true home, tender without fitfulness, and constant without monotony, the human heart shows more of its divine richness than in all the parade of passion that makes the staple of romances. So, too, in the steadfast fidelity with which the heads of a true family pursue the even tenor of their way, never swerving for a moment from their fixed aim, the best welfare of those committed to their charge, there is more true heroism than in all the protestations of disinterestedness and the oaths of eternal friendship, that so dazzle the youthful imagination. God himself is the great exemplar of an even mind. He holds the mighty worlds in such noiseless equilibrium ;—He melts the prismatic colors into this sweet, uncolored sunshine, emblem of his own mind ;—He who combines all thought, all emotion, all power, sits serene upon his throne, gives his signet of quietude to his divinest messengers, and more than in wind or tempest or earthquake, speaks in the still, small voice of peace.

O learn of God equanimity without indifference—

learn of Him, the Infinite Love, how to be even tempered without being unfeeling. Look up to the calm heavens; to the marvellously balanced stars; to the divine repose in the face of Jesus, and pray for the true spirit of maturity, —say, " O my God, take me not away in the midst of my days, until I have learned it, and when I have learned it, let me live to breathe into others its surpassing peace."

In its train comes progress, such as belongs to the noon of life—progress without instability. Too much of the boasted stability of many men comes from sheer obstinacy, and they escape the charge of fickleness, by not moving at all, except in a narrow and monotonous round, thus falling into a morose conservatism, as bad as reckless radicalism, and boasting of being finished because they have ceased to improve, like the English town which was called the most finished of any in the kingdom, because no house had been built there for a hundred years. The true man will shun instability, by having decided principles, which of themselves commit him to generous progress, and because he is on a good substantial road, he will ever press on.

It is one of the most cheering views of life, that we may always be improving, and especially cheering is it, when we are in the very midst of the gravest work of existence. This fact is not always seen, and a distinguished poet, in apologizing for the haste in which his autobiography hurries over the events of his life after the thirtieth year, the time of his marriage, says: " Comedies and romances usually terminate with the marriage of the hero,

and most biographies should also. The strange and event·
ful period, the period of psychological development which
makes a narrative entertaining, then chiefly ceases, and it
is the contest and onward striving, not station and attain-
ment, that most interest in communication." This principle may do with romance readers, but not with sober students of the book of life. The thick of the battle comes
at noonday, and if we are cowards then, the morning triumph but emphasizes our defeat. Great things indeed
have been done in youth and manhood. Colburn con-
founded the mathematicians at six, and Pascal was a philosopher at sixteen; De Vega wrote plays at twelve, and
Pope says of himself:

" I lisp'd in numbers, for the numbers came."

To take examples of more substantial power; Pitt was
premier of England at twenty-four, and Napoleon was the
conqueror of Italy at twenty-seven. Yet these are excep·
tions, and the rule of life assigns its chief triumph to the
meridian, or after the meridian. Even the greatest poets,
whose imagination is supposed to be one of the illusions
of youth, have borne their noblest fruit late in life. Dante
began his immortal poem in the very meridian, and Milton
won his place at the great Italian's side, when nearly three-
score; and our chief moralists and statesmen have used
their early years but as the basis of their noblest erections.
Our Webster made his greatest speech at forty-eight, and
after forty, our Channing began the campaign that gave

him his spotless fame.   Measuring life by it moral worth we call that the most critical time for progress, which is to decide whether a man is to keep or break the promise of his starting, whether he cherishes to the end his best convictions, or is broken down by base lusts, or consumed by unholy ambition.   True to his better genius, every man may expect, surely, deeper experience of religion, wider openings of spiritual life, as years ripen his sensibilities.

Press forward ever—be ever a learner in the school of life—learn more clearly and deeply by what you already know, and make the stern facts of the world, serve you as texts in the wisdom that is divine.   Remember that in life, as in warfare, the shortcomings of the outset, may be made up by a braver purpose in the sequel. Many a noble life is a Marengo, the defeats of the morning covered by the triumphs of the day, and cheered by some new purpose, even as those battered legions were cheered, by the advancing plumes that told them of the approach of their chief and his peerless guard.   "The battle is completely lost," said the most courageous officer to his general, "but there is time to gain another."   So Marengo was won.   Improve not merely by reading and thinking, but by acting, and let action give point to books, and life add fire to thought.   Improve not merely in your capital of knowledge, but also in your method of living.   Look well to it, that your method leads you upward as well as onward, and with all your anxious striving, you lean more upon God, and bring his blessed Spirit to be the solace of your worn and weary will.   Then noon will have a blessing deeper than the spontaneous joy of the morning, and in firm experience, and calmed passions, and fixed habits, and devout aspirations, you will find that you have put your feet upon a path that God himself hath made for you —even the way of the upright, that shineth more and more unto the perfect day. Somewhat for yourself in sense of such mercy, but more for others who lean upon you, you will say: " O my God, take me not away in the midst of my days."

Such is the burden of our thought concerning the middle-age :

Experience without worldliness.

Equanimity without indifference.

Progress without instability.

The subject under consideration has interest for all — for the young, since their meridian is near, for the aged, since their meridian is a fresh remembrance—but for many, perhaps for most of us, because it is noon with us already.   Our sun has climbed to the zenith, and will not change much until it sinks towards evening. Be it so. Blessed be God for this favored time of life. Let us hold stoutly on to all the good to which heaven has called us, and with brave, cheerful heart, work while it is day. It is high time for us to know, and make others know, on what ground we stand, and bear our open resolute testimony to every worthy principle and good institution. We have no years to waste, no excuse for folly or vice now. In God's name press bravely on, and whenever the hour calls for fidelity, let not the man be wanting to his post. Instead

of less heart, put more heart into our work, and with full
experience, and calm judgment, and clear conscience, grasp
the helm of our destiny. Instead of less faith, let us
have more, more of God in our purpose and our trust
Let truer, deeper life bring us nearer the Father, and so
interpret, not so much for continued existence, as for purer
living, the prayer for length of days, that we may serve in
the noonday heat, the benign Master whom we hailed with
our morning song. More than for the breath of life itself,
strive for that spirit, without which, what we call our life,
is but an animated death.

X.

Cloud and Fire

Night's sad cadence dies away
   On the yellow moonlit sea;
The boatmen rest their oars and say,
   " Miserere, Domine! "

Morn's glad chorus swells alway
   On the azure, sunlit sea
The boatmen ply their oars and say,
   " Te laudamus, Domine! "

COLERIDGE, altered.

CLOUD AND FIRE.

ҬHE Mile Stones on our way seem to come nearer together now, and as we look back upon them in the distance, some that were wide apart when we passed them, come into almost the same line of perspective, so that the stone that was covered with summer vines and flowers, seems to stand by the side of the stone that was bared to our gaze by winter winds, or half covered by winter snows. What man of us who has passed the middle age needs to be told that life is full of vicissitudes, and that upon our journey, as upon the great Hebrew Exodus, the angels of God appear sometimes in cloud, and sometimes in fire.

That ancient story of the Hebrew wandering relates one of the chief facts in the history of the human race, and suggests thoughts for the guidance of every man's career. However much or little we may interpret the past through theological eyes, nay, looking merely from the secular historian's point of view, we must regard the Exodus of the Israelites, from Egypt to the promised land, as one of the great events of civilization, and the law which they bore with them, we must consider as the groundwork of all ethics and jurisprudence. At present, we dismiss the historical relations of the event, and speak of its moral significance for each individual life.

There is great moral beauty in the story of that forty years' march through the wilderness. No wonder that so many hymns, and prayers, and sermons, have for ages regarded it as the most significant emblem of the journey of life. Poetry has illustrated, and not created, the expressiveness of that simple narrative. Onward the great company went, providentially guided through all their devious wanderings. Their sanguine hope was sobered by a hallowed memory, as, seeking a new home, they bore with them the bones of their great ancestor, and so their future was consecrated by their past. By day, the cloud guided their march, by night, the pillar of fire. Interpret these images wisely, and the Exodus of Israel becomes a lesson for us all when we think of

The Cloud by Day;

The Fire by Night;

And the Sacred Relics borne through Cloud and Fire homeward still.

The Cloud by day! In the bright daytime — the hours auspicious and hopeful — would we walk wisely, we are not to roll the eyes in giddy rapture over the broad landscape and the blue sky, but look rather for the cloud that offers its warning or its promise. There is wisdom and peace in the disposition that takes this view, and tempers hope with caution in the bright hour. Miracle apart, the dark spot in the horizon, generally marks something of importance for our guidance, and the little sailor of the air, that bears in its bosom the wind or the rain, has greater practical significance than all the fields of transparent azure through which it floats. Is it not so with human life? When all things go well with us, and it is bright day, may we not wisely look round for signs of some darker visitant than the flashing sunbeam—think soberly of the omen of our exposure or disappointment, the monitor of our danger and our duty? So thinks the good pilot always, whatever be his ship or sea. The sagacious statesman so regards his own position, thinks less of the crowds that dog his steps and shout his name, than of the wily foes who would thwart his plans, or the foolish friends who might cajole him into folly. The great leaders of nations, from the day of Moses to that of Washington, have known how to see and follow the teachings of the guiding cloud. Never beguiled into ignorance or presumption by success, sobered by the honors that make weaker heads drunk, they have heard the warning before the danger came, and the pillar of cloud has been the angel of their deliverance.

The man of business reads the same lesson in his peculiar province, and cautiously watches the skies, which to the thoughtless, promise only blessing. He studies the doubtful fortune of trade, and looks for the cloud, when, to less observant eyes, the whole horizon is flooded with golden light.

The Christian moralist, taught by the study of history and observation of mankind, never parts company with this same caution. For himself, and for others, he never will be thrown off his guard by appearances of prosperity without bound, or of virtue beyond fear. The watchman's trumpet he keeps ready for its uses, and the very tones that speak the " All's Well," carry vigilant warning in their sound. But why single out specific classes of persons? Who is there whose experience is not full of such teaching? whose life is not deeply marked by passages that teach the wisdom and the necessity of looking well to the cloud, and making a guide of what might else be a judgment? The significant thing that we need most generally to observe, stands in contrast with the horizon at large, and tells us of trials to come. When we think that we are doing well, there is some hint for us to do better, even to make that well secure, and to prevent the giddy successes of to-day, from becoming the bitter disappointments of to-morrow.

A just self-discipline will make this truth a part of our habitual thought for ourselves and our children. It is harder to think soberly for our children than for ourselves, so much do we enjoy making them happy, and so strongly do we desire to protect them, even from the thought of trials. But the best kindness seeks for them an honest discipline, for life as it is and must be. It is unkind to blind them to the truth of things—unkind not to teach them the lesson of the cloud-pillar—not to train them to see divine leadings in the shades, as well as the lights of human life. It is well to make childhood and youth happy, but its present happiness is rather fretted away, than secured, by constant indulgence, and certainly future years of care and exposure cannot but be the worse for expectations wholly extravagant, and energies wholly unschooled. 'Let children learn early to see that their will is neither God's law, nor the world's, nor the household's. Let them learn to own the divine uses of self-denial, discipline, the subjection of impulses to principle, of clamorous desires to well-considered good. Let the very air which they breathe, be laden with the spirit of faith and patience. Let the love, that beams upon them in its thoughtful cheerfulness, express the true character of the life opening upon them, and so shade hope with wisdom. Is it not well, nay, essential, to educate children in view of either extreme of fortune? to prepare them for self-reliance, however many their friends, or brilliant their prospects? Wretched, surely, the policy that makes affluence the occasion for enfeebling the energies, just as if high privileges did not rather increase, than lessen, the demand for the best powers. The son, however fair his prospect of wealth and friends, is poorly off, if he cannot use fortune wisely, and bear reverses bravely. The daughter, however radiant in beauty or grace, however protected against want, is the nobler woman from being schooled in the utilities and the temper, that can dignify reduced fortune by self-reliance, or adorn a brilliant position by good sense and energy. Let the annals of courts and commerce within our own times, impress upon us the worth of an education which is adequate to either lot, and which, in the brightest day, looks warily towards the cloud-pillar, and accepts God's hand in its guidance.

But is not this teaching a gloomy philosophy, to insist on caution when present prospects are bright, and to speak of the cloud, when the sunshine seems a sufficient guide? Not gloomy, but the reverse, for this philosophy gives the most cheerful view of divine providence, and calls out the most elastic energies of man. It brings God's love to bear upon our perils, and invigorates the soul when most tempted to slumber away its force in false security. It gives depth to our happiness, and drives despair from our adversities. He who learns caution, when courage is tempted to be presumption, will the more abound in courage, when caution is tempted to become cowardice. Sobered into prudence by the pillar of cloud, he is all the more ready for fortitude, when night brings the pillar of fire. In short, the very spirit that takes from pleasure its giddiness, takes from trouble its frequent despair.

So think of the Pillar of Fire, whenever we need its light in darkness, as we all must do. Every day little vexations come, and in every life great griefs appear There are probably times in every one's experience, when the burden is too great, apparently, to be borne, and relief would be hailed as a mercy, if Heaven should take life itself away with the pressure. Such seasons, whatever their circumstances, leave their mark, and it is well, if they sign their cross upon us in blessing. Little blessing comes, if grief brings despair instead of resignation. We sometimes hear people speak of being discouraged, and with tones and looks in keeping with their words. There is no such word in the Christian vocabulary, and the saddest psalm or prophecy, ends ever in jubilee or blessing. The very essence of faith, to say nothing of hope and charity, forbids despair. We may indeed, and often must, abandon particular plans, and be baffled in important undertakings. Yet even these should show us something encouraging, either in themselves, or their lessons. Life is always a militant estate, and to use defeats well is as important as to follow up victories. Every true man's diary, reveals Heaven's mercy in many an apparent discomfiture, and when read with the commentary of years, the record proves that a defeat may be a true victory, the spur of an energy not to be put down, or the incentive of a devotion, winning peace and power from humility.

Certainly we owe much of what is best in our experience to the true use of seasons that have seemed peculiarly hard, and which interpret the night of our own Exodus by the pillar of fire. Every man has trying times in his business or profession, and is much the better or worse, as he bears them well or ill. Every home has its days of tribulation, and the relations of its members depend much upon their use of the ordeal, for their union or estrangement must needs connect itself closely with the result. The critical periods of history have been times of trial, and the leaders of science, freedom, faith, virtue, have been those who have followed the fiery pillar through a night that has filled feebler hearts with despair.

All mental and moral conflicts especially illustrate this truth. Speak not merely of the militant heroes of Christian history, but of our own ordinary stature of experience. Our religion, or what we ought to call such—the sum total of our thoughts, feelings and purposes, regarding God and his providence; does not whatever is deepest in it come most fitly under the emblem of the cross, that chosen symbol of peace through conflict? Many a man not fond of using theological terms, and not technically called religious, can tell from his own experience, that God's love comes to cheer him as he strives well through darkness and struggle. In every Pilgrim's Progress, the Valley of Humiliation is on the road to the Delectable Mountains. Some there are, indeed, who break down at that passage, and sink into despondency when they should be cheered by humility into new faith and hope. Be of good cheer always, the Divine voice says. There will be some light to guide us out of the shadowy valley, and God's providence does not war with his creative hand by denying the hope native to the human heart. God has put into our natures a spring of courage, as also a spring of caution, and life is arranged so as to call ever for the action of both.

As Creator, and as Redeemer, too, he calls for all our courage. The courage, which is a natural instinct, he would confirm by heavenly grace. Surely Christ came to quicken this power anew by renewing the affections that make a man brave, and revealing the aims that make the prospect always cheering. His own Gospel, Heaven's love in his life, so fully incarnated, was the fire-pillar in a dark night, and its warmth and light have not ceased to bless us. In some way good will come; believe it—the light will shine on our path as shall seem best to God, and be best for us, if not always as we may desire. Within the mind surely, and in the outward condition, the good angel shall come. When has it been otherwise to a true seeker? What lesson is taught more decidedly by the best experience than the wisdom, as well as the power of a hope that never fails?

So life should interpret the old Exodus, and hold up to us the pillar of fire by night, as the cloud by day; thus rebuking the poor frivolity which swings to and fro between gloom and glee; thus illustrating the reasonable equanimity taught by our blessed Exemplar in word and deeds.

Cautious, courageous by fire and cloud, onward still from bondage to promise,—bearing with them Relics of sacred Remembrance, the company divinely guided went on in hope. Dwell a moment upon this last image presented—memory, not the enemy, but the friend of hope.

With us, as in that eventful march, one treasure can never be left behind, unless we are utterly heartless and ungrateful—one treasure that need not be shut up in any funeral urn, nor appear in visible form—the treasure of sacred remembrance—the memory of wisdom or goodness passed away—a trust as hallowed as was the dust of their great ancestor to the Hebrew heroes in their march. In a man so strong and resolute as Moses, how interesting this spirit of tender retrospection appears in view of his indomitable enterprise. The great lawgiver, in presence of the remains of Joseph, and bearing with the ark of promise the urn of remembrance! Fact virtually renewed always when a right mind meditates upon the tombs of the faithful. Wisdom does not lead us to borrow any creed of despair from the dust of heroes, or the ruins of empires. Whatever has been well done, teaches even in its crumbling monuments the worth of well doing ; and a true heart gathers treasures ever increasing from the riches of memory. What in fact is mightier as a progressive force, than the influence of the wise and earnest men who have lived for their race and their God? What is the Christian Church itself, but the great companionship that keep sacred the Divine Master's memory, and unite remembrance and hope in a life reverent and progressive? Forward for ages, that great company has journeyed, cautious and courageous, as cloud and fire have been witnesses of God's presence in light and darkness, bearing with them the mystical body of Christ, and pausing at stages in the march to commune with the spirit of Him who died that men might live. In all its solemnity, what power and peace there is in this commemoration! It brings near to us the heart of Christ, and connects with his death and rising all the loved and lost who have trusted in his name. Such remembrance, instead of leading us to languid and indolent reverie, gives a high companionship, refreshing and quickening the soul for striving and progress.

More and more, I must confess it, the Communion service has beauty and meaning. More and more it allies with itself whatever has been best in experience, and whatever is most blessed in hope. More and more it is enriched as enlarged studies interpret the good minds of the Church universal, and as our own life deepens its own peculiar revelations. How much of our wisdom, strength and inspiration, comes from remembrance? The sages and benefactors of our race who have blessed us by their eloquence and heroism—the companions who have cheered our homes and friendly circles by their kindness and fidelity—who can part with these treasures without renouncing his birthright and forsaking God, the giver of such good? Sometimes in our career, regret is so bitter and overwhelming, as to make us pause and shrink from further toils and cares, now that so much of the joy of life has been taken away. Who has not sometimes been ready to say, with the classic poet, in view of some sad bereavement, " Alas, how much happier to remember thee than to converse with others." But heavenly mercy teaches us a truer spirit, and turns mournful memory into a cheerful hope. Consecrated by Christ, remembrance is the handmaid of progress, and the light that shines over its treasured dust, cheers the faith to the land of promise.

How wonderfully, even in merely earthly limitations, God enlarges his promises as life goes on, and kindles new interest even from the wreck of fond hopes! Study the plan of Providence; and how full of benignity it appears, as each season and age brings out its peculiar hope. Within and above all lesser promises, the great hope rises supreme, and has its august manifestation in Him whose life was the light of men.

Before us, O Beloved of the Father, be thy spirit and truth, shading our gladness with sacred thought—cheering our grief with blessed faith, joining in one precious union all worthy memories with the remembrance of thyself! The years are pushing us forward without asking our consent, and startling us ever with the sight or the story of changes. We hardly can recognize how we ourselves are changing, until perhaps some sudden shock strikes those next us, or when we are led to compare our present self with the self of some time long past. We look at an old picture or friend long absent, or revisit some old homestead, and in some face or tree or building, we find a tongue to tell us how rapidly we are passing on and away. So let it be! God does this for us, and not we ourselves; the change is well, unless marred or hurried by our sin. So let it be with us, as with our fathers! Onward still; whether by cloud or by fire, follow the living God, and in our smiles and our tears raise the old psalm of blessing to Him whose mercy endureth for ever.

> " Weep, O my soul! yet in weeping be still;
>   Not like the worldling's wild sorrow be thine;
>   Even thy tears flow at God's holy will:
>   Weep then, my soul, but in weeping be still,
>   Weep as seems good to thy Father Divine.

"Smile, O my soul! but in smiling be still,
    Not like the scorner's proud smile shall be thine:
Even thy joys wait on God's holy will.
Smile, then, my soul, but in smiling be still,
    Smile as seems good to thy Father Divine.

"Smiles, tears, He appoints, we strive to be still;
    Storms rage, and for peace in vain do we pine:
Yet moves on triumphant his mighty will.
Thou too, O my soul, at last shall be still,
    Still in thy home with thy Father Divine."

XI

Old Age.

" As I approve of a Youth, that has something of the Old Man in him, so I am
no less pleased with an Old Man, that has something of the Youth."

CICERO.

Depart awhile, each thought of care,
   Be earthly things forgotten all;
And speak, my soul, thy vesper prayer,
   Obedient to that sacred call.
For hark! the pealing chorus swells;
   Devotion chants the hymn of praise,
And now of joy and hope it tells,
   Till fainting on the ear, it says—
      Gloria tibi Domine,
      Domine, Domine.

LYRA CATHOLICA.

OLD AGE.

WHEN evening comes, and dim shadows gather over the earth, we look gladly to our homes, in whose cheerful light and friendly faces we see the whole day reflected, and find new and serener comfort given. Happy is the evening whose light is brightened by the face of some guest who has been the tried and loyal friend of years, and whose presence is at once a charming remembrance and a radiant hope. So was it with the two disciples on the day of the resurrection, when, in their walk to Emmaus, they invited their mysterious companion home with them, and found their risen Lord revealed to them in the guest of their frugal table. Rich and sacred lesson, to guide our thoughts upon the Evening of Life. As our Sun sinks from its meridian, and the shadows fall more heavily, and labor pauses in its task, what comfort and power is there in the presence of the most tender and constant friend, of Him sent by the Father to keep us ever in his love! He walks in darkness who walks without God in the day of life, and in double darkness, unless, as the day declines, he wins him to still nearer companionship, and so repeats the invitation—" Abide with us, for it is toward evening, and the day is far spent."

Here is our subject in this paper—the evening of life —its true Light, Peace, and Power, a subject coming home most seriously to us all; for although few of us may rank among the aged, all of us, however young and sportive, make a sad mistake, if we forget that the sins of youth are visited upon age, and that a true life is of itself the only good art of winning a happy age. We would treat this subject cheerfully, more cheerfully, perhaps, than any other, for each season is of God's making; he who made the evening and the morning called them both good, and surely nothing on earth is fairer than a peaceful, spiritual old age.

Consider first its true light, or the proper wisdom which should come with age. Of course it is no time then to begin to be wise, for if the true light has never shined upon a man's pathway before, it will not be likely to shine upon him merely because the world's light is waning. Use life well, study its facts, employ its opportunities, shun its temptations, meet its dangers, appreciate its blessings, as they come, and it will not fail to teach heavenly wisdom. Of worldly prudence we are not speaking now, for this generally comes of itself, without respect to fidelity or character, and the worn-out profligate of threescore can commend self-control as the best expedient, and the broken-down defaulter can praise honesty as the best policy. Not of worldly prudence, well as it may be in its place, but of that higher wisdom we are speaking, which finds a divine purpose in our existence, and studies experience by the light of God. We need this always, but especially in age, when our life becomes like a book of remembrance, and memory is a garrulous babbler, unless her facts are ranked in true order, and led forward to the music of cheerful hope. The life of a faithful man is a Scripture written by the hand of God, and to be interpreted only by God's own love. All its labors and perplexities, all its pleasures and triumphs have a meaning in themselves, and as parts of a providential whole. We are wise as we discern this meaning. Glimmers of it we may have all along our career, but when we pass the fifth decade, and enter the last score of the allotted term of usual age, we are sadly in the dark without its shining. Then most of our earthly experience is a remembrance, and we are benighted, unless we can carry with us from the past a light that does not fade.

In the walk to Emmaus, Jesus interpreted to the two disciples those Scriptures which recorded at once the history and the hopes of their race, and made the past shin upon the present and future. Their hearts burned within them as they listened, for he told them that their own lives touched directly the great plan of Providence, and He who came to be the Light of the World, had been the light of their life. Blessed revelation, not confined to them alone, not limited solely to the Jewish books thus unfolded! Abide with us, Messenger of Heaven, Incarnate Word, and open the book of our lives, and show how Chronicle and Prophecy meet together there, and every ffliction has a lesson, and every remembrance a hope, and every labor a reward. Abide with us not as a stranger for the first time received, but as a familiar friend new welcome and interpret to us our experience, that we may interpret it to others!

Pleasant and profitable should be the talk at the evening of life; and such it must be when the calm, cheerful, wisdom of the Master is its guide, and touched by him, every reminiscence opens some bright prospect, and the bread broken in his spirit quickens anew the sources of joy. How much we do need him to save us from the worldling's desolation, when he sees his boasted light fading, and the world becoming to him "a banquet hall deserted," with vacant seats for company, expiring lamps, and smouldering ashes, and empty cups for cheer. Even the shrewdest worldly prudence is a miserable solace, and the most successful man of the world, as he fights over his battles, or talks over his times and fortunes, is but a hollow-hearted, benighted chatterer, unless a light from above shines upon his experience, and he has something of the spirit of him at whose word the hearts of the two disciples so burned as they walked to Emmaus. Such is the true wisdom for age, and they who would have it at evening, when other lights fail, must seek it at morn and noon, when other lights shine.

And how can it abide with us, without bringing cheer-fulness in its train ? There is no cheerfulness worth nam-ing, that does not spring from the light of God's love in the soul, and therefore our Saviour, who most manifests that love, is the most cheering of all companions for the evening of life. We need his genial spirit always alike to give us patience in trial, and true joy in our blessings, for all our years, however youthful, call for some resigna-tion, and tempt us to some discontent. But when solemn monitors tell us that the daylight is fading, and our vigor lessening, and our labors must be lighter, and our familiar pleasures fewer, and the great night is not far distant, then especially do we need Christian cheerfulness to give us patience under the change, and to make a willing offer-ing of the exacted sacrifice. See God as Christ reveals him in the earlier seasons of life, and we shall not fail to see him during its closing years. He whom we sought as Guide, will stay with us as Comforter, and his glory will shine out at sunset even more blessedly than at noon-day.

Our Saviour does not only teach us cheerful patience under the privations of age, but he enables us to win from them peculiar blessings, and make each loss open into a gain. With the gospel before us, with God's love and life's meaning so revealed, why mourn at the passing of years? God has made every thing beautiful in his own season. Does the frame lose something of its elasticity, re-member that infirmity does not belong to age alone, and that temperate old age, in its moderated force, has a calm pulse and subdued strength most congenial with its quiet pursuits and reflective temper. Do the cares of business press so heavily as to call for young energies to come to the relief of overtasked age, remember that each season has its own appropriate work, and that age has in ripened judgment a full compensation for the decline of muscular vigor. Do what are usually counted as the pleasures of life fail the aged, remember that the purest pleasures cease only with rational life itself, and that in the gift of treasured remembrances and reflective wisdom, and moderated passions, and ripened faith, serene, deep enjoyment of nature, man, and God, age may have full recompense for all the fleeting joys of youth and manhood—more than recompense surely for the loss of all those pleasures which tempt excess more than they offer happiness. Is death near to age—so near as to give uncertainty to every hour, and thrust its spectral head into every scene ? Say, what season is free from death ? Remember that more, far more persons die young than old, and that death deals gently with the aged, alike in the manner of his approach and in the solaces which God has commissioned Christ to bear in that visitant's footsteps, that he may be the king of terrors no more, but the usher of the soul to the cherished company gone before. No. Mourn not over the passing years, but fill them with true affections and worthy works, and God will bless us even to the last. The interest of life will not cease; and instead of doting petulance, or what is quite as bad, shallow frivolity, a cheerful sense of God's love will go with us to the last, and open fresh com ˎ

fort as the night shades come on. Even that charming
sense of novelty which gives such zest to youthful curiosi-
ty, will not cease ; for how can the knowledge of God and
his providence be exhausted in our span of years ?   Nay,
the more we know, are we not earnest for still more, and
does not a cheerful religious spirit enjoy the best attribute
of genius itself, and see the universe as an ever new and
ever opening revelation of divine wisdom and love ?   Who
will not seek the Father betimes in his chosen Messiah,
and welcome anew the Divine guest as night draws near ?
Abide with us, O Christ, in thy holy joy, for it is toward
evening, and the day is far spent.

Need we say that such light and peace cannot come
without bringing power with them ?   We need power at
every season, yet never more than when bodily strength
begins to fail.   He who makes our strength according to
our day, has not left the close of our day to helplessness.
He is ready to give full balance for the force withdrawn
by the new power granted.   Piety, which is the safeguard
of youth, is the old man's staff and stay.   Let him lean upon it, and he leans upon what is divine.   Let him lean upon
it with all his mind and heart, and his mind and heart
will be strong enough to make up for the decline of muscular force.   Resting upon God in all the maturity of the
judgment, and all the calmness of confirmed experience,
and with all the confidence of affections not bound to the
earth, age rests upon the Rock of ages.   The work to be
done it cannot but do, and in some form of cheerful activi-

ty, useful by advice, if not by continued labor—useful by peaceful example, if not by more obtrusive service, the aged man stands ever at his post of duty, and awaits his Lord's bidding.

Strong for action according to his vocation, he is strong in believing, and in that grace which comes to him through faith. Joy and crown of a true life—new childhood—second morning of our being, so exemplified in the experience of the ripest men! A return to youth, not merely by the strange renewal of young remembrances, but a regenerating of the affections, a renewal of that spontaneous trusting reason so beautiful in childhood? Blessed old age, so entering the kingdom of heaven like a little child, and winning youth and childhood to itself by its holy wisdom and loving counsel! Nearer God than ever, it partakes more largely of His grace, and all past experience and labor, all thoughts, affections, purposes, seem but to have been shaping the mind and heart into a vessel for holding the precious effluence from above. The disputing reason, the impulsive feelings, the daring will, all seem to kneel down then in faith before the mercy-seat, and be ennobled by the service and exalted by the obedience. Imagination itself, before so wayward and sometimes rebellious, becomes the servant of faith, and true to the Infinite Creator, joins him in creating the new heavens and the new earth, wherein dwelleth righteousness. The noblest genius ever seen on earth joins with the simplest piety in the invitation to God's Beloved—"Abide with us, for it is toward evening, and the day is far spent." The thinner the veil of this earthly tabernacle, the more need of the light that can chow the Divine glory and the eternal world through its perishable material.

What can be more practical and cogent than our present topic—Age and its Preparation ? Take it to yourselves, children and youth, for your parents' sake and your own. Deal gently and reverently with your elders, as you hope to be dealt with, if your years are as many. Begin to live not as for the present pleasure, but as for the term allotted by your Creator, and judge all your conduct by its bearing upon the whole. Do not waste your years in folly; do not spend your strength on vanity; do not, by exhausted health and perverted passions, sow in youth the seeds of a bitter harvest in age. " It is a most amazing thing," says the grave John Foster, " that young people never consider they shall grow old. I would say to young women, especially, renew the monition of anticipating every hour of the day." Exchanging his habitual solemnity almost for jesting, he adds : " I wish we could make all the criers, watchmen, ballad-singers, and even parrots, repeat to them continually, you will be an old woman, you will, you will." We would not be so extreme as this, but surely we must say to all youth, seek God in a sober wisdom, and cheerful temper, and devoted purpose in your day of strength, and he will bless you with his brighter presence when the evening comes. You, too, who are in the high noon of life, and too prone to measure your security by your gains, remember that gold is not God, and nothing is more melancholy than the grasping covetousness so habit-

10

ual to the old age of a life given to godless gains. Use your means and rule your care under the Master's guidance, and he will be your guest when your working-day ends.

Some in my circle of readers allow a more direct appeal, for their evening is already coming on. Little favored indeed would any circle or company be without such presence, and the charm of childhood itself is never complete, without some counterpart of venerable years. And art itself, as the interpreter of nature and of God, finds no completeness in its grouping, unless youth and age combine in the beauty of the scene. It is not well to think sadly that we are growing old, for such is our lot during our whole lifetime, and the man of sixty does not feel older than the youth of eighteen. Probably the truest life has least painful consciousness of age, and takes every season as a progressive blessing. Yet they who have entered their probably last score of years, have a work to do appropriate to their season, and right faithfully should they do it. Touching examples from classic and Christian sources urge the appeal. What beauty in the group pre sented in Cicero's charming dialogue on Old Age, where he presents the venerable Cato, at more than fourscore, nstructing and delighting such brilliant young men as Scipio and Lælius, with his cheerful philosophy of living, and welcoming the day that shall take him from this earthly tumult to the great company of souls, and especially to his dear son, as noble a man as was ever born. What higher beauty, when the sage's desire is strengthened

into the Christian's trust, as in home scenes that we all
have known, and which make the old man's festival, at
eighty, more beautiful than the play of rosy children, who
gambol at his feet. Wisely let the elders interpret their
years as a revelation from the Father—cheerfully let them
bear their privations, and use their privileges—piously let
them lean upon the divine arm, and walk in peace towards
the curtain that hangs before the dark valley, already quiv-
ering as if to rise. He whom God sent to be their guide,
has passed through that gloom. Let him not be a stranger. Elders, slight not your Saviour—slight not his dying love—say now with new earnestness, and in response
to every early impression of his gospel: " Abide with us,
for it is toward evening, and the day is far spent."

It is late autumn now with nature, as I am writing,
and the leaves lie withering at our feet. It seems like autumn with mankind, and the tree of life itself has been
dropping its fairest fruit and foliage, so treasured for years
The earth stands now, as if at one of the evenings of her
great day, and the night shadows were falling upon an entire age. Our fathers have fallen, and are falling. Can
we not almost hear the muffled drum beat of a mighty nation, circling the world with her great soldier's funeral
march, and keeping company with the word that our great
civilian is no more? It is evening now; but instead of
complaining, raise gently, joyfully, humbly, the Christian's
vesper hymn, responsive to the matin song, and as the daylight dies, welcome anew the bringer of light uncreated
and undying. Join, join our souls with the dying prayer

of the mighty!   Say: " Abide with us, Beloved of the
Father, for it is toward evening, and the day is far
spent."

" My heart doth feel that still He's near
To meet the soul in hours like this,
Else — why, O why, that falling tear!
When all is peace, and love, and bliss!
But hark! that pealing chorus swells
Anew its thrilling vesper strain,
And still of joy and hope it tells,
And bids creation chant again—
Gloria tibi Domine!

XII

Prospect and Retrospect.

My Father's hope! my childhood's dream!
  The promise from on high!
Long waited for! its glories beam
  Now when my death is nigh.

Blest scene! thrice welcome after toil—
  If no deceit I view ;
O might my lips but press the so^{il}.
  And prove the vision rue!

Its glorious heights, its wealthy plains,
  Its many tinted groves,
They call! but He my steps restrains,
  Who chastens whom He loves.

Lyra Apostolica.

PROSPECT AND RETROSPECT.

Every man is looking forward to some coming good, and a large part of his happiness is from anticipation. From the very outset of his journey, his eye is fascinated by some distant object, and no amount of disappointment is sufficient to rid him of the fascination. Nay, the loss of one fond prize, serves but to sharpen the desire for a fonder prize, and throw added enchantment over the distance. God has ordained that it should be thus with us, and that by many an illusive chase, we shall strengthen our faculty of enjoying substantial good. "He," says Coleridge, " is the best physician in the treatment of ner vous diseases, who is the most ingenious inspirer of hope.' Our Creator then, is the greatest of physicians, for he is ever treating life's fitful fever, that chronic disease of mankind, with the medicine of hope. Poor indeed is the man who enjoys only what he possesses, and has nothing to hope for. Says Shakspeare :—

"True Hope is swift, and flies with swallow's wings,
Kings it makes gods, and meaner creatures kings."

Let us be willing to bless this charmer, although we have so many times been deluded by the charm.

The leader of the hosts of Israel, and the giver of their laws, had guided his people from the land of their captivity to the land of promise; and now, without being permitted to set foot upon the long sought Canaan, he was to die. He had freed them from the Egyptian yoke, led them safely across the sea and the desert; he had preserved them amidst the perils of famine, and disease, and the enemy, and from the far worse moral perils of discord and idolatry. Forty years he had sought to prepare them, by the hard ordeal in the wilderness, for their home in the happy land. He had tried to imbue them with reverence for the One God, the God of their fathers, and for the law given by his hand. Now, on the plains of Moab the hosts were encamped, the desert passed—the foe conquered. All was joy and hope. The tents of Israel, that had been borne through so many perils, and pitched in the desert, often among murderous tribes, were now spread in peace. On one side rose the mountains of Abarim—on the other side rolled the long looked for river. From the peaks of those mountains, the banks of that sacred stream were visible, perhaps its waters could be seen gleaming in the light, like a screen of silver, between the wanderers and the land flowing with milk and honey :—

> " Sweet fields beyond the swelling flood
> Stand dressed in living green."

Who should be so happy in all that host as their leader?   On the shores of the Red Sea, so safely crossed, his joy was overflowing, and his voice and his sister Miriam's, had led the thanksgiving song of the redeemed nation :— " Sing ye to the Lord, for he hath triumphed gloriously, the horse and the rider he hath overthrown." Now a happier day had come, and should not his strain be yet more joyful? Were not the deserts, with their fires, and serpents, and more savage enemies, far behind? and was not Canaan now in sight?

Far otherwise than joyful, was the lawgiver now.   In much sadness he made the proclamation : " Hear, O Israel, thou art to pass over Jordan this day." He knew the impulsive and superficial character of his people.   Their past errors taught him their future dangers.   He knew that prosperity was a harder trial than adversity, and that many who cross the desert in safety, find their ruin in gardens of peace and plenty.   He knew that the day of triumph is ever a day of trial, and instead of gay festivals, he appoints a solemn meeting; instead of songs of jubilee, he utters serious counsel; recalling the sober lessons of experience, he repeats the law with especial adaptations to their future position.   He embodies in a poem his most important lessons, and intrusts it to the charge of the elders of the nation.   It is a rebuke of the people's sins, yet a rebuke mingled with the heartiest encouragement—

10*

the whole breathing a sadness that would be overwhelming, were it not for the deep faith and hope that rise above the tones of mourning. This poem was the swan-song of the great prophet. His mountain-throne of triumph was his tomb. He died with a benediction upon his lips. It had been decreed : " Thou shalt see the land, but thou shalt not go thither." His eye, as it was closing, rested upon the tents of Israel in the plains beneath—on the sacred river and the promised land, which the Lord showed to him, from Gilead on the east, to Dan on the west—from northern Naphtali, to the south, and the plain of the valley of Jericho, the city of palm-trees.

Thus died the man whom God had raised up to do a work, second only to that of Jesus Christ. His fate is that of all his race. He saw the land but was not permitted to go thither. No man, in this world, is to see the full result of his own labors. Each, whatever his success, must die with the land of promise only in sight.

Learn now the lesson of the great lawgiver's history in its relation to things present and to come.

Observe its application to the most obvious forms of human enterprise—the sphere of ordinary business. He who labors from morning to night to hoard up wealth, never finds his Canaan of content. He has been dreaming of the time, when care and fatigue shall be at an end, when wealth shall bring leisure, and leisure satisfaction. A land of promise has been ever before him. But when he approaches the long sought home of rest, new cares and new labors rise before him. Long before the six-score years allotted the lawgiver, the stern decree that he must die finds him still toiling, still unsatisfied. He looks upon his cherished treasures, and knows that they are to pass into other hands. With sore misgiving, he questions the future: " What use shall be made of the goods which I have earned? May not temptation lurk amidst the very bounty I bequeath?" Happy indeed for him, if, in view of the Canaan opening, not to him, but to his children, he can be assured that from himself—alike from his word and example, a law of integrity and fidelity has gone forth which will be a safeguard through plenty as through privation. Happy the parents, who having brought their children to a position of competence, leave them with a good education, a sound mind, and an earnest heart, that can make them equal to either fortune. No heritage, however large, can be fatal, if the sense of responsibility be transmitted with the sense of privilege. No heritage can be small, that carries with it a noble remembrance, and an example of energy. Sad indeed the land of promise without such guidance—sad for those who are guides to its border, and for those who survive to enter into its domain.

The same principle may be applied to all those who have labored not solely for themselves and for their children, but for the future welfare of their country and their race; to all the lights and leaders of our race, to the patriots who have striven for their nation and died before the hour of triumph, or lived to see new perils in the national prosperity—to discoverers in art and science, who have met with envy and ill will from the very ignorance and prejudice which they would cure—to moralists and philanthropists who have found their blessing returned by cursing from the vice which they would reform, and the darkness which they would enlighten—to teachers of pure religion, whether those who were sent originally to reveal the true Light to the world, or those who strove to revive its brightness in opposition to the despot who would darken, or the denier who would quench, its glory.   Read history superficially, and as we meet with the names most honored, we say, "these men were successful; they did their work and had their reward."   Scan their lives more critically, and we find that they had not crossed the threshold of their hope, and the aureola that gilds their fame, has most of its radiance from the gratitude of posterity.

Still farther we are ready to carry the idea of the text. The noblest kind of progress is that which is estimated by its kind rather than by its degree, and which looks to elevation rather than to mere extent.   Every right-minded person desires to grow up in true mental and moral stature He desires to be wise in the knowledge of himself and of God, and whatever God has made.   We have all looked more or less earnestly, in our young enthusiasm or our mature sobriety, for a virtue untarnished by a fault, or a peace of mind untroubled by a doubt or fear.   This is the upper land of promise. In this we cannot but believe, and towards it, unless we are utterly unfaithful, we must ever press. Do we find it?

We surely trample upon the gospel, unless we believe in perfection and happiness as the proper end and aim of the human soul. Nay, in a true mind, this faith is as indestructible as faith in God's goodness.

Perfection!—we do not find it on earth. The best men have the clearest sense of their own deficiencies. The best workman sees most the incompleteness of his work. The greatest artist, whether poet, painter, orator, is least satisfied with his own production, and laments the vast distance between his aim and his doing—between his reality and his idea. The wisest and most fervent Christian is humblest of men, is sure indeed that he is on the right road; yet counts himself, like Paul, not to have apprehended or seized the mark, but to be still pressing on.

Happiness!—who finds it here below? Yet the truest man believes in it more and more. Nay, seeks for it in a faith ever calmer as life is teaching him to distinguish between the shows and the substance of things. His hope is no hectic fever of his soul, but it is the throb of its most healthful pulses. The leaders of humanity up the heights of the spiritual life have never despaired. Leaving to others the cheering lessons of their example, they have urged their followers to begin where they ended, and, passing within the veil, they have trusted there to know things not seen by earthly vision.

The topic that we have treated has decided connections with the season of life now under consideration, and with the century in which we live. We are just passing beyond the summit of the nineteenth century, and are thus prompted to look behind and before. How can we help thinking of the many benefactors whose lives and labors have tended to make our own future, and that of our race, so auspicious. The men who begun this century at twenty years of age, are now over three-score and ten. Fifty years form a very significant portion of the individual's experience and the nation's history. It embraces the active period of a life extended to what is usually called the limit of age—the period from twenty to seventy. They who at the opening of the century were just coming upon the stage of affairs, are now passing away. A land of peculiar promise was before them. The new generation, then just reaching their majority, were led in this country towards a future by one whose name may, in some respects, be connected with that of Moses, and who died just as our century began. Our Washington was their leader, and he did not live long enough to realize the greatness of the heritage which his fortitude and wisdom did so much to win for others. Chief of his country's armies in the wars of liberty, in time of peace, firm guardian of her laws, he saw the nation freed from the foreign yoke, and subject to a civil order based upon the convictions of the people. The duties of the soldier and magistrate faithfully discharged, he sought repose in his peaceful home. But the quiet shades of Vernon proved as the hill of Abarim. Rumors of wars disturbed his retirement, and when the peril of war was over, faction clouded his horizon, and the last hours of the great patriot were not without anxiety as to the solution of the momentous problem of free institutions. Constitutional liberty was the theme of his anxiety and his prayers. He looked to the land, but was not permitted to go thither into its fairest regions. His people were to cross the river and enter a realm of untried plenty. He was not to go with them, and Vernon was the Pisgah upon which our lawgiver died. And now the generation that followed him is passing away. Eventful indeed has been their history—not ignoble their work. Who in the most general way would undertake to tell the lessons of the last fifty-four years, without overflowing gratitude to the Ruler of events for the men raised up to be our benefactors? Calm reflection now should check the violence of party prejudice, and recognize the hand of Providence in each of the two great lines of influence that have shaped our national destiny. How large is our heritage through the labor and enterprise of the statesmen, pioneers, navigators, inventors, orators, poets, moralists, divines, who have conspired to bless the nation and the home? The old world has not withheld its bounty, and its leading minds are now a portion of our inheritance.

One by one, our guides and guardians have been passing away—some of them lamented by the millions—some of them known only to the little circle whom they have befriended, and by those blessed in their death with a benediction as worthy in the sight of Heaven, as if pageants and marble spoke to the world of their honor. Who is there among us who will not now cherish tender thoughts of the benefactors who have led us to this hill of vision and who have gone, or are going, from our side ?

Fair, indeed, the future before us—fairer, perhaps, and more exciting than any ever before promised to mankind. What is to come of it—of all this working of powerful principles, of liberty, order, education, in connection with those mighty material agencies, which human invention has bestowed upon man ? A half century to come, like that which has lately passed, to what will it bring us ? The imagination asks no fictitious theme, but reels in wonder before the omens of simple truth. Sober history is enthusiastic prophecy.

Yet be quieted, our souls. Pass on cheerfully, resolutely, but still expect no exemption from the universal lot. Who of us can reasonably expect to realize what we have promised to ourselves in life ? We are all engaged in some pursuit which we hope will lead to peace and comfort. Many work hard with head or hand, or both, in the hope of one day living at ease, free from the imperious command to toil. But, believe it, we shall never find the promised land of leisure or contentment. We must in some way strive as long as we live, whether compelled by necessity or by desire. Many look to future riches, towards which they have been travelling through a forty years wilderness of privation and fatigue. The pleasant region seems near at hand. The desert is passed, there rolls the long-sought river, and beyond, the fields smile with plenty.

" Joy, joy, is the cry. Let us enter into rest. Let us and our children cross the waters and revel in plenty." But no. Thou shalt not go over, nor enter the land flowing with milk and honey, where pleasure comes, and not care. You shall have care and anxiety to your dying day, quite as much anxiety in keeping and using your gains, as in winning them. You shall die as upon Abarim, on the verge still of a promising future, and your joy in the prospect will not be without misgivings as to the lot of those who come after you, lest their triumphs may have more peril than your trials.

Yet nevertheless press cheerfully on and do our part faithfully. We are debtors enough to the past to be creditors to the future. Grateful for all that has been done to bless us, we repay the obligation by benefits to those who come after us. For our own individual souls, we are shaping a boundless hereafter. Let this fact teach us the coherence of all time, whilst we take heed lest any narrow notions of individual isolation may lead us to repudiate our relations to our neighbor or our race. Our home and kindred—our community, our church, our nation, nay all humanity has a future connected in some measure with our own. Let the memory of those who have blessed us, guide us in view of things to come.

The world to come! Thither a greater than Moses is the guide of the faithful. He who died on Calvary opened to his followers a new earthly future, which he did not enter. He is the great interpreter of all earthly hope

—the solace of disappointment, the consecration of success. He offers not indeed to stay the flight of time, or give every fair prospect its earthly fulfilment. The Canaan that he opens is the realm in which he with the Father dwells. Honor to all them who have enlarged the *surface* of human life, and been the leaders of humanity in its onward march. Glory unto the Eternal Father for the gift of him who came to open the *depths* of the spiritual world, and whose swan-song was not like the ancient lawgivers, and did not treat of earthly conquests and fears, but was a prayer of immortal trust, a call to heavenly mansions. Let each dying year be soothed by his word, and let its requiem speak of the hope that does not die. The land of promise is never found, because the soul's true home is not on earth, and all our seeking, as it is true, serves but to lead faith towards the unseen and eternal world. The true ideal is not a dreamy fancy, or ever-wandering plan, but it rests upon a spiritual faith. From that world came the archetypes of all things fair on earth—to that world all true hope and effort lead. By our disappointment and our success, it is the part of wisdom to learn at once patient waiting and filial trust. Human life is not a master delusion. Jesus our guide, the gravest experience responds to the most enthusiastic youthful confidence. Thus the noblest of aged men of our time have passed away. The Holy Spirit has put the new song of the redeemed into their hearts, and the disappointments of past life seem but as the withered blossoms which fall that the fruit may ripen.

XIII.

Death.

Into the Silent Land !
Ah ! who shall lead us thither ?
Clouds in the evening sky more darkly gather,
And shattered wrecks lie thicker on the strand !
Who leads us with a gentle hand,
Whither, O whither,
Into the Silent Land ?

O Land ! O Land
For all the broken-hearted,
The mildest herald by our fate allotted,
Beckons, and with inverted torch doth stand,
To lead us with a gentle hand
Into the land of the great departed,
Into the Silent Land !

VON SALIS. Translated by Longfellow.

DEATH.

At the tombstone we now stand, that last way-mark of our earthly life. There standing we read the words of gospel faith, from that apostle who was snatched from the darkness of Pharisaic prejudice by him who is the Resurrection and the Life : " O death, where is thy sting ? O grave, where is thy victory ? " These are the words not of a dying man, excitable by overwrought nerves, or enraptured by delirious visions. They come from a man in the fulness of active life, and the very master-spirit of the greatest enterprise ever undertaken on earth, an enterprise that struck at the empire of the world. Nothing can be more practical, nay more business-like in its bearing than this letter of the apostle Paul to the church at Corinth, that metropolis of commerce between the East and the West—that New York of old, in which the merchandise, the people, the manners and creeds of all nations combined their pride and their misery. Advising them how to settle their disputes, remove their scandals and adjust their church offices and affairs, the apostle rises in tone as he proceeds, and closes with those sublime passages on the paramount worth of charity, and the truth of the immortal life, which reach their climax in the words just quoted. Here, as everywhere, the truly practical man shows himself to be the fervent spiritualist, and in the midst of his labors contemplating death and eternity, not to disparage, but to cheer his work.

Let such a spirit guide us now in our meditation upon death in its practical bearing. We have been considering the Circle of Life, and now in a few papers upon the close of life and the future state, we are but completing the theme. Now our topic is Death.

Death as a fact Natural and Providential; as demanding preparation, general and special; as to be met soberly and hopefully when it comes.

In common with many theologians, even of opposite creeds, we regard death as an event quite in the order of Nature and Providence—not in itself, but only in its incidental fears and penalties, as an extraordinary arrangement for the punishment of mankind. Our race were evidently born to die, and the very structure of the body, the increase of population, and the relation of human life to outward circumstances, compel us to believe that, from the very first, man was not intended in his bodily organization to be an exception to the usual course of nature. The coal that burns so cheerfully in our grate, bears marks

of wood and foliage that died years before man was created; and the stones of our houses, often embed shells
whose tenants breathed out their life before earth was
eady for man's dwelling. When he came, there is no
proof either in reason or revelation, that he was to escape
the universal lot of decay. It was decreed that he should
die if he sinned, but this dying was, we believe, not natural death, but a spiritual decline, such as sin ever brings
and salvation removes. The death which Jesus came to
do away, was not the ceasing of bodily life, since Christians must die as surely as other men, but it was that decline of faith and love which deadens the soul to God and
immortality. Taking the Christian view, we are to accept
death as a fact of nature, and by a right spirit make it
also a fact of Providence which reveals the will of God,
as well as the laws of matter.

The physiologist has his place in the investigation of
this great change, and has much to tell us of the phenom-
enon of life and death. Yet he can go very little into
the deeps of the subject, and whilst the race of shallow
materialists pretend to hunt out the mystery of our being
on the point of the dissecting knife, the true man of science calls their philosophy empty chattering, and stills his
voice into devout silence, as he contemplates this wonderful structure tenanted or untenanted by its soul. The
higher it ascends in the scale of being, the more devoutly
does science look above material laws to an overruling
mind, and see a Providence within and above nature.
The Christian begins where science ends, and interprets

the facts of nature by the mind of the Creator. If without God's will not even a sparrow falleth to the ground, surely without his will no rational creature dies, and death so intertwines itself with the uses of life, and with the whole economy of the universe, that we must consider it eminently as a providential as well as a natural fact.

As we cross the threshold of the subject, then, be ready to regard this great change as among the ordained events of our being, and instead of shrinking from it as from a sentence of execution passed upon us in God's anger, on account of original sin, let us accept it as part of his benign plan from the very beginning. "O death, where is thy sting?" Not in the fact of death itself, but in the fact of sin, the only fatal sting is found, for by this sting the soul's peace is poisoned, and her vision is darkened to the light of God and heaven.

If death be thus one of the ordained facts of Nature and Providence, it is reasonable to prepare for it upon the same principles as for any other great change or transition. Each season of life has its beginning and close ; nay each year is born at its beginning, and dies at its ending, so that every thoughtful man conducts his affairs in view of his yearly account. He not only endeavors to manage his business upon judicious principles in general, but he has also an eye to rounding off the concerns of the year in particular, that the past may be without remorse and the future without fear. Now our earthly life itself is but a great year in our existence, and the change that comes at its close, is but one of a series of changes which begin with our birth.   Prepare then for death, as we prepare for every great transition, as we prepare in youth for manhood, or in manhood for age, by a life true to every obligation and duly mindful of the change to come.

This principle rebukes at once the superstition that regards preparation for death as something ghostly or magical, wholly apart from true living, and the philosophical indifference that is content to set death down as but one among the fatalities of nature, about which we are to give ourselves no concern, because we cannot help them. Strangely the superstition still haunts the world, that the service of God is something separate from practical rectitude, and that actual usefulness is no preparation for meeting Him at last. " Prepare to meet thy God," is a command that should be heard not merely in books of devotion, and chambers of sickness, and sanctuaries of faith, but in all the active scenes of life, in our places of business and enjoyment, in our pleasant home and quiet meditations. " Prepare to meet thy God,' by the faithful use of every power and opportunity intrusted to you. See God's signature on every faculty of our mind, and every day of our existence, and do not defraud him of the reasonable service due from what is his own. Say not that it throws a gloom over life to have this service constantly in view, for we cannot use life for its true worth, unless we interpret its meaning through its Creator's will; and our best happiness as our just responsibility is of his ordaining. The recollection will many a time rebuke our

11

worldliness, and spur our sluggishness, but should it not far more frequently cheer away our despondency, and renew our strength, to be assured that we are called to serve Him who is so merciful to every infirmity, and so encouraging to every effort as our Father in Heaven? Remember that under his kingdom all fidelity is true service, and worthy living is preparation for worthy dying.

And yet however purely and devotedly a man may try to live, death is a change so peculiar and so solemn, as to call for some preparation peculiar to itself. No man can be so conscious of rectitude as not to feel a decided need of forgiveness, or so clear in his spiritual vision, as to have no desire for an assurance better than his own thoughts. In various modes this need has been supplied, and by the gospel only has it been fully supplied. Law of true life, the gospel is also the true preparation for death. In Jesus Christ it brings God's love so near that the soul may cling to it in faith, with full assurance of pardon, and in him the immortal life is so revealed, as to be no more an opinion but a fact. The sting of death is sin, and the strength of sin is the law. He who took away the rigid law, and breathed the spirit of life in its stead, and brought immortality to light, has taken away that sting. Know Jesus and trust in him; follow him in his mission and in his cross, by the practice of his charity, and in the worship of his church; and then we find that his gospel is working into our whole mind and heart a power able to overcome the grave. He sadly neglects his duty and interest, who overlooks this fact. We call him an unjust man who lives so unmindful of dissolution, as to make no just provision for those to whom he owes property or protection, and it is one of the essential duties of an honorable citizen, to leave his affairs in such a state that his family and neighbors shall not needlessly suffer by his death. Does the duty end with care for worldly goods, and is it not every man's solemn obligation to think as much of God's testament for his soul, as of his own will and testament for his property? Central in the providential plan of God, stands the mission of Jesus, as the mediator between the visible and the invisible worlds. Central in that mission stands his death of sacrificial love, and as central in his gospel and his church, stands the command to keep that death in remembrance. Remember Christ loyally, if we would share the peculiar comfort which his death imparts, and every approach to the table of communion shall be, far more than you may be conscious of it at the time, a season of preparation for the last hour. Without gloom, without any sepulchral chills, the spirit of the Master will come near to you in blessing, and if you receive him worthily, his peace will follow you through every trial. We cannot have too much philosophy, yet we need more than philosophy, we need the gospel with its grace, to give life beyond theory, and a victory over death.

Draw still nearer the solemn subject, and consider the very presence of death, that time when the word comes to us, " This night or this day, thy soul will be required of thee." How should we ask and strive to meet that hour?

Much of its circumstance must be wholly beyond our control. In an hour that we think not, the Son of Man com-
eth, and the time and the mode of our dissolution are not
set down in any horoscope that we can read. Yet generally men may have warning when their time has come, and
they always should have warning when friends can give it,
that the last hour may not be lost to charity and faith.
Surely as civilization becomes Christian, and deeds of
violence cease, death approaches with gentler step, and
sends more reliable word of his coming. The views and
habits that we usually cherish, will in great part decide
our temper and bearing in his presence, and in this as in
every emergency, the true character will be likely to show
itself. If it is not always true, that the ruling passion is
strong in death, and the brave are sometimes timid, and
the timid are sometimes brave in the last conflict, it is
true that the ruling principle may be expected then to
show itself when disguises fail. It is not best to insist
much upon the importance of appearing well, since if it
is well with the soul the bearing cannot be otherwise. Yet
there is a natural self-respect, which may justly move a
man to give honorable testimony of his convictions, and
fold his mantle in peace around him as he falls. The noble
wishes to die with a dignity worthy his name, and the same
instinct appears in the poorest laborer. Old Siward, the
Northumbrian, cried out from his death-bed to be clothed
in mail, and armed with his sword and battle-axe, that he
might die like a brave soldier; and we have accounts from
the survivors of the English war ship Centaur, that many

of the crew who had labored incessantly during days of cruel suspense, attired themselves in their best clothes, when assured that the sea must be their grave. Apollodorus carried to Socrates a cloak and tunic of fine wool for his dying dress, and Mary of Scotland, and Charles of England, went to the scaffold in their stateliest array. Such externals a Christian man may think little of, yet he will not be indifferent what witness he leaves behind him as he goes from the world. I have known a circle of friends who formed themselves into a society to pray for a happy death, but no such narrow society is needed, since every true prayer spoken or unspoken has the same aim, and every church is virtually such a circle.

In all simplicity and truth, in all tenderness and wisdom, we should pray to meet the last hour. Away with the hard stoicism that is ashamed of every natural sensibility—away with the ghostly cant that presumes to scorn this earth which God has made, and to hurry the approach of the fatal messenger. Let the soul be wholly honest and true at the last hour of its earthly witness. While life lasts, it is not without great blessings to every sane mind. We read that during the prevalence of a malignant fever, a venerable minister found an old man sick with the disease in a subterranean stable among rags, without any other furniture than two saws and a hatchet, which he could no longer wield. " Courage, my friend," said the priest; " God is about to show you favor to-day, for you will leave a world where you have known nothing but troubles." " What troubles ? " answered the dying man, with feeble voice. " You are mistaken ; I have lived very content, nor have I ever complained of my lot. God be praised for having given me life, and for closing my days, that I may join him. I feel the moment—it has come, father, adieu ! " Let us, who are so much more favored, be not less grateful. Be not afraid to say, that there is much in this life worth living for, and that the eye is to close upon blessed privileges, precious friends, glorious works of God and man. Let the regret not sink into repining at the good we leave, but rather rise into gratitude that we have enjoyed it so long. Let life come before us in solemn review, and all its mercies unite 'their testimony in praise of that sovereign love that has watched over us, and is to watch over us still.

In that love we can, if we will, be strong, and strengthen others. It is our only dependence then, for however wise or affectionate our friends may be, they cannot go with us where we then are going, and there will be a sad sense of loneliness and desertion, if we cannot lean upon one who can and will go with us, and will make the dark valley light with the glory of his presence. Humbly, yet earnestly, in lowly confidence rest upon the everlasting arm—contemplate Jesus as he was on earth, and as he is ow with God—seek the Father in him, and him in the Father, and our dying whisper may swell with its feeble breath the strain that in every age has repeated the apos tle's jubilee : " Thanks be unto God, who giveth us the victory through our Lord Jesus Christ."

The experience of mankind is after all a secret history, and every day's sunshine falls upon scenes of faith and sacrifice that the world knows not of. The great emergencies of nations do but call out reserved powers, always alive in obscurer scenes. How touching is that passage of the Reign of Terror, when the sisters of a religious house went to their death calmly, singing praises to God, and the hymn became fainter, not sadder, as each voice was silenced by the axe, until the Superior alone continued the strain, and the infuriated mob were awed by her tone whilst it lasted, and appalled by its pausing, when the slaughter was complete. Yet without the magic of such common sympathy, and the inspiration of such historic heroism, many a lonely sufferer lifts the voice of praise and prayer as bravely as that army of martyrs, and as acceptably to God. Every hour multitudes are passing away, whose last thoughts are not for themselves, but for those whom God has committed to their charge. This parting, and not physical pain, gives death a sting to the Christian. Probably most persons suffer far more many times during life, than in the pains of dissolution. Hunter, the celebrated physician, so long observant of others, turned to a friend during his own dissolution, and said: 'If I had strength to hold a pen, I would write how easy and how pleasing a thing it is to die." Not pain of body, but of mind, may be the sting of death to a soul whose sin is forgiven, and to whom life has ties all the closer, because of the love cherished, and the sacrifice made. In a way that we know not, God can take away the sting, and his goodness, which suits its ministry to each season of our being, will not leave us desolate at the last hour. In Him put our trust.

Thus we meditate upon death as a fact, as an event to be prepared for, and as a trial to be met. It implies a morbid state of mind always to be haunted by its presence, and to have our pleasure dashed, and our enterprise enfeebled by its spectral vision. Yet it is equally morbid to try to shut out the thought, and to live as if this world were all. Let death teach us wisdom, and give us peace and power too. Let it show the pleasures and cares of the world in their true proportions, and rebuke our vain strifes and anxieties. Let it calm all the fever of our passions, by the promise of its rest, and stir the best energies of our being by its limit to our labor, and its crown to our fidelity.

Learn to live as if we were to die, and we shall die as if we were to live the life eternal.

XIV

Immortality as Fact.

" In legitimacy of conclusion, strong and unexceptionable is the argument from Universality of belief, for the continuance of our personal being after death. The Bull-calf *butts* with smooth and unarmed brow. Throughout animated Nature, of each characteristic organ and faculty there exists a pre-assurance, an instinctive and practical anticipation; and no pre-assurance common to a whole species, does in any instance prove delusive."

COLERIDGE.

" And lo! above the dews of night
 The vesper star appears
So faith lights up the mourner's heart,
 Whose eyes are dim with tears.

" Night falls, but soon the morning light
 Its glories shall restore;
And thus the eyes that sleep in death
 Shall wake to close no more."

W. B. O. PEABODY.

IMMORTALITY AS FACT.

Our life, whilst we are on earth, is of itself a fact far greater than any of our opinions about it; and every thoughtful man, as he reflects upon his own experience and consciousness, upon what he has felt and thought and done, is more and more convinced that his being is, after all, a mystery constantly surprising him with its developments. We have been surveying the Circle of Life from birth to the grave; and has not the feeling been growing within us that each season brings with it a revelation of ourselves, of that interior self which we can never exhaust, and which passes our understanding, however much we may try to understand it? So striking has this truth been to some of the chief thinkers of our race, that they have supposed our whole life to be but a remembrance of a pre-existent state, and that all our new notions are but the old ideas revived. Wiser far it is to interpret the progressive development of our being here as promise of more perfect development hereafter, and to regard the fact of the present life as no less mysterious than the fact of futurity. Who will review his own career, and say that it is more strange that he should live hereafter, than it is that he has lived here? Does not our whole existence in its successive stages tend forward still, and does not the hope that lights the grave begin at the cradle, and gather brightness as the years increase?

Of the Future Life, we treat in this meditation :— the Fact, the Form of the Fact, the Appreciation of the Fact.

The Fact of the Future Life—how do we prove it, by what class of evidence or method of argument? Every thinking man has many a time exercised his mind upon the subject; and our philosophers, from Pythagoras downward, have been piling up volumes of high discourse on the immortality of the soul. Yet who of us does not see, that the fact is far deeper than all reasoning about it, and that its roots are not touched by the critic's pruning-knife or the logician's spade? The fact is part of the organic being, and the providential training of the human race, standing among those first truths which have their best evidences in themselves. Try to prove it logically, and still the best proof is better than our logic; try to disprove it logically, and our chain of reasoning refutes itself when touched by living experience, as the iron rod which man lifts against heaven, becomes a conductor for the divine spark.

More or less clearly the truth of immortality has always been held by man, and the peculiarity of the Christian religion was not so much in stating it as an abstract idea, as in bringing it into full light and true life. The fact of Christianity itself is therefore the fact of the immortal life, since Christianity accepts all the light of Nature, and concentrates all other proof in its own divine witness. Does any one ask, how Jesus proves the doctrine of immortality, and to what class of evidence we assign most value, the evidence of miracle, or of reasoning, or of inspiration? we reply that we can make no such distinctions, that Christianity is to us a living whole in Christ himself, and the gospel is in every part the glad tidings of eternal life, as truly as there is clearness in every part of a diamond, and attraction in every fragment of a magnet. To Jesus Christ it was given to present our humanity in its perfect state and true destiny. In him the soul has its true consciousness of God and immortality. His own life, in such communion with the Father, was and is the living proof of the gospel. He spake with authority, and not as a scribe. Go to him as he asks us to do, and we learn of him the fact of eternal life. That life was in him a conscious possession, and it went out in all his words and works; was sealed by his death, and crowned by his rising body and the descending Paraclete. I will never attempt to prove the future state from the gospel, until I attempt to prove that the sun is bright, or that the blossoms of spring are promise of the fruits of autumn. I accept Christianity as the central fact of God's providence; and instead of trying its doctrine of futurity by less evidence, I would use the greater to confirm the less, and rejoice to see every deep yearning of the soul and every generous aspiration of the mind, and every sacred lesson of nature so met and fulfilled in him, who is the Resurrection and the Life.

Sit at the feet of the great teacher, and straightway all other worthy teaching becomes luminous. The analogies of nature, interpreted by him, illustrate God's plan for the soul's welfare, and up the ascending scale of natural transformations we trace the way to the spiritual world. The metaphysical argument from the very being of the spirit has new force, when by the Word of Christ that spirit comes into clearer consciousness, and experience becomes the heart of reasoning. The moral argument drawn from the survey of life as a discipline under Divine Providence, and requiring retributions here and hereafter, is taken by him out of the region of speculation, and speaks as with the trumpet of judgment in every serious Christian conscience. So in the fact of Christianity, all other evidences of the fact of immortality have their consummation; and the life of Christ, whenever truly discerned, is the light of men.

In him the Father's purposes shine forth as clearly as does the perfection of our humanity. He is the living proof, that God has created at least one order of beings to receive his favor and to glorify his goodness, not solely within the limits of earthly existence, but through life eternal. So in Christ, the mind of God and the needs of mankind, combine their testimony to the fact of futurity.

The question now comes as to the form of the fact. Paul stated well what all have asked or thought, when he said, " How are the dead raised up, and with what body do they come ? " The answer may be satisfactory without being specific upon every point, since even in the near realities of this present world, we are not allowed to see precisely the form of the future until it comes, and every man's fortune and mental development show results that are a surprise to himself. As we do not presume to know all about our appearance and destiny hereafter on earth, we cannot expect to know all about the future of the soul and its position hereafter. Enough, however, we may know to silence denial, and to confirm faith by rational anticipations as to the two chief points—the future person of man, and the sphere of his existence, or the spiritual being and home.

All existence of which we have any knowledge has some form ; and God himself, although his essence is infinite, and therefore indefinable, manifests himself through the various forms of creation, and especially through his Son. He made man in his own image, and gave the human body a form corresponding with the faculties of the mind. What form the soul within us has to the All-discerning eye, we cannot say, without claiming his attributes ; but we have reason to believe that it has either some form, or the capacity of developing such. There is a natural body and a spiritual body, says the apostle, and the sages of the world have said the same. Why not follow at once the Word of Inspiration and the hint of nature, and believe that the soul bears the germ of the spiritual body, which, after death, is to be developed in accordance with the nature of its faculties, and the elements of its future sphere, by the power of God?   Accept this view, and we shun two extreme errors; we are saved from the pantheism which asserts immortality only in name, and destroys all personal identity by merging man's being in God's infinitude; we are saved also from the materialism that knows no future existence apart from this present bodily fabric, and places all hope of immortality solely upon the resurrection of the body.   So man is secure of personality without sinking into materialism, and has hope of a future that shall continue his conscious existence without continuing his physical limitations.   The form of the spiritual body is a subject fairly within the domain of philosophical analogy, but does not belong to the positive ground of Christian faith.

The idea of continued personal existence raises the question, where—or what is the place of future abode? Where is the world of spirits?   That there is a world to us invisible, is as obvious as that there are beings to us invisible.   God is every where, yet we do not see him. Christ and the spirits in fellowship with him, still live, yet we do not see their abode.   Our Saviour, when on earth, had communion with heaven; yet the everlasting gates were not revealed to the eye, nor was the undying anthem heard by the ear.   Where then is the spiritual world?   It is quite enough to say, in answer to all infidel denials of a spiritual state, that we see but a small portion of the universe with our senses, and that the portion of it most important to us here, the domain of our thoughts and emotions, we perceive not by the senses, but by our con sciousness. The finer and more powerful elements of nature are least tangible; and such forces as electricity, magnetism, and the odic current, are so subtile and mysterious, as to seem transitional elements, between the material and the spiritual worlds. It is enough to disarm such gross infidelity to affirm that nature, instead of denying, gives analogies in favor of a spiritual world, which must be the interior life of the universe, as the soul is the interior life of the body.

This analogy has been developed with great fulness by various philosophical writers in all ages, and by none with so much system and persuasiveness as by Swedenborg. In him we see the universe exhibited as the external of the spiritual world, all the orbs of creation having their invisible atmosphere of life, each having its own heaven, and God being the sun and centre of all. Isaac Taylor has comprehended all theories of the spiritual world within three classes. The first of these makes out the home of souls to be within the present visible world, upon some purer planets or central suns. The second regards the spiritua world as all around us, and pervading all existence, especially surrounding every orb. The third theory regards the home of the soul as to be provided by a transformation of the visible universe into a more glorious creation, or by the end of this world, in order to the rise of a new creation, with new elements, and new and higher expressions of omnipotence and intelligence. These theories show possibilities, and may develope probabilities. However wanting in positive proof either of them, or any combination of them may be, they present analogies for the service of faith, and show the folly as well as the sin of the godless view of the universe that denies the soul a lasting home in some mansions of the Heavenly Father.

So then we speak of the form of the fact of the future state, affirming the continuance of personal consciousness with such organism as God may give, and in a sphere of being provided by him, and we leave the particulars alike of the spiritual body and the invisible world in the region of pious contemplation and scientific analogy.

To bring the whole subject down from the abstract to the practical, let us now look at it for ourselves, and speak of our just appreciation of the fact of futurity; not of the future state as a motive, for that will occupy a paper by itself, but of the way to make the fact a reality to us. If a man die, shall he live again? In our creed, and with our best convictions, we say with more than the patriarch's light, yes, he shall live again; and sometimes to us, as worldly as we are, the unseen world is the reality, and this earth is but the shadow. But generally it is not so, and we live as if immortality were a fancy, and heaven a fond dream. How shall we rebuke such worldliness, and make futurity an ever-present fact?

How do it except by treating it as a fact in our conduct, until it shall make itself a fact to us by its spirit?

Work and wait. As we work for the true aim, that aim shall be clearer; and as we wait upon a heavenly power, that power shall draw ever nearer.

Work as under the divine kingdom, and its reality will constantly grow upon us. Does not all faithful earthly service illustrate the worth of religious obedience? Upon the stormy ocean, with death upon the waves and mutiny in his fleet, Columbus was true to his noble queen, and her majestic smile was then as near to his sense as when he knelt before her a poor suppliant repelled in scorn from other courts. In dark times, with cold and famine in his camp, with murmuring among his countrymen, and the threat of a traitor's doom from the repudiated throne, our Washington kept his allegiance to his country, and her approving countenance was as clear to him as when he laid his sword at her feet, and took the oath of fidelity as the chief magistrate of her constitutional law. Even so in our relations to the Divine Sovereign and the spiritual world, every act of obedience fixes the attention, and clears the vision. Working for the life eternal quickens the faith which is the substance of things hoped for, the evidence of things not seen.

And the more we work, the more reverently we wait; for much as we may do to make heaven near, we only put ourselves in a position to allow its spirit to approach us. We knock at the gate, that it may be opened to us. There is a life which we do not form, but which we can only receive. That divine life was manifest in Christ in its fulness; and its influence, through him and all means of grace, still flows through all worthy faith, affection, work and prayer, into the souls of men. We live not by bread alone, but by every word that proceedeth from the mouth of God. That Word is proceeding still from the Infinite Wisdom and Goodness, still from the heavenly world and the eternal throne. Receive it; receive it by every receptacle in our spiritual nature, by all thought, feeling, fidelity, devotion, and the life of God and heaven within our souls shall interpret Christ's saying, " As I live, ye shall live also."

Futurity—eternity—is not the thought too glorious to be cherished by our poor nature? There is not presumption, but humility in the faith. In lowliness we most truly secure the good of the present life, and the mind is exalted by adoration of him who lights the earth for our path and fills it with plenty. We live now only as we receive his bounty. So live the life eternal; and even now, accepting God's free Spirit, we may pass from death unto life. Reverently accept it. If we feel a reverent and lowly gratitude when we lift our eye to the heavens, and know that the gentle ray which touches so benignly its delicate nerve has been on the way from its remote star ages before man came into being, more reverent and lowly be our gratitude when the soul's vision is touched by th light uncreated, and the God who has filled the visible world with his bounty, opens to us the glory of his unseen and eternal home.

" This world I deem
But a beautiful dream,
Of shadows which are not what they seem:

Where visions rise,
Giving dim surmise,
Of the things that shall meet our waking eyes.

" But could I see,
As in truth they be,
The glories of Heaven that encompass me;
I should lightly hold
The tissued fold
Of that marvellous curtain of blue and gold.

" Soon the whole,
Like a parched scroll,
Shall before my amazed sight uproll;
And without a screen,
At one burst be seen —
The presence wherein I've ever been."

XV.

Immortality as Motive.

Eternity! Eternity!
How long art thou, Eternity!
Yet onward still to thee we speed,
As to the fight the impatient steed,
As ship to port or shaft from bow,
Or swift as couriers homeward go.
Mark well, O man, Eternity.

Eternity! Eternity!
How long art thou, Eternity!
As in a ball's concentric round
Nor starting point nor end is found.
So thou, Eternity, so vast,
No entrance and no exit hast.
Mark well, O man, Eternity.

Tersteegen.   Translated by C. T. Brooks.

IMMORTALITY AS MOTIVE.

THERE are some passages of our career in which the fact
of the future state comes out from its shadowy mystery,
and startles us with its solemn reality. A thoughtful
man cannot enter upon any momentous enterprise without
some intimations of the bearing of his conduct upon his
spiritual welfare, and no man who has not wholly imbru-
ted his soul by beastly sensuality, can do a marked wrong
without some instinctive sense of the judgment to come.
Over all the mile stones of our journey, stands the majestic presence of Eternity, like the mighty heavens, while
lights and shades are the emblems of its decrees. Fully
convinced as we may be of the fact of the future state,
we may fail, however, even by the very greatness of the
fact, to feel its power duly as a motive. The spiritual
world is too often allowed to remain at a vast distance, a
magnificent, but very remote reality, like that starry way
above our heads, milky in color from the dim light of un-

12

numbered suns, whose whole radiance thus beheld, gives us less guidance than a lamp in the street through which we walk, or a taper in the chamber of our vigils. No small portion of the thought and labor of theologians has turned upon this very point, and of old and of late the great question has been, how most effectively to bring the powers of the world to come to bear upon the present life. The old priesthoods and the new radicalisms have had the same end in view. Whether by prayers over the mystical wafer, or by manipulations in the mesmeric circle, they have tried to call forth spirits from the vasty deep, and prove each in their own way, that human life opens into the unseen spheres. The ages of faith have not passed, change as they may in the character of their faith. There is faith enough in every living heart, to give great interest to the inquiry how ought a reasonable person to live in view of the fact of the future existence ? This is our topic now—the Future Life as a Motive, or more particularly,

The Reality of the Motive,—the Nature of the Motive,—the Urgency of the Motive.

The Reality of the Motive ! How can the Immortal Life be a fact without becoming a motive ? It cannot be, unless the future life be so disconnected from the present, as to exclude the very idea of any influence proceeding from our actions and character here into our lot hereafter. Even supposing such total disconnection, and regarding the resurrection merely as a physical change, without any moral accountableness, like the transformation of a creeping worm into a winged moth, without the transmission of conscious identity, the change, if it could be foreseen, could not be contemplated without great interest, although in that case the chief motive would be in the mind of God, the active agent, and not in man, the passive subject of the transformation. That ultra form of theological doctrine, which comes very near this belief, and which looks to the fact of the resurrection, to make all men at once holy and happy, without respect to their character in this life, does not wholly exclude the idea of motive from its creed, since its champions maintain that the prospect of such boundless joy, and the conviction of such infinite love must needs subdue repining, and awaken gratitude and obedience. But take what we regard as the Christian view of the future state, in connection with the present life, and the fact of a conscious and responsible continuance of being, is the motive that crowns every other, and subjects all aims to the one master aim.

The very nature of things leads us to believe that our future in all its extent, hereafter as well as here, must depend upon our conduct as truly as upon God's power. There is something in conscience itself which declares the eternal sacredness of the right, and bids us accept it for our present and future trust. The very sense of personal identity moreover implies such continuance of personality hereafter, as to connect the mind here with the mind hereafter, by a bond which God himself cannot break without breaking his promise of a personal immortality. Allow as much as we may for the regenerating power of divine grace here and hereafter, the individual's own will is not destroyed, and the responsibility of its own acts still re mains. So obvious is this truth becoming, and so import ant is it to every earnest appeal to men, that it is finding favor with the sects once inclined to deny it, and those two extreme classes of dogmatists, those who maintained on the one hand, that some are to be saved and some to be lost hereafter, without reference to their works, and those who maintained on the other hand, that all are to be saved without retribution hereafter, without reference to their works, are disappearing ; and the leaders of both these extreme sects are preaching moral accountableness here and hereafter.

The Bible is very clear upon the point, and from beginning to end it holds man responsible for the deeds done in the body. In the Old Testament, the fact of the spiritual world is less distinctly set forth, yet is constantly implied, and although often identified with the continued national existence of the Jewish people on earth, the accountableness of each man in the future is declared perhaps all the more powerfully to a sensuous and ignorant people, by being associated with such temporal and material imagery. But when we come to the Divine Teacher himself, we find every word and act imbued with the doctrine of responsibility to the heavenly throne and the unseen world. All the parables in their visible figures, and all the discourses in their spiritual truths, rest upon futurity as the great fact and the great motive. There is in the very mien of our Saviour a solemnity like the majestic shadow of the coming judgment : there is in his tone a .deep authority that speaks of justice as well as mercy, and holds all men accountable for their talents, whether many or few. Say if we will, that most of his declarations regarding future judgment are figurative expressions borrowed from temporal affairs, and therefore not to be applied to the future state; does not the same shallow reasoning apply equally as well to the promises of peace and blessing hereafter, and destroy the motive of grateful hope as well as that of rational fear ? Reject from the Bible as merely figurative, and not referring to the future state all material imagery, and we take the life out of the whole book ; we have the body without the spirit, the blue sky without the eternal heaven. In the most expressive imagery, borrowed from external objects, as well as conveyed in direct and unequivocal words, our Saviour declares the accountableness of man to God for his deeds. His very mission to save men from sin, implies the doom of sin unrepented of, and his condemnation of wickedness around him, in its very tone, proves that he distinguished between guilt and misfortune, and in God's own name arraigns the transgressor. Nay his most gracious offers of privilege, his call to men to receive eternal life, have a startling earnestness about them, which proves that men have a part of their own to perform, and what is offered in mercy must be received by fidelity.

On the ground of reason and revelation then, there is

reality in the motive drawn from the future state, and we are solemnly called of God to live in view of the world to come. We proceed now to inquire into the nature of that motive.

We cannot take the course so prevalent, and regard this motive as very different in kind from all other good motives. Much less can we contrast the present and the future state so sharply as to consider contempt for this earth, as in itself any preparation for heaven. We cannot regard the spiritual life as demanding a nurture essentially different from the nurture of all pure affections, nor can we believe that salvation means any thing much more mysterious in kind than the true health and peace of mind, which we may begin to know here. We do not believe in the mere ritualist, who hangs the whole of our hope upon receiving a consecrated wafer, which has become heavenly food under his hands, nor are we persuaded by the extreme dogmatists of a now very limited class, to rest our only hope upon the transfer of an innocent sufferer's merit to our account, without any reception of that spiritual life which is the reconciling and the atoning gift. We do not cherish the best of our earthly affections by such means; we do not recognize God's present love, nor nurture pious gratitude by such means. As pure mind and heart must be essentially the same in all worlds, we are moved to judge of God's nearer presence by what he shows of himself now, and of true life hereafter, by the truest life here. The plainest sense, and the most direct philosophical argument from the very essence of mind, would lead us to this view of the nature of the motive. Is not this view wholly confirmed by the example and word of Jesus?

What can be more clear than that Jesus came and labored, and died and rose to throw open the spiritual world to the affections and practical use of mankind. The Heavenly Father whom he reveals, is the God whom our own hearts yearn for. The divine life which he lived is the consummation of our highest ideas of what is good and pure, true and lovely. He won the hearts of his disciples to himself by imbuing their devout reverence with the tenderest affection, and when he went away from them, he tried to have them continue in the same feeling towards him, just as if he, their friend and Redeemer, were with them still, and heaven were but the completion of their earthly fellowship. Mark his words and bearing at the most solemn moments of illumination—as at the Transfiguration, when souls departed came from the unseen state and stood by his side—or as at the table of communion, when he desired that he might be always remembered there even as when with them in the body;—note the words of the Cross, in which with his dying breath he so tenderly commended his mother to his beloved disciple's care— note his bearing after the resurrection, when, notwithstanding the mysterious change that was transforming his body, he kept the same heart for his friends, and said, "peace be with you," to his disciples, and called to the true-hearted woman who had followed him to death, " Mary," and drew that reply " My Master," which proved that the heart is essentially the same in both worlds, and its best affections have truest life beyond the grave. Nay, more; that witness of Jesus gaining strength and beauty in all ages; that promised Spirit, which men call Comforter, given in his name, what has it been doing, but always testifying of the community of life between the two worlds, calling men to follow the gospel of love, and win peace unspeakable by all worthy affections and faithful obedience?

Christ then joins his word with the evidence of our reason, to prove that the motive to be drawn from the future state resembles in kind, however it may differ in degree, from the motives that give the present life its purest peace and joy.

So obvious and practical in its nature, is not the urgency of the motive clear? Our plainest reasoning, our conscience, our honor, our affections, move us to live for the future, whilst we are in this world; and what greater madness can there be, than to shut from our view the infinite future beyond? Shut it not from view; but like practical Christian men, give attention to its solemn interests.

Is there any thing to fear in the developments of futurity? Yes, much to fear, although there should be more to love—much to fear, unless we can, by true life, rise above fear into love. True to the gospel and to the Christian consciousness in all ages, we must preach the retribution of God against all evil doers. There is judgment against the wicked, although he may escape the penalty of human laws, or drug remorse to sleep by vicious arts and excesses. He who oppresses the feeble, robs the poor, despises the widow and orphan, watches in order to ruin the innocent, pampers his passions on human misery, tramples upon God's image in man, or profanes God's name and word, shall not go unpunished. There is terror in God's majesty for the wilful offender, and fear is most salutary when it wakens penitence, and so inflames the love which alone can cast out fear. Among men not wilful offenders, there is a chastened fear of God which always remains after the fear that hath torment departs; a devout awe in view of the Almighty, and All Holy One, a shrinking from the very thought of arraigning his goodness or slighting his law, a godly fear that clears the very fire of love from its clogs and ashes. Let no man be ashamed to say that he fears God, for the fear of the Lord is the beginning of wisdom. Fear him if we are doing wrong, because we offend the very love that is trying to bless us, and which wounds us to reclaim us from transgression. Fear him if we are trying to do right, for he whom we serve is not our equal, although we call him Father; and our loyalty cannot be true, unless its very love be mingled with reverent awe which leads our loftiest virtue to bow with trembling before the mercy-seat.

Such fear is the minister of that sacred love, the crowning motive flowing from the spiritual world. God is love, and we are prepared for his presence the more we partake of that which is the essence of his being. Here the glory of Christianity opens upon us who believe that the whole

12*

of life should rest upon a spiritual basis, and that heaven opens around and within us now whenever we practically accept God's love, and breathe it into all the uses of our sphere. True heavenly-mindedness only can interpret the real urgency of the motive flowing from the unseen realm where God dwells, and where the spirits of the just are with him. He that seeks this frame of mind cannot be proud, cannot arrogate aught of the blessing to his own personal merit. His highest joy is in being willing to receive what God so freely gives. He does not presume to originate or create that sacred fire which inflames every worthy affection, or that heavenly water which refreshes the soul's inmost life. His best faculties are to him but receptacles of blessing; and the more deeply he enters into heavenly peace, the more he adores the might of heavenly love. Over the retributions of God, he acknowledges the rule of the Divine goodness, and he cannot but believe that there is a love deeper than any abyss of woe.

Who does not sometimes feel the force of this motive, and oftener deplore its absence? Is it true that God has created us in his image, and called us to live in his love and truth, and sends out precious influence to win us and keep us within his kingdom? Then what manner of persons ought we to be? What becomes of our petty pride and insatiate vanity, our repining, our petulance, if we will but recollect ourselves, and cherish the sweet temper and friendly service proper for the subjects of a divine kingdom! What becomes of our poor selfishness, if we

bear in mind the bounty that has blessed us with enjoyment and hope! The faith, which is the substance of
things hoped for, the evidence of things not seen, instead
of being a ghostly spectre, horrifying us with sepulchral
terrors, becomes a cheering, benign angel of God, throwing
over all our labor and trial and joy here the light of life
eternal. Such words, indeed, shame our unworthy living,
and it may seem presuming even to speak them. But
frail as we are, are we ready to abjure all part even now
in the power that comes from the unseen world, and to
shut the everlasting gates that open more blessings than
we can number to us and the children of men? No. We
will not part with our birthright. Strive and pray for
greater fidelity—for more of that true spirituality which is
at once practical and devout—which makes life strong and
beautiful as it brings heaven near—which moves men to
be heartier and braver as they are wiser and purer—which
translates all prayer into action, and all action into prayer,
that God's will may be done on earth as in heaven.

Here, readers, we approach the close of our course of
thought on the Circle of Life, which has occupied us in
most of these pages. Circle we call it, because it begins
and ends in God's Providence, and the same great events
are constantly recurring. Yet strictly speaking, nothing
returns to its beginning, and the path marked out for us
by our Creator is towards infinite progression. Forward
in time we are tending, pilgrims of a countless multitude,
most of whom have gone from sight into the unseen world.
If we are alive to true humanity, our heart must beat in

sympathy with the vaster humanity that now lives beyond the grave—if we are alive to friendship, its holiest affections cannot fail to have some cherished objects there—if we are alive to God and the Beloved of God, we shall feel the attraction of their hallowed presence-chamber within the veil. Along the advancing ranks, from the unseen portion of the company to the portion at our side, living influence even now comes to us and bids us beware of all unfaithfulness, and enter into life eternal.

XVI.

Home Evermore.

Mine be Sion's habitation,
Sion, David's sure foundation:
Form'd of old by light's CREATOR,
Reach'd by Him the MEDIATOR.
Peace there dwelleth uninvaded,
Spring perpetual, light unfaded:
Odors rise with airy lightness;
Harpers strike their harps with brightness;
None one sigh for pleasure sendeth;
None can err, and none offendeth;
All partakers of one nature,
Grow in CHRIST to equal stature.
Home celestial!   Home eternal!
Home uprear'd by power Supernal!
Home, no change or loss that fearest,
From afar my soul thou cheerest;
Thee it seeketh, thee requireth,
Thee affecteth, thee desireth.
Grant me, Saviour, with thy Blessed
Of thy Rest to be possessed,
And, amid the joys it bringeth.
Sing the song that none else singeth.

HILDEBERT, A. D. 1133   Translated by Neale.

HOME EVERMORE.

In our meditation upon Immortality as a Motive, I spoke of the influence coming from the vast array of Humanity, that has passed into the spiritual world. We give the whole of this meditation to a fuller consideration of the subject. God himself is ever bringing it near to our affections, by removing our own companions by the way to the eternal spheres, and thus planting the amaranths of immortality among the decaying flowers that bloom along our path, and climb upon our Mile Stones.

When a tyrant ruled the land, and the march of his minions was wet with the blood of the faithful, the thoughts of the early Christians turned gladly towards the eternal throne, comforted indeed as they contemplated the great multitude who had passed from the trials of earth to the triumphs of heaven. Not to that primitive age, nor to such tribulation, has the same disposition or the same need been confined. We are so constituted that whether happy or sad, we cannot live wholly absorbed in things present, nor be unmindful of the unseen world.

Our nature forbids it. Creatures of memory and of hope, we must in some measure remember all events and persons who have had power over our lives, and we must interpret the future somewhat in the light of the past— the present hour cheered or darkened by the things that have been or promise to be. A man may try to stifle the disposition, or hide the need of living above the present, by cutting himself off from all human associations, or by drowning his thought in the deluge of worldly cares. Yet even in the lonely wilderness, the solitary is still haunted by the faces that he has known, and they that have gone from the world to the unseen land, seem to hover around him, and things unseen become the greatest of realities to him. He too who seems engrossed with the pressure of secular affairs, has his part in the invisible. He is driven on in his career by a force of habit or association, whose origin is among things invisible : he is attracted by visions of future success or ease, which have not and may never have any visible fulfilment. Nay, the mightiest men of action have been possessed by some dominant principle or influence entirely beyond themselves or their position. The Alexanders and Napoleons have been influenced by historic examples, that live only in the intellectual horizon. Better counselled, better cheered, the heroes of Christian history have lived and labored, as surrounded by heavenly presence, as members of a family part on earth, part in heaven. Every true household shows the working of the same spirit, and we look upon all as belonging to our home, and as having relations with us now, who have been taken from our side, and called to the unseen mansions.

What nature craves, the gospel sanctions and teaches. Our Saviour revealed the eternal world as the soul's true home. They that were with him, and who lived after him, rejoiced in that heavenly household to which he called them, and deemed it a breach of faith for any Christians to be as strangers and aliens in that spiritual commonwealth opened to their love and communion.

What nature thus craves and the gospel urges, the Christian Church has never failed in some measure to recognize. There may have been, there doubtless was, much narrowness in the ideas held concerning the spiritual world, and the claims to its blessings. Yet what beauty alike among the lowly and the strong, in the cottage and the church, what beauty and power too have been given to human life, from its associations with the heavenly company on high. Indeed there are few occasions in which a Protestant feels himself more disposed to fall in with the spirit of the Ancient Church, than in respect to the festivals which open this month of November, in which we are now writing. The Ancient Mother, in many things so stern and ungenial, seems quite winning and amiable, as she calls her children to close the ecclesiastical year with the feasts of All Saints and All Souls. We cannot ask the Saints to intercede for us, nor are we taught to pray for the souls of the faithful who have gone from the earth. Yet to us not without instruction, comfort, and incentive, is our thought of the heavenly company who have gone to their rest, left to us their example, and call us to their fellowship.

We need to think of them surely, and the thought which meets this need cannot but have power, great power over us. Consider its influence first in enlarging and elevating our views. That great multitude not to be numbered, of all nations, kindreds, people, tongues, around the eternal throne! Meditate upon them, and how can we have a bigot's creed or a worldling's scorn? All exclusive nationality, clanship, caste, speech, there disappear, or if any traces of their influence remain, they remain only to add to the beauty of that divine union in a harmony more perfect from its unity of spirit in diversity of gifts. The feuds of sect, often more bitter than those of nation or clan, are not found there. The various kindreds and tongues that divide the theological world, do not convene their councils or prepare their anathemas. In one great kindred of filial love all unite; in one language of spirit and truth all join. There is the man of the ritual who trusted so much in the baptismal water and the sacramental wafer to impart divine life, and whose walk was nearer to God than any mere ritual could lead him; there, too, is the man of the doctrine who made a secondary thing of the outward form, and who trusted to be saved by imputed righteousness, not, however, without earnest striving for the righteousness which he claimed not as his own by merit, but as of faith; there, too, is the man distrustful of ceremony and dogma, trusting in the power of good-works, and yet by a faith working in love, saved from the perils of a proud and superficial morality. Thus the Churchman, the Puritan, and the liberal Christian little inclined to take the ground of either, are there. They stand in near companionship as they speak, not in the old tongues of technical theology or sectarian habit, but in the language of that heavenly grace, which is better than the tongues of men and of angels; beyond the gift of prophecy, the understanding of mysteries and all knowledge.

How can it be otherwise with the great communion on high ? The lives of the faithful, the word of Christ, the nature of the eternal life, warrant our saying, To what narrow border of Christendom, or to what great hierarchy have those qualities been confined, that give the soul peace and have promise of heaven ? Go for the standard, not to Papal calendars or Puritan codes of discipline, but to the Master. We cannot acknowledge any narrow standard, such as opens heaven to the Dunstans and Dominics, and closes its gates against the Fenelons and the Howards of Christendom. Do we ask who form the company of the Blessed ? The Beatitudes are the reply, and the blessings of the Sermon on the Mount have their consummation in the Heavenly Zion. The meek, the merciful, the pure in heart, the peace-makers, they and such as they, are blessed. To what kindred or tongue, nation or people are they limited ? They who were Christlike in the world, amid its stripes and separations, shall they not be more so, nearer the Master, nearer each other, as partial vision is enlarged,

and no longer seeing through a glass darkly, they know
even as they are known? Enlarging indeed is such a contemplation, and exalting too. It has all the elevating influence coming from the study of the gifted minds who
have adorned our race, whilst it throws a divine light upon
their earthly experience, and connects the brightest pages
of human history with aims eternal, and with life in heavenly mansions. We are morally and spiritually elevated,
not so much by our labor as by the use made of our
inheritance. If we stand high it is because the toil, suf-
ferings, virtues, wisdom of so many generations have
placed us there, and the work of ages has combined to
give us our home, our culture, our vision. Who so base
as to be willing, were the thing possible, to renounce his
share of the great heritage of humanity, his birthright in
the great domain of time—to cut off that stream of living
water that flows to him through the great channel of life,
beginning in God, and flowing through the ages, its golden
sands enriched by all that has been good, and true, and
lovely in the world? View history thus, how exalting is
the survey. How much more so when we connect its developments with the spiritual world, interpret the treasures of earth in their relations with the treasures of heav-
en! The wisdom that has here communed with the Divine mind, the love that has here soothed the sufferer, and
yearned to rest in God, have not died. They live, and
Cherubim and Seraphim, the angels of light and love scorn
not their presence. The lowliest virtue and the sublimest
intelligence there dwell transfigured. In one edifice, Im-

perial Rome gloried in gathering all the treasures of the world's faiths, and in the temple reared by Marcus Agrippa, collected all the symbols and idols of the dominant religions of mankind, from the monstrosities of Egyptian superstition, to the beautiful creations of Grecian taste, and the stately forms of Roman heroism. Alone of the old temples that of the Pantheon has been preserved, and in the seventh century it was dedicated to the memory of the saintly names of the Christian church. " The capital of Paganism," writes Count de Maistre, " was destined to become that of Christianity, and the temple which in this capital concentrated all the forces of idolatry, was to unite all the luminaries of faith." To a better, a nobler, loftier temple even than that thus purified, the spiritual Christian looks—even to one that gathers the faithful of all creeds, and nations, and kindreds. Is the study of what has been noblest in man on earth exalting ? Look to the heavenly company, and how is the view exalted, as well as enlarged?

Does intellectual greatness most win our reverence ? Then behold its consummation, not its apotheosis, but its Divine adoption : not its pride claiming to be God, but its reverence, the more exalted as it is more filial. Aye, genius itself, true to its sacred mission, not groping its way in feeble reasonings, but seeing truth in the light divine—not fashioning its conceptions of the lovely from things perishable and fragmentary, but from open vision of the Divine Archetype itself! Even the genius for action is there yet in being, and in more potent energy. For the highest action even in this world is moral and spiritual, and survives the body. The mind builds the home of charity, or gathers the nations into peace and order, before the hand touches the stone, or the arm of the law arrests the offender. The nearer that men approach to the Almighty will, the greater the power and the sphere accorded to them. Not in ignoble indolence do men live the life eternal. Theirs indeed is peace, but what peace is so great as the serenity of earnest and harmonious action, even the peace of Him who said, " My Father worketh hitherto and I work," the peace that beams out from the works of the Father, and from the face of Him in whom the Father stood revealed ?

We must not dwell more upon this theme—the power of the heavenly company to enlarge and exalt the views. Theirs is another ministry, and one still dearer. It is to attract and quicken the affections in part towards themselves, indeed, but none the less towards God through themselves. The order of Providence is that the longer we live, the larger and closer is our relation with the unseen world—the greater the company of those who have gone from us, leaving their mark on our minds, and their memories in our keeping. Poor indeed the lot, and wretched the spirit of him who counts friends and benefactors only among the living. They that have gone in peace care for us, and we ought to care for them. They care for us, because Christ did and does; and they that are near him are like him. Nay, is it not one of the characteristics of a perfected mind, to care more ever even for scenes and persons connected with its own early development? A wise man thinks more earnestly and tenderly of his early home, the fields of his sports, the companions of his pastime, the parents and friends who counselled him, than he did when he was himself a child. The more we advance, the more we interpret and dwell upon the beginning, so that the analogies of human interest here below would seem to teach us that there is no Lethe rolling between us and the better land, to shut the living from the memory and regard of the departed.

But God is our teacher, and in Christ he has opened a school for the heart which can reach depths that no human wisdom can penetrate. Many a rough nature learns a lesson of faith and love there, which it is sometimes too proud to confess. God opens to our minds and hearts a high and holy realm of contemplation, to which few are wholly indifferent. As we contemplate that goodly company, so vast, so imposing, and yet so winning in some aspects that come near to each soul, a feeling arises, half of earthly friendship, half of heavenly communion, mingling all that has been fairest in memory with all that is loveliest in hope; so that we cannot say as we linger whether the power that attracts us is of man or of God, until our fidelity unites both elements in one, and by a sacred humanity we are drawn nearer to the Father, and both loves unite in one.

The affections are thus engaged, and so too are they quickened. Looking thus upward, we feel the power of all worthy examples. The life that once animated them seems still to enforce them, and the annals of virtue and devotion seem to live anew as sacred preachers of fortitude, comforters of grief. The source of that power which comes from communing with the faithful in the unseen world, we need not be too anxious to analyze. How the departed act upon us, we may not say with dogmatic certainty, until we can say with the same certainty how the living act upon us, sometimes to lead us to God, sometimes to sink us in sin. Who is not willing to own a power above the ken of a sensual philosophy, in the influence that has come to him from those whom he no more sees in the world? Who has not found in some sacred remembrance, in the cherished image of some benefactor, a ministry to his soul passing the aid of any abstract precept, passing the range of the material understanding? God works upon us more and more by the ministry of the departed. In our homes they meet us in how many influences, in the sanctuary they speak to us often how mightily. In hymn and gospel we hear the words of souls now departed, in prayer and meditation we use their wisdom, and utter their love. The ministration is more effectual, as we connect what they have done in the world with what they are now above the world.

We do not deem ourselves now as occupying the region of dreamy sentiment or idle musing. Active force comes from the thoughts we have been urging—power to cheer and animate the will, as well as to enlarge and elevate the views, and to engage and quicken the affections. To do well the various works of life, we need to know well the great work of life. Who shall teach us, if not they who have done its work faithfully, and gone to their rest? As we seek them, they come near to us, and their words live for us, and their deeds act for us. The world's time-servers will not meet our want. They may show us how to look upon the expedients of the hour, but they know nothing of the great and solemn interest of life. In transient disappointments, we need associations that lead us beyond the transient to the eternal—in present perplexity we require counsellors, from whose spirits beams the brightness of the eternal light. When we feel pain or sickness, we would feel also the assurance that they bore all this and more in peace. When we are on the verge of that gulf which to the senses is darkness or void, shoreless, cheerless, when things earthly are fading away, and friendly hands here below do not help us, do we not need the solace of that great company who can make us feel—not alone—but among brethren, more in number, than we leave—Him chief in the company who went to prepare a place for the faithful? Read soberly the annals of the strong of the earth, whether among the lowly or the illustrious, and then say, confidently, that man is never so strong, in life or death, as when cheered and strengthened by faith in unseen power, and communion with invisible minds. Christ meets the want in his promise to be with his own. The promise is fulfilled in all agencies that repeat his gospel and bring the Comforter near.

Take home this doctrine each of us in the measure of

our experience and needs.   In some of the ancient church-es, I have read that there was a beautiful custom of calling upon the most venerable person present, to begin the service at the festival of All Saints, in remembrance of the departed, and of varying the age of the individuals succeeding, until the last sentence was spoken by a little child; thus expressing the great range in the ranks of the faithful, so commemorated in summoning age and childhood to celebrate its various benefactors.   Not thus in form, but in true spirit, elders and youth respond to the truth inculcated.   In our own circle let all, from venerable age to lisping childhood, light the memorial taper to cheer with its light the tombs of the beloved that stand along our pathway.

How much of the influence that has made and is making us what we are, comes from the invisible company? Let any one of mature years think of his relations with the unseen world—think of all who have tried to help him in word or deed, in his early home, or in his varied intercourse with the world, through books that have nourished his soul, or deeds that have made clear his pathway.   Does he not find himself rebuked for his too habitual worldliness, and addressed by a power that is attractive, ineffably winning even in its solemn rebuke?   Is not earthly life— I will not say despised, because of its baseness—is it not by this spirit redeemed from its frivolity, and consecrated anew as the gateway of heavenly mansions?

Let not youth shrink from the contemplation.   In that great and innumerable company there are those whose presence may win the young heart to dwell with home affection upon the unseen land, not there, alone and desolate, but among friends. In every circle, and surely among our circle of readers there is some child who bitterly needs such solace, to take the sting from the bereavement that has quenched to the vision a light and love which God has kindled in a parent's face. Life will have purity and power as that image is remembered. To how many such remembrance at once rises, perhaps of some devoted mother, or cherished wife, or darling daughter, of whom it is not too much to say :—

> " Another hand is beckoning us,
>   Another call is given;
> And glows once more with angel steps
>   The path that leads to heaven.

> " O, half we deem she needed not
>   The changing of her sphere,
> To give to heaven a shining one
>   Who walked an angel here.

We will not leave the topic without recognizing the stern moral which it urges by the very pathos which it moves. Do they that pass from the world still act upon it ? Are they remembered—does their example and spirit still speak ? No man liveth to himself, or dieth to himself. What is our example—what our spirit—how are we living—how shall we be remembered ? They in this world, who are the happier and better because of our living in it, are witnesses that we have some hold upon the higher world. Our lives may repeat the beatitudes, and by blessing others we may win a place among the blessed.

Thus the heavenly company point a stern moral, as they hold out a cheering hope. Power and peace meet in their benediction and their appeal.

XVII.

The Great Cycle.

Happy those early days, when I
Shin'd in my angel-infancy !
Before I understood this place
Appointed for my second race ;
Or taught my soul to fancy aught
But a white celestial thought ;
When yet I had not walked above
A mile or two from my first love ;
And looking back at that short space,
Could see a glimpse of his bright face ;
When on some gilded cloud or flower
My gazing soul would dwell an hour,
And in those weaker glories spy
Some shadows of eternity ;
Before I taught my tongue to wound
My conscience with a sinful sound ;
Or had the black art to dispense
A several sin to every sense ;
But felt through all this fleshly dress
Bright shoots of everlastingness.

   O how I long to travel back
And tread again that ancient track !
That I might once more reach that plain,
Where first I left my glorious train ;
From whence th' enlighten'd spirit sees
That shady city of palm-trees :
But ah ! my soul with too much stay
Is drunk, and staggers in the way.
Some men a forward motion love,
But I by backward steps would move ;
And when this dust falls to the urn,
In that state I came, return.

HENRY VAUGHAN.

THE GREAT CYCLE.

WE have travelled some distance together, kind reader, and have taken notes of various aspects of human life, from its beginning to its close. We have not bounded our vision by our footsteps, and have had some glimpses of the everlasting hills, and now our journey ends with their ethereal heights in the enchanted distance. Lest the guide might of himself be too tedious, he has secured the company of some of the sweet singers of our great Israel, and as we started upon each stage of our pilgrimage, we have had a strain or two of song to cheer the way. The sweet poem of Vaughan, " The Retreat," that makes our closing motto, expresses a sentiment that we must all of us at some time have felt, as we reflect upon our career We cannot help casting a glance behind us as we journey on, and it is an essential law of every sound mind, that it shall revert constantly to its own experience, and like the revolving wheel of a chariot, turn constantly back to itself, as it goes forward. We must return to ourselves thus

whether we choose or not, for we can no more rid ourselves of the orbit of our being, than we can rid ourselves
of being itself. Our own will can do a great deal for us,
but it cannot do every thing, and even when the will strives
the most bravely, it can only strive upon a path or tide
which God has fixed for us. We may guide the horses,
but we do not make the highway; we may ply the oar or
tend the sail, but we do not create the tides or the winds.
It is well for us, as we close these meditations, to think
somewhat seriously of the orbit in which we are placed,
and remember that the strongest man is moved by a higher
power, when he is apt to think that he is but moving himself. At the outset of our career we are tempted in the
giddy pride of young blood to suppose our will to be every thing, and when we have travelled far, and are perhaps weary and dispirited with fatigue and disappointment, we are tempted to regard our own will as nothing,
and to sink down into utter fatalism. Combine our young
enthusiasm with our mature experience wisely, and we
shall see the sweep of our own will, and of God's agency
also in the great cycle of our being.

There is surely something more than our own volition
in the power that so binds our past and future with our
present, and gives a retrospective turn to our most sanguine anticipations. Not only in his repentance does the
wayfarer, like the returning Prodigal, *come to himself*,
but also in all his just obedience and healthful progress.
More than in a literal sense the pilgrim is ever returning
to his starting-place, and whether his path be upon the

globe or any other sphere, he who starts from the East, if he goes far enough towards the setting sun, finds himself at the East again, with his evening hymn welcoming the morning dawn. The evening star that shone so mildly upon his twilight musings, will become the morning star that flames in the forehead of some distant sky, that meets him in his course, and Hesper may kindle into the Phosphor, whose dawning he implores :—

> Let those have night, that love the night:
> Sweet Phosphor, bring the day:
> How sad delay
> Afflicts dull hopes! sweet Phosphor, bring the day!

The first and most familiar application of this principle to human life may be made to our remembrance of our own early days. It need not be argued, for it is plain enough, as before set forth, that our childhood is never so fresh to us as in old age, and that every true life in some way repeats the prophet's words : " He shall return to the days of his youth." What the psychological law of this fact may be, we are not anxious now to set forth, since we are concerned only with illustrating its truth. It may be that first impressions last the longest, not merely because they were made upon a fresh and sensitive surface, but because constant retrospection has been all the while deepening the image, just as the object longest held before the silvered plate, takes the strongest picture under the sunshine ; and surely childhood is always in the sunshine as it stands within the chamber of memory, and is always

13*

thus deepening the transcript of itself. But whatever may be the explanation, we may be sure of the fact, and the wisest and the simplest men cannot but recur to their early days. We have already quoted Gray's charming Ode on revisiting Eton College, so full of touching reminiscences, and we may borrow a still stronger illustration from Goethe, who so prided himself upon his artistic coolness, and who yet could speak of his early days, in such tender strains as this in the Inscription to Faust, that wonderful creation which embodies so much of the meaning of our modern life :—

" Once more, sweet visions, are ye floating hither—
    Forms, who of old oft gladdened my dim sight?
Shall I now hold you, beautiful, together?
    Yearns my heart still for that illusion bright?
Nearer ye throng!   Let not your beauty wither,
    As from the misty cloud it bursts in light.
How with the joy of youth my bosom springs,
Breathing the magic air shook from your dewy wings!

" Old days of gladness in your train come sweeping,
    And shades of loved ones start up all around,
Like some old tale which set our young eyes weeping,
    First Love and Friendship come.   Each inward wound
Now bleeds afresh ; the old complaint unsleeping,
    Laments life's mazy course with echoing sound,—
Names the good spirits, who, when joy shone o'er me,
Smiled round me one short day—then took their flight before me.

*   *   *   *   *   *

" What I possess now seems no longer real,
    But in the Past I live, in my soul's first Ideal."

We suppose that the same law of our being moves the more diverse natures, and that the play of the memory, like the beat of the heart, is pretty much the same in this majestic demigod of the German Parnassus, as in the lowliest reader of his verse. With us all, life, as it travels on, recurs ever to its beginning, for it has received its appointed orbit from the same hand that formed and guides the spheres.

But this recurrence to our early days is but one form, and perhaps one of the most superficial forms in which the orbit of our being indicates its revolving movement. We look back in our better moments, not so much to a certain period of time past, but to a certain spontaneous experience, and, to a true believer, childhood has its chief attraction in the retrospect, as revealing so much of God's image in the instinctive play of the spiritual faculties. We were made originally in the divine image, and the most extreme teacher of the doctrine of the Fall of Man and Original Sin, although it be Augustine himself, will not deny that there are in our nature some traces of that primitive constitution or selfhood, which came from the Creator's own hand. As we go on in a true life, and through repentance and faith win spiritual peace, we cannot but attach more importance to the earliest gleams of the divine light within; and thus the farther the pilgrim travels, the nearer he is to his first home, and in coming truly to himself, he comes nearer to his own soul. Surely all that strengthens the mind, or quickens the affections, or in any way improves the man, faithfully interprets him to his own consciousness, and introduces him to himself. A great many writers, as already remarked, have spoken of the fact, that when we meet with any exalted truth or noble sentiment, we are apt to receive it as a familiar thing that we seem to have met before, in spite of plain evidence to the contrary. With some minds of no mean philosophical pretensions, the inference has been that our souls have lived in a pre-existent state, and that thus all experience appears like a reminiscence of that state. A noted American theologian has startled the sober orthodoxy of his brethren in New England, by insisting upon the reality of a pre-existent state, in order to justify God in bringing the human race into this world under a curse, which in his view can be only cruelty and injustice, unless all those thus born under wrath have sinned somewhere before this earthly probation. · But we prefer the poet's version of the psychological fact, and Dr. Edward Beecher's dialectics are far less persuasive to us than Wordsworth's verses :—

> " Our birth is but a sleeping and forgetting:
> The soul that rises with us, our life's star,
> 　Hath had elsewhere its setting,
> 　　And cometh from afar :
> 　Not in entire forgetfulness,
> 　And not in utter nakedness,
> But trailing clouds of glory do we come
> 　From God who is our home."

But without yielding either to the poet or the theologian, why is it not enough to say, that every noble truth and sentiment that excites this sense of reminiscence, by appealing to the soul that God has given us, reveals the true or inmost man to himself, and developes vague instincts and dim intimations into conscious sentiments and positive convictions? It is very certain that the farther we advance in true culture, in wisdom, virtue, faith, devotion, the more this feeling grows upon us, and the pilgrim, instead of going into a far country, seems to be entering more fully into his own home, and getting acquainted with himself. The ripe apple is but the blossom matured; the sturdy oak is but the acorn unfolded; and so the best development of a cultivated mind is but the bringing out of its own powers, under providential influence, or in other words, the coming of man to himself.

But where is our need of God, and what becomes of religion in this view of the great cycle? If life appears thus to turn upon itself, what need of the Divine Mind and the Eternal Ruler? Much need every way; for if we study the orbit of our being wisely, we see at once that whilst like the rotating globe on which we live it is turning ever upon itself, this movement, like that of the globe, is part of a majestic economy that rolls each sphere loyally about its central orb. The soul is drawn by its primeval nature, by its own inmost wants, by the revealed Word and the Holy Spirit towards God, the Parent of its being, and the Sun of its Righteousness. In fact its most signal experience of the spiritual life is called by a name expressive of its true birthright, regeneration, or the new birth. Thus the soul lives its true life, and is fully born when born of God, and becomes his child, not merely by creative power, but by redeeming and renewing love. It comes to itself in coming to God. It cannot live truly for itself until it moves in its due path about the Divine Light, and turns each phase of its being to the heavenly warmth and radiance. In its power, as well as in its weakness, the soul needs God, and bears witness of him. True to Him, we have growing experience of his own attributes, and of his sufficiency for our peace. We have true life only as we live in Him. The Mission of Christ was an approach of the Father to men, and an opening of the souls of men to the knowledge of the Father. They that received him had life, even the life of the sons of God. As they beheld his glory as of the only begotten of the Father full of grace and truth, they read their own being in that divine light, and saw that God's love is man's true life. All Christian experience but developes that great truth, and shows that man can come to himself and know the full capacities of his own being, only by turning to God in a filial faith and living obedience. However brilliant his genius or vast his knowledge, no man can find out the best that is in him without seeking God, and without God he who thinks to gain the whole world loses his own soul. True growth is thus an awakening; true progress is thus a returning—not in a monotonous and servile round, but in a revolving ever advancing cycle, like the vine climbing towards the light, in an ascending spiral, that turns ever

upon itself, and bends its ripened clusters towards its parent root.

The state of mind thus cherished by a true relation
between the soul and God, is the true life which the gospel
so commends. It is the life eternal that may be begun
here on earth, and into which every true believer passes
from the death of sin. Who of us shall presume to define what this eternal life is, when the deepest philosophers
are utterly at loss to define what time is? As, practically,
we may say that we measure time by succession, or by the
passing of objects, or events, so we may say, practically,
that we can estimate eternity by our experience of the
Absolute Good, or of those truths and affections that live
without decay, uniting the intensest vitality with the deepest tranquillity, like the God in whom they have their being. Perhaps all of us, however frail, who have tried in
any measure to be faithful to our calling, have had some
gleams of this experience, when we have been lifted above
all chances and changes into that ethereal current, in which
the soul is not utterly absorbed and annihilated, as the pan-
theist dreams, but lives and moves in God, as the gospel
teaches, all the more alive to its own being from having
its life in Him, the Infinite and Eternal Love. The most
spiritual and exalted minds of our race have had most of
this experience, and in their seasons of fullest inspiration
they have felt themselves consciously drawn away from
their own self-will into the sweep of that eternal cycle, in
which the creature freely moving, yet divinely moved,
earnest yet tranquil, enters upon the eternal state, and in-

terprets better than any dogmatic argument can possibly do, the prayer of the divine Saviour for the fulfilment of the great Atonement :—" That they all may be one : as thou, Father, art in me and I in thee, that they also may be one in us : that the world may believe that thou hast sent me."

The very clod beneath our feet may, if we will but listen to its oracles, teach us a far deeper lesson than any base materialism can give, and may expand into a far larger wisdom many a dogmatic champion of the schools. How many and what mysterious currents of influence act upon that little piece of clay on which we tread ! To say nothing of the magnetic and electric properties which may act upon some of its particles, we know very well that each of its atoms feels something of the attractive force that sweeps the spheres in their cycles, moons around earths, earths around suns, and probably suns and systems about some distant central orb, perhaps the chosen pres-ence chamber of the Eternal Word. If the dust bears witness of such a majestic cycle whose times rise into eternities to our limited understanding, what shall we say of the soul and the recurrent yet progressive cycles of its divinely ordained orbit ? Surely the dust that goes to the dust as it was, falls not without bearing by its analogies some witness of the spirit and its union with the God who gave it.

So then in closing these notes of our life-journey, we take our stand upon the rock that cannot change, although every mile stone on our way may crumble into dust. We measure life not by the course of years, but by the character of its experience, sure as we are that quality as well as quantity must enter into our numbering of our days. The object is not to travel fast, but to travel wisely and well. We need in this impatient age, and in our fretful, restless country, to look carefully to the dominant temper, and in our vagaries of folly and passion to *orient* ourselves by the true light. There is something in that word " orient " that we Americans need to study, for it tells us of a clime and a wisdom that we are apt in our bustle and haste to forget. To us, the children of the impatient West, it speaks of the East, and of the divine light that there dawned upon the nations. The East has been the providential school of the divine life, and its commissioned prophets have borne witness that a profound rest of the soul in God is the essential mark of all true power, and that they who walk with God have a peace that the world can neither give nor take away. Do we not yearn for more of that true leaven with which God of old blessed his chosen servants, and with which the Divine Son was sent to bless the world ? Does not our best culture show some relentings of our rebellious pride, and some fond and filial yearning towards the birthplace of our best faith, the home of our deepest humanity ? Certainly by what is best as well as by what is worst in our American temper, we are called to check our unrest, and calm our passions, and quicken our faith in the still yet living waters that flowed of old from Siloa, and flow ever from the oracles of God.   We complete our own lives and round the orbit of our own being, whilst we complete the circle of civilization by bringing our own Occidental energy into reconciliation with the true Oriental faith.   Our race, like the individual man, is stronger and wiser by tempering self-will with loyalty to God's will.   The race, like the individual, can enter the kingdom of heaven only by being converted and becoming as a little child.   Let our indomitable energy ally itself with spiritual faith, and the Star of the East will shine upon us without eclipse in the path of its empire Westward.

In some respects I am as ready as any man to glory in our country and its institutions.   Nay, I think that we honor our country even when we most candidly criticise its failings, because we use the liberty which is our noble birthright, and thus recognize our blessings in exposing our defects.   Certainly nothing can exceed the folly of the prevalent disposition to measure power and prosperity solely by quantity, count our strength by number, and estimate our progress in the main by speed.   We are undoubtedly the fastest people on the face of the earth, but it by no means follows that we are the wisest or the happiest.   A man may travel fifty miles an hour, but if he is upon a bad or foolish errand, the faster he travels so much the worse for him, for he is sooner at the accomplishment of the wrong.   We spoil every thing by hurry, whether it be the dinner that we devour without quiet digestion, or the land that we exhaust by impatient tillage, or the health and strength that we waste in our haste to be rich, or in the mind and heart that we fret and fever away by the constant round of excitement. In the opinion of some medical men we are wearing ourselves out as a nation, by our hurry and intensity,—too eager to get a living to be willing to stop to live. The statistics of insanity show an alarming increase of that fearful scourge, and ten thousand pale and anxious faces are writing their sad commentary upon our temper and habits. I am not fond of croaking, and believe on principle in the power of a cheerful heart. Precisely because of this power, I insist upon the need of a more tranquil faith, and more peaceful and steadfast method. We may all rejoice in the prosperity of our country—in the vastness of our domain—in the numbers and intelligence of our people, and nevertheless remember that we are but human, and are exposed to all the perils that have been the wreck of nations in the old world. Whether for a nation or for an individual soul, true progress is to be measured by the character formed, not by the distance travelled. Not without meaning we close our notes of the Mile Stones on our way with those hallowed words that Jesus, the great Mediator between time and eternity, as well as between man and God, spoke when he embraced all men and all nations in his parting prayer:

This is Life Eternal, that they might know thee the only true God, and Jesus Christ, whom thou hast sent.

XVIII.

After Thoughts;

A FEW CLOSING REMEMBRANCES.

OCTOBER.

Ay, thou art welcome, heaven's delicious breath!
  When woods begin to wear the crimson leaf,
  And suns grow meek and the meek suns grow brief,
And the year smiles as it draws near its death.
Wind of the sunny south! oh, still delay
  In the gay woods and in the golden air,
  Like to a good old age released from care,
Journeying in long eternity away.
In such a bright, late quiet, would that I
  Might wear out life like thee, mid bowers and brooks,
  And dearer yet the sunshine of kind looks,
And music of kind voices ever;
And when my last sand twinkled in the glass,
Pass silently from men, as thou dost pass.

BRYANT.

It becomes
  A man, if aught delightful to his soul
  He hath received, to bear a grateful mind;
  Kindness gives birth to kindness; in the heart,
  When grateful Memory holds its seat no more,
  The Man to every generous sense is lost.

SOPHOCLES.

AFTER THOUGHTS.

A FEW CLOSING REMEMBRANCES.

TWENTY-TWO years ago in the summer of 1854, I arranged for the press the papers that make up the substance of this volume, and introduced them with an introductory sketch of " Companions by the Way." I remember well the day when that sketch was finished, the last day but one of summer, and just before the close of vacation, when the stern call to work was sending its whisper before into those last hours of play. Those years have brought so many changes in thought and affairs, in life and history, as to make the book an old story, and perhaps to hint the wisdom of letting it alone, or of trying to make it over anew. But there are notes of places and persons enough in its pages to move friends to ask for its republication, and there are records of experience and conviction that speak best in their own proper words and would be weakened, if not falsified, by being written over under new conditions. Therefore the author, without claiming any especial importance for his efforts, or expecting any great number of readers, complies with the request for a new edition and adds these familiar remembrances of the later years.

If it is an awkward matter, and may seem an ungracious task, to venture upon personal reminiscences after dealing with general topics of high interest, it is well to remember that the simplest is likely to be the best way out of trouble, and that any sincere and truthful remarks upon the drift of the last score of years, will be sure to rise above personality into principle, and to open private experience into generous fellowship. Certainly we are all travelling on together, and more and more we are made to feel how much we share each other's lot, and our fate is bound up with that of our race. I cannot recall the cherished companions, to whom this volume was dedicated in 1854, the class of 1832 of Harvard University, without associating the nation and the world with their personal career, since they have served upon so many fields of peace and war, and done good work in so many spheres of science and art, letters and religion. We meet now even more regularly and loyally than then so long ago, and on the last Wednesday of every October we dine together, as many as are able to follow the welcome call, to see the old faces, and to sing the old songs ; to shake hands with the living, and to remember tenderly the dead, who now number more than half of the seventy-one names credited to us on the Triennial Catalogue. Many names on that list have already risen into historical importance, and with these sober years and gray heads, the end of usefulness has not yet come with the surviving. The two class-mates who last left us, the Rev. Oliver C. Everett and Dr. Stephen Salisbury, were gentle and faithful souls whose lives are a lesson to us all, and I name them here tenderly.

Those of us who have lived in the great cities cannot live to ourselves only, and even our country rambles and restings are sure to keep us face to face with the eventful scenes and significant persons that are constantly shaping our experience. I cannot tell a long story now, even if I had one to tell, and I must be content with writing down a few remembrances of conspicuous aspects of recent life, that may perhaps interest old friends whom I do not see now as often as is desirable, and be of some use to young people who sometimes ask counsel of years graver than their own. For these I wish to make these pages instructive, even if I fail to make them entertaining.

I. — UNDER THE TREES.

Within the last twenty years, we Americans have been thinking of country life as never before, and private gardens and public parks are memorable marks of the progress of rural taste. It was very sad, that Andrew J. Downing, after laying out so well the public grounds in the city of Washington, in 1851, lost his life the next year in the river Hudson, and there is comfort in believing that the banks of this river, in their homes and surroundings, will be a lasting remembrance of the founder of American landscape gardening.   Happily his mantle fell on Frederick Law Olmsted, whose tour in 1855 through Europe, with an especial eye to parks and ornamental grounds, prepared him to take charge in 1856 of what was to be our New York Central Park, for which he made the accepted plans in 1857.   That enterprise has told upon the taste of the whole nation, and in nothing have our people improved so much as in appreciation of natural scenery, and in the method of keeping the charm of nature under the hand of art.   We have become a nation of travellers at home as well as abroad, and every beautiful region in our land not only attracts hosts of summer visitors, but warrants the building of public houses for guests.   In one way and another we all live part of the time under the trees, and it would be well if there could be a general and judicious comparing of notes as to the best way of doing it.

But experience here in the woods has, in some respects, had little variety, and may not on that account be worth telling.   Our home has been these twenty-seven summers upon this little hill that overlooks Long Island Sound, and the only change of place that we have made here in that time, has been in buying the eight acres next below the cottage in which we were boarders, and in building the house which has sheltered us for nineteen summers after due enlargement for children, grandchildren and kindred. Our friends generally, and people at large, do not like such stability, and not a few sell their country places and wander at their sweet will, and sometimes to their sour discontent, into new quarters or rambles, when the summer heats begin. I prefer a fixed home with liberty of course to leave it a while, whenever duty calls, or wholesome pleasure invites. It seems to me, that the advantages of this course far outnumber those of the wandering life. For ourselves, we can say that for twenty-seven years we have found health in this air and in those waters, and, in a frugal way, we have found in this quiet old village the characteristics of country and seaside combined. There is a fine beach for bathing, there are beautiful drives and sightly walks, with neighbors near at hand, and with a thriving and growing city within a smart half-hour's drive.

This place itself is somewhat distinguished over other American places in the fact that it does not grow much, if any, and that a new house is seldom built among our well-to-do people, whilst most of them constantly improve their grounds. There is far less business here, at the old centre, than in 1779, when the British troops landed from their ships, and burned the town to ashes. Yet the old character remains, and the solid citizens date their pedigree years before New York grandeur began. The minister of the Prime Ancient parish, as it was called, lives in the parsonage that was left to the church by the nephew of Roger Sherman. He has had such predecessors as the Rev. Andrew Eliot, President Humphrey, and Professor Lyman Atwater; and the parish dates from the coming of Roger Ludlow, in 1639, whilst the line of clergy began with the Rev. John Jones, an Oxford graduate, who, after a long ministry here, died in 1664, the year that saw New Amsterdam accept the English flag, and take its present name of New York. The Episcopal church here has a record of more than one hundred and fifty years; it gave to King's Chapel, Boston, its last rector, the Rev. Henry Caner (1747–1776); it had the service of the first Episcopal clergyman ever ordained in this country, the Rev. Philo Shelton, and now with two parishes it prospers under the charge of two clergymen, one of whom is a poet and scholar, and the other, in the next village, is a muscular Christian, a bold thinker, with a liking for sea and land adventures.

If asked to state what are the advantages of having a summer home in a place like this, fifty miles from the great city, I can truly say to men who are occupied most of the year with business or professional cares, that it seems to me the best thing in the world. A parish minister can be here under the trees, and at the same time within call of his people, and he has the satisfaction of being always at their service, and they always know where to find him if sickness, or death, or occasions less sorrowful make his service essential. Then there is health of body and mind in the quiet of this country life, as contrasted with the excitement of cities, and the dissipation of the great watering places. The true life depends upon the just combination of constancy, with change, and he who lives most of the year in the great city has stir and strain enough to make him need an interval of tranquillity, such as settled country life gives. In fact, you may have virtually four separate seasons by a good combination of town excitement with country rest. In the winter, and the weeks before it, and after it, the work is hard, and the excitement is unceasing ; then comes spring, when you can lighten your work a little, and run now and then into the country, and spend some days there when not kept at your post ; then comes the summer vacation with its full rest ; then the autumn call to go to work again with at first lighter, and then heavy care, as the busy season opens, and the world and the church are in full life again. I have found great satisfaction, as well as health, in this division of the year, and twenty years of close parish work, without any serious interruption by sickness or travel, were a fair commentary upon the wisdom of such method. Then, too, you secure good opportunities for study by this course, and you can find time during your spring and autumn retreats, and your summer rest, to take with you into the woods the important books of the year, as well as enlighten and edify yourself and your parishioners by studying some of the great masters of thought.

There are certain points of economy that are to be looked to in choosing and carrying on a country place; but without discussing these at length, I will only say with prudence you can be sure of having solid value for the money that you spend, and that with a good right-hand man to manage the place, such as has served us here for near twenty years, you need not have much to worry you. You will have abundance of vegetables for the table, as much fruit as you are willing to cultivate with care, plenty of milk for winter, as well as summer, and a play ground for yourself and your children to your heart's content. In fact, the out-door school is the best for the little ones, and the true kindergarten is under the trees with the real objects about them to name and to study, and the merry birds to pitch the tune for their songs. The day is not long enough for these little ones, that make play of work and work of play, and hardly know the difference between the two, whilst kind mother nature looks on benignly to see the muscles swell, and the senses brighten.

As to the influence of the country upon the mind of a student, or upon any thoughtful man, there is a great deal to be said in various directions. It is not wise to say that the fields, and trees, and rivers are sufficient companions of themselves, and that it is the part of wisdom to forget, or try to forget, the town and its people, mankind, and their life in the green woods. You cannot do this if you try, and the pastoral poets, who make so much account of fellowship with nature, always show that they have been schooled in society, and that they carry society with them at heart into their retreats. In fact, when you go into the country and quit the present excitements of the town, you have the town before you more vividly than when in the midst of its pressure, you have not time to consider current events and persons, because new experiences crowd them out. But under the trees you recall your social experiences. Events and persons appear before you, with peculiar distinctness, and nature seems to be the camera which reflects unbidden the images in your memory, and sometimes tells you of what you thought that you had forgotten. For a time you find this office of nature most exacting, and she does not allow you to leave the busy world, whilst she saves you from new distractions.

It is not true then, as a recent Pessimist philosopher has said, that the modern rural tastes are proof of the cursedness of our social life, because delight in the country implies hatred of the town ; for the town is ever present in the country with every one who has had recent experience of its stirring life, and one charm of the rural retreat is pleasure in watching, or remembering the distant agitation, without being in the midst of its whirl. This nature, indeed, which is so ready a medium for our memory and thought, and so ready to write out before our fancy the secrets of our minds, is by no means a passive material like paper, but has a charming life in every vein and leaf. Her kingdoms of plants and animals are not company enough for us, but they are a marvellous companionship that deepens and exalts other society; and as with the persons who please us most, such as bright children and genial women, the great charm is not so much in what they say and do, as in the exuberant spirits in which they say or do it; so it is with the spontaneous life that beats at the heart of nature. In the town all in comparison seems to be planned and mechanical, and life is set to clock work, and its business is done with calculation; but among the trees an involuntary genius seems to rule, and these mysterious creatures, the flowers, the grasses, the vines, the birds are moved by a spirit of which they are not conscious, and you feel its power over your spirits. Whether we know it or not, this experience has much to do with the charm of nature, and in spite of the great shock which has been given to the spiritualist school of pastoral philosophy and poetry by the new theory of the play of atoms, and the explanation of all growth by mechanical agencies, the spiritualist thinkers are regaining the lost ground, and bringing the atom itself to establish the fact of the ever present and ever active force, that lives in nature and joins nature to God. Here, within these recent years, the masters of the new science have been carefully read and considered, not without some perplexity of mind, and some disturbance of the old faith. But the trouble is not lasting, and the result is to lead us to discern in nature the rising path to higher life, and to delight in every feature of the landscape that hints of the aspirations of man, and the condescension of God to his needs.

I have hardly dared to tell how constantly the landscape here, with its inclosure of groves, and its distant view of the sea, insists upon suggesting visions of history and life, and how inevitably the prospect has shaped itself into a grand abbey, with its chapel and cloisters, with stones older than Muckross, and roof higher than Westminster, in which every sacred truth has its record, and every worthy act has its monument. But so it has been and is. I do not ask others to accept my notions as their own, or to see the spirits of the great men of literature and heroism, where I see them. I am willing to say that for me, more and more these trees seem to be like cathedral arches, and to take to their keeping, upon every hill and rock, the names that deserve best of mankind, and bring heaven near. God himself does not disdain to own his temple, nor frown upon the cliff that is sacred to his name, and the rock that bears the Cross, which these cedars have furnished, and the native woodbine has been so eager to clothe with beauty. He prepares us by the rising steps of nature for the Incarnation in which earth and heaven, humanity and divinity meet together, and that sequestered grove is the shrine of meditation and prayer, that throws light upon the whole temple.

It is not idle dreaming thus to give historical and spiritual significance to the landscape, but a real power goes from the practice. Cut the name of Shakespeare or Dante, or Milton, or Wordsworth upon a mossy rock, and let some of the natural growths of the ground, the clematis, the woodbine, the bittersweet or honeysuckle embroider and illuminate it, and the man himself is presented to you as an objective presence. He is there, and you no longer rack your own brain to bring his image forth from its secret chambers. This fact comes out this week, which recalls the death of Dante, September 14, 1321. Put a wreath above his name, as our child who so loves nature has done, and take his great poem to the place, and see how he rises before you in his blessed sadness, and he helps you to interpret his trials and your own, and points the way from Purgatory to Paradise, as where the spirit of St. Bernard was his guide towards the Beatific Vision where

> Within the deep and luminous subsistence
>   Of the High Light, appeared to me three circles
>   Of threefold color and of one dimension,
> And by the second seemed the first reflected
>   As Iris is by Iris, and the third
>   Seemed fire that equally from both is breathed.
> O how all speech is feeble and falls short

Of my conceit, and this to what I saw
Is such, 't is not enough to call it little !
O Light Eterne, sole in thyself that dwellest,
Sole knowest thyself, and, known unto thyself
And knowing, lovest and smilest on thyself!
That circulation, which being thus conceived
Appeared in thee as a reflected light,
When somewhat contemplated by mine eyes,
Within itself, of its own very color,
Seemed to me painted with our effigy,
Wherefore my sight was all absorbed therein.

These words breathe the life of the old Catholic faith, I know, but they come to us through the father of our modern letters, and our new times that rejoice in this liberty cannot well do without his religion.

II. — ON THE PAVEMENTS.

It is pleasant always to go from the pavements to the shade of the trees, and in due time it is pleasant to go back from the trees to the pavement. The city is the centre of human life and where men most congregate, they ought to find God in the midst of them. It is hard indeed to live as we ought to do in the great crowd, and those of us, who have passed the most of our time for more than a quarter of a century in New York, need not any stern moralist to tell us in what a world of care, and trouble, and temptation we have been. Such a multitude of interests and excitements, such intensity of motive, and such incessant pressure of care, who can try to recall all this flood of affairs and experiences without wondering, that he ever could stand it at all, and that he has come out of it with a whole head! Yet there is another side to the picture, and we must not forget that if the city makes many calls upon our time, it encourages the habit of organization that brings the many particulars into one system; that if the pressure upon us is intense and incessant, the encouragement may be as intense and constant, if we make the best of our position and bring into play all the best helps of business and society, the refinements of culture and art, and the incentives and comforts of religion. The forces that assail a man there are many and strong, and ever at work, and he must be many sided, strong and unfailing. It is a great thing to know how to live there in the face of all these difficulties, and they who go through the ordeal unscathed, should thank God humbly, and show their gratitude by encouraging and helping others who are more tried and tempted.

We have had so many changes of times and fortune, that it has been very hard to know what to depend upon in the great city. And even the seasons of apparent prosperity have unsettled principles, broken up old neighborhoods and brought on frightful reactions. The saddest aspect of the city now, as contrasted with twenty years ago, is the diminution of the middling class of residents, and there have been times when this class seems almost to have been driven out by the increase of luxury, taxation, and rent in order to make the way for the domination of the extremes of the rich and the poor. There has been promise of improvement in this respect of late, and there is good reason to believe that more steady times, sober thought, and moderate living, will bring back some of the thousands of families whose modest tastes, and frugal habits, and serious temper, make them good citizens, and earnest helpers in all good works and institutions. The war fever, with its financial craze that went into every circle and movement, did a great deal to demoralize our people ; and even our churches were led by the pride of caste and the swell of ambition into extravagances that are now regarded with surprise, and repented of with deliberation. Dives is called to bring his chariots and his coteries within the small space that is marked off as the charmed district, whilst the less favored children of God are left in the larger part of the city to the uncertain mercies of missionary chapels. Old Rome only keeps her trust unbroken and cares for all, with jurisdiction as expressive as it is imperial. Her catholicity, in this respect, is finding acceptance elsewhere, and old Trinity Church has not yet bowed the knee to the new snobbishness that sacrifices the many to the mode, and such movements as bear the name of St. Augustine and St. Chrysostom are in the line in which those old saints loved to walk. Good Doctor Muhlenberg and his associates have not toiled in vain; and St. Luke's Hospital and the Holy Communion Church are blessings to all, and Christ is ever near where the churches meet together thus in charity and in prayer. Nor must we forget how much all churches, who open their doors freely to all comers, even if it is for the evening service only, are doing for those who seek them. The pewed churches are, in some respects, free gifts, and in the course of the year, thousands and tens of thousands enjoy their eloquence and their music without any return. Those of us who have year after year spoken to crowded assemblies at the evening service, and who are constantly meeting the hearers who were not parishioners, have reason to believe that the minister of the regular city parish does not limit his labors to the proprietors of the pews. A hard working body our clergy on the whole are, and they need their summer rest to save them from utter wreck. Their work apparently on the whole prospers, and the pulpit and the religious press of our city are pillars of strength and fountains of light to the nation. The remark is sometimes received with derision, but it is none the less true, that institutional religion has its centre and stronghold in New York, and whilst ideal thinking prevails elsewhere, here the church as an institution, has its strongest defences, and for years it has been a power throughout the land. The spirit of the world is strong here, but it is not unchecked. There are indeed not only persons but congregations where the commercial temper supplants all spiritual loyalty, and the church consists only of a financial committee, a treasurer, and a smart man who is hired to preach as long as his preaching pays. But this is not the principle of the leading churches, for they recognize in the pastor a certain official power, and they help him to success by keeping loyally open the path of his usefulness. Those who have done their work under such encouragement, and retired when the years of moderated vigor come, should own gratefully the kindly auspices under which they have labored, and not be impatient of the law that gives to every man his day, and calls him to quiet places when the evening shadows fall. It may be that the man, whose pulse no longer beats with the electricity that belongs to the metropolitan pulpit, may find as large a field in the calm studies, wide fellowships, various labors of pen and voice that retirement brings. One who has had three parishes in widening circles of numbers and labor, and done his best for them each in spite of defects and shortcomings, does not rightly complain at finding himself at last in the largest of all parishes though it may look as wide as the wide world, and he may seek not wholly in vain for the church that is without sect, and the brotherhood that is without bigotry or uncharitableness.

The state of things in New York city is apparently more hopeful than for many years, and the superior men there seem to take more interest in public affairs. These men have been very remiss in this respect, and the wealth of the city has been lacking in refined taste and far-seeing enterprise. Many men of affluence have lived and died there in our time without making any mark of noble manhood upon their generation, or leaving any lasting memorial of faith or humanity. There has hardly been any dominant public opinion which embodied the sober sense and general conviction of the educated classes and acted upon the mind of the multitude. Our colleges and universities there have had little of the heart of the community, and in society at large money has lorded it too much over intellect and culture. Perhaps the break between the old residents and the resident population has come in part from the influx of strangers who knew nothing of old New York, and cared as little as they knew. The new times may change all this; and the lessons of the war and the wreck of the public treasury by monstrous frauds, and the dread of further outrages in this direction, may combine with a better culture, and truer taste, and gentler humanity, and more earnest faith, to bring together the heterogeneous elements of our city life; and under the lead of our powerful journals, schools, and churches, they may give New York a nobler position before the world than it ever had.

Certainly it is a very pleasant place to live in; very healthy with its boundary rivers and fine parks and plentiful water, and generally mild climate; very winning in its social tone, so tolerant, so genial, and, in its best circles, so charitable and devout; so orderly in its characteristic citizenship, and so safe from fire and from tumult. I may be laughed at for saying what I do, that I found more roughness in Paris and London in a month, than I have found in New York in over a quarter of a century. There are streets here, undoubtedly, which it is not safe to frequent; but where in London can a gentleman walk in the evening without being grossly offended if not rudely assailed? I have never been robbed, to my knowledge, in New York, but I cannot say as much for the country, where hen-roosts and orchards are sometimes plundered, and there is little if any police. We have suffered indeed from monstrous abuses; and the taxation, which all pay who own houses or hire them, is frightful. Let this be reformed, and the rule of expense be moderated, and no city homes can be more desirable. The schools, colleges, art galleries, literary and historical societies, are gaining in magnitude and character, and when all these privileges shall be duly organized, and wisely used by our people, and brought within the range of the common lot, our healthful and beautiful city will be the comfort of its inhabitants, and the delight of strangers, as well as the pride and strength of the whole nation.

III. — OUR FLAG.

No matter how retired or studious a man's life may have been for the last twenty years, there is one thing that has been sure to meet his eyes, and be very clear and vivid, as he looks back upon his path. We Americans all know that we have a flag, and we have all more or less suffered for it. The national heart was undoubtedly in our people before, but they never felt its beating fully, till the blow was struck at the life of the nation, and with all our habits of peace, our love of industry and our instincts of good neighborhood and humanity, we found ourselves at war, because war was made upon us by an insurgent section. It is not well now to try to revive the old quarrel, but one may fairly venture upon a passing reference to the great struggle from a non-partisan point of view; and only good can come from speaking a candid word of the part taken by men of moderated temper and conservative principles, and of the part which they are now called to take in the reconstruction of the national order.

The war has been the tragedy of our civil history, and, to a great extent, the tragedy of our domestic and personal life. Most of us have suffered in heart and fortune sadly by the conflict, and it has left us overburdened with debt; and our young country finds herself under a load of taxation and embarrassment, that was thought to belong only to the oppressed and superannuated nations of the old world. Had the result of the strife been foreseen, it would not have been begun, and even the mad pride of South Carolina would have shrunk aghast from the vision of impoverishment and ruin, that have followed the assault upon a national fortress. Had the result been foreseen in the other quarter, certain provocations would have been withheld, and whilst the conscience of our serious people would never have consented to the extension of slavery, there would have been more caution and forethought in dealing with the evil. The doctrinaire school of reformers, who took it for granted that the world goes by opinions, and who seemed to think that a declaration of the rights of man secures to them their rights, would have thought better of the grounds of solid progress. They would have seen that true liberty is not merely an opinion, but a power, and that bondage is not cast off by a word, or even by a nominal law, but by new conditions of liberty and new characters of intelligence and motive. The Rousseau theory of naturalism which makes it out that human nature is perfected by being let alone, that civilization is a grand blunder, and that historical continuity is the lineage of tyranny, has done a great deal of mischief . amongst us, and it went from the early visions of Jefferson, the philosopher of the Old Dominion, to fever the brains of the idealists of New England. These men have learned wisdom in a sober school of experience, and they see now that we cannot jump out of history any more than out of nature, that races have their historical roots, and that civilization comes in the historical line of law and education, without break or repeal. The African cannot be made Anglo-American or German by vote alone, and he must be what he is, and keep a subordinate place, until trained for something better. We are all seeing the fact, that the slave spirit may remain after emancipation is declared, and that demagogues in the name of liberty may rule as malignly, and perhaps more wastefully, than the old masters. Better sense of the need of education to secure liberty, and of the dependence of the backward race upon the advanced race for guidance, would certainly have moderated the rancor of the assault upon Southern institutions, yet might not have changed the final result.

It is important now alike for the just understanding of the great conflict, and for the true success of the present peace, to discern clearly the two points at issue between the parties at strife, — the one point being the sovereignty of the states, the other point being the continuance and extension of slavery. The first of these had more to do with the logic of the dispute, and the second entered more into its motive. The question of jurisdiction was more one of reasoning and of pride, whilst the question of property was more one of interest and passion. He surely was a sagacious statesman who tried to separate these two points, as far as Charles Francis Adams did, and to suggest a way by which the southern point of honor as to jurisdiction could be saved without opening the new area of freedom to the inroads of slavery. But the suggestion was of little avail, except perhaps in showing in advance the temper that we need now in the work of reconstruction. The slave power died of its own madness, and of the sycophancy of the demagogues and money makers, who played into its hands, and led its leaders to believe that their audacity would be safe as it struck at a peaceful and industrious people. Slavery is gone, and God be praised for overruling the madness of men to the glory of His Kingdom. It is gone and in a way that its friends expected as little as its enemies. Those of us who never favored aggressive measures, but who believed in evolving the spirit and acts of liberty by the method of civilization, not by revolution, but by evolution, saw revolution accomplished without our design. We only refused to consent to the extension of slavery, and when the flag was assailed, we stood by it as the standard not only of the nation, but of civilization and humanity. We could not and would not see our birthright of Anglo-American nationality lost, and whilst some preachers went to the war as chaplains, or as soldiers, more kept to their post and preached and prayed, and wrote for the triumph of the nation, and for its firm and benign rule over the whole land and people. Some of us suffered not a little loss of friends and power, whilst all the while we were earnest for peace and good will, and we never forgot that the brave men who fell on both sides in battle were our countrymen, and that their wounds were ours and their children were precious to us, and to share with our own the blessings of the nation.

The end has come and now let us have peace. It is well that the two great parties who now seek the control of our government have set forth platforms so just and comprehensive in this respect, and so full of hope and strength for the states that seceded. It is well that men of culture and character are candidates for the highest office. What is wanted as much as anything, is a comprehensive, far-seeing, and earnest public opinion under the lead of men above partisanship, and beyond suspicion of self-seeking. This high council of the nation may not be definitely organized, yet it may none the less exist, and speak and act. The professional men of the country, not excepting the clergy, the solid business men, the professors of ethics and social science, the weighty representatives of the permanent industries of the nation, the conductors of the great journals and reviews, all ought to belong to this fellowship, and constitute an outside senate that will strip the mark from all villainy in high places, and by a just public economy give light and strength to every worthy principle and measure. The present aspects of our American religion promise well for such tendencies, and the great denominations that have territorial extension, as well as moral force, are gaining in union and influence. The Methodists, the Presbyterians, the Episcopalians are rising national forces, and the Roman Catholics, whilst their priests are to be carefully looked after in their relations with our public schools, are not to be set aside as aliens, nor is their wholesome influence over unruly people, and dangerous socialist tendencies to be ignored. We are not indeed to confound church and state, yet we may nevertheless defend, and nurture civic institutions by moral and religious principles, and regard the nation as the body of which the church is the soul. The Holy Spirit rejoices in all the good fellowship of man, and is ready to breathe into them the breath of divine life, as when the City of God arose from the ideas and institutions of the old Law and Temple in the vision of Augustine, and Hildebert saluted the Paraclete as " Melodia civium gandentium," the melody of joyful citizens. We have heard something of that melody in the hymns of our people, and we shall hear more of it, when they all rejoice together under the old flag, and march to the same airs of liberty and union.

Fourteen years ago, in 1862, when our conflict was most intense, a stone cutter on the way to the war carved in deep letters on the cliff overhanging our road, the words " God and our Country." He won honors in battle, and had an officer's commission in keeping with his merit. The inscription remains and means more than ever now. When I look at it, I often think of what has happened to interpret that saying. A single remembrance speaks volumes, and I can hardly believe what I know to be true, that the two groomsmen at a marriage which I was called from the country to perform in my own house in the city, the summer before the war, the two grooms-men, I say, were afterwards strangely associated with the two war presidents ; and one of them, afterwards in this service, wrote the life of General Grant, and the other in a fit of melo-dramatic madness took the life of Abraham Lincoln. That blonde bride is in her grave, and seldom have the marriage bells had more eventful echoes in their sound. Yet the church bells still ring in the nation's jubilee, and God and our Country ring out in their notes.

IV. — ABROAD.

Our American people at large seem to have gone or to be going to Europe, and a considerable part of them are ambitious to go round the world. A considerable propor-tion of travelled Americans have written and published letters from abroad, and whilst the writer acknowledges his share of that often infirmity, he is not weak enough now to venture to do it over again ; but he aims only to give a few notes of the impressions left upon him by a visit of less than a year, at the time of life when experience has sobered enthusiasm, and the study of books has made it as instructive as it is charming to compare the old world itself with what has been said and sung about it.

They are not wise who expect that voyages or travel will take them out of nature, or away from mankind and from the old Adam that marks man everywhere. The American finds in Europe much of what he left at home and most of all he finds himself and his kindred and essentially familiar ideas and usages in the lands from which his fathers came. Yet the old world, because it is old, differs from the new, and a thoughtful observer sees at once, that things are more taken for granted, and manners and habits are far more fixed there than here. It is acknowledged abroad more than with us, that every one cannot do everything, that there is a limit to a man's reasonable expectations and powers, and in spite of the shaking of old dynasties and the rise of dashing upstarts, the sense of caste is very strong; and most people seem to expect to live and die in the rank, and generally in the calling, of their fathers. There is an acquiescence in position, however lowly or lordly it may be, that is quite in contrast with our new America, where every boy may expect to be president and every girl may dream of being the president's wife, or sharing a millionaire's palace, purse and equipage. The comely young woman, whom you see with her mother digging the hard soil with the mattock at Interlachen, has the look of mild acquiescence

22

quite as much as the soldier who rides to the daily drill over the Rhine at Cologne, or is trained at the guns in the mountain fortress of Königstein. The baker, who sells you his gooseberry tarts near Westminster Abbey, is as easy at his counter, as the dean in his stall or the bishop on his throne. The landlady at the Grosvenor Hotel in old Chester, accepts her position as graciously as the Duchess at Eaton Hall, and in both of them you see the heritage of time and the traits of loyalty that long ages have settled. If life in its lower estate there may run in dull ruts, in the higher plane it moves in stately paths or flows in graceful channels, where the waters may none the less dance and sparkle because the way is worn, a bound is set, and mud and rocks and quicksands do not interfere.

This characteristic of the old world appears in the predominance of institutions over individuals. With us the individual, the personality is everything; and the very sanctuary of worship is likely to bear the name of the man who preaches there, and who may be praised for the eloquence of his prayers as well as his sermons. There the man is second to the institution, and in the Church of England you can often hardly tell one voice from another in the drawling rhythm of song and prayer, and sometimes of sermon. Mr. Moody was a marvel, because he stood out so bravely as a man in preaching and in prayer, and much of Spurgeon's success comes from his bold individualism in face of the uniform cut of manner and tone which marks the rank and file of the regular clergy. Even when thinking is bold, manner may be monotonous, and no one can appreciate the reform now introduced into the English pulpit by such stirring preachers as McGee, Bishop of Peterborough, who has not observed the prevailing monotony of the English clergy. This fault does not of necessity come from the use of a liturgy, for the liturgy may be read with vital expression, and may give the devotional rest and comfort that help fervent utterance, when the preacher has his own word to say, whilst there can be no doubt that the great length of the service in the Church of England tends to take the life out of his voice, if he is obliged to be the reader, and to substitute rapid gabble for articulate expression. The liturgy, like all other institutions, requires life in the minister to save its constancy from stagnation; yet take it as it is actually rendered with the average fidelity, it cannot be charged with deadening devotion. It embodies the organized faith of ages, and the English homes that have been nurtured under its influence need not shrink from comparison with any other homes in Christendom.

Institutions may be called the art that rises in history, for they show the heart and mind and work of communities and centuries; and they are history embodied. It is well to interpret all art somewhat in this way, and to regard poems and pictures, statues and buildings, as being quite as much expressions of history as are laws and schools and letters. Europe becomes peculiarly interesting when interpreted in this way, and art is evidently gaining power by presenting the main points of history in living personality. It is no longer the sycophant of kings, as at Versailles, or the master of ceremonies of Sacerdotalism, as in so much of sculpture and painting of Rome, but it is the interpreter of God and humanity as they appear and speak in time. There is a union of calmness and force in its great works, that remind you of the Word and Spirit that give peace and power to everything that is divinely human. The culture that is thus presented is not assailing, but befriending religion in many ways, and especially by teaching that the great things have been done by struggle, that every victory is won by sacrifice, and we who set up the statues of saints and sages and heroes, must not condemn ourselves by forgetting their valor. It is well for Italy to see Dante in visible form at Florence and Naples, and to trace from him to Cavour the lineage of liberty. It is well for Germany to set up Hermann and Luther in bronze before the nation, and not to forget Goethe, and Schiller, and Humboldt, and Stein. Bunyan and Baxter are out of prison, and with Cromwell and Milton, among the great teachers in England, they speak to the eye as never before. France is revising her record and giving her metal and her marble to do honor to principles, and men that her kings and emperors set at naught. She sends the statue of Lafayette to America, and sets up the grand figure of Liberty in the harbor of New York.

To an American, especially to a New Englander, England is the great attraction abroad, and to an American of Puritan origin, her church is more interesting than all foreign churches. One asks many questions as to the Church of England, but the main question is, how stands the old quarrel, and how far is the son of the Puritans, called upon in honor to turn away from that mother church, in respect for the fathers who came out of it to find a new home and church on these shores. The reply cannot but be explicit for a man of a comprehensive mind and a generous temper. Instead of Laud and Strafford, the English Church now presents Tait and Gladstone as the leaders of clergy and laity, and it is not only in the breadth, but in the height of her communion, that her excellence lies. She secures the liberty of her bolder thinkers and encourages the charity and piety of her most earnest devotees. Lord Falkland and Provost Whichcote of two centuries ago would find her friendly to their aspirations, and John Wesley would never have been cast adrift by the present leaders of her opinion. It is surely a great reach of intellectual and spiritual emancipation, when you can, under the auspices of this Church, range from the charming scholarship of Dean Stanley to the grave eloquence of Canon Liddon,

go from the Platonic culture of the Master of Baliol to
the ascetic discourses of the Warden of Clewer, and have
the influence of bishops like Trench, with his rich learning, and Wilberforce with his vigorous statesmanship, and
whose latest comers have presented such varieties as the
liberal Richard Temple, and the conservative Harold
Browne.   Nor is the English Church let down by the
fact that she has been able to spare such men of power
as Newman and Manning, the latter the most wide awake
prelate that I have seen.   A New Englander who goes
to England with experiences of the narrowness of sec-
tarianism, and the uncertainty of individual purposes, and
the necessity of institutional order and historical faith,
cannot but be impressed favorably by the aspects of the
church of his fathers.   He who sees the undoubted fact
that at home and abroad the choice of people for themselves and their children, must be between the organized
historical church in some of its leading forms, and what
is called Free Religion without creed or law or clergy,
cannot but look with hope and affection upon the Church
of England.   That her method is not perfect, and that
her system needs reform, her clergy and laity know perhaps better than any outsiders, and their humility is not
their weakness.   But imperfect as in some respects the
administration of Church affairs may be in England, her
Church has order as well as faith, and to men who have
had experience of the caprice of opinion, and the inso-

lence of voluntary lords over congregations and clergy, there is something very winning in impartial law.

It is not strange that a descendant of one of those pilgrims who went from the south of England and whose kindred had worshipped centuries ago in Salisbury and Winchester Cathedrals, should find peculiar attraction in that region — not strange that after visiting at Bemerton, Hurst, and Brighton the churches of George Herbert, John Keble, and Frederick Robertson, he found the old birthright restored to him, and that he left England for France at heart within the church of his fathers, at once sure that he had not deserted the humanities of the new times and that he had a deepened sense of the worth of the old catholicity. There was not a little in the character and culture of the English dissenters,[1] especially of the Liberals, whom he saw so pleasantly, that tended to favor the English Church. Their genial homes and their personal accomplishments were proofs of their affinity with the old faith and manners. A broad church liberal like Charles Beard, not only expressed much of a devotee's love for the ancient shrines, but publicly protested

---

[1] George Herbert Curteis, in his Bampton Lecture of 1872, speaks thus of the Unitarians of England : "In personal character many Unitarians represent the very highest type of Christian manhood. In ability and learning, their ministers are often on a par with our own. To theology they not unfrequently make valuable contributions. In ecclesiastical matters, their tendency is rather towards the Church of England than away from her."

against assailing their rightful endowments, and a scholarly pastor like Thomas Sadler and a profound theistic philosopher like James Martineau had as much of the English liturgy in their worship as their doctrines and their position would allow.   An American who had given commemorative discourses upon such old English reformers as Wycliffe and Milton, and such new men as Milman and Keble, Robertson and Maurice, as well as upon the evangelical German leaders, Schleiermacher and Rothe, need not be thought capricious or inconsistent for finding so much to please or instruct him in quarters, ecclesiastically so wide apart in England, or for remembering so gratefully the kindness he everywhere received.

V. — STUDIES.

Not only for the importance of the thing itself, but to meet the wishes of earnest young men who have entered upon new ethical and theological studies, I may venture to give a few notes of the men and principles that have had most to do with what has been wisest and best in experience.   It is as false and foolish to say, that a man ought to think and act and live from himself alone, as it is wicked to say that he ought to live for himself alone; and the great champions of individualism refute themselves by their study of the great masters, and by their delight in docile followers.   We New England boys of a half century ago, lived in a time of rising independence, and we saw in our days every yoke of authority laid aside, and in time the protest against precedent was carried out into the assertion of the absolute supremacy of the private conscience and the individual soul. Yet the new liberty but changed the leadership without snapping the leading strings. Those of us who were not radicals by temperament or training, need not be ashamed to own our guides.

Where should a Massachusetts boy find his model man, his guiding thinker and his constant friend, but in his pastor? I have spoken of our pastor in the introduction to this volume, and I can now say, that he, whose voice I heard when a little child in the burial service that prayed for God's blessing upon us as fatherless, was my adviser and friend to his death, a period of more than fifty years. He was a master of practical wisdom as well as of speculative philosophy, a judge of human nature, and no novice in the world's prudence and thrift. His mind was logical, ethical and judicial, rather than emotional, æsthetic and executive. Perhaps his best power came out in the pulpit, where his remarkable manner gave weight to his remarkable words, and both manner and words told together in certain sentences that hearers can never forget, and which often give point and force to the close of his sermon, as when an arrow is shot to its mark by a strong hand from the bowstring. James Walker died December 23, 1874, aged eighty years, after some years of retirement and of limited bodily vigor, but without loss of mental power. His conversation was never more keen and witty than in his later years, and the last time that I saw him, although suffering somewhat from a local difficulty, he was full of interest in life, and he spoke with much emphasis of the great struggle in Europe between the human mind and the old despotism, with hearty indorsement of the liberating champions, strong for Bismarck and Germany against Antonelli and Rome. A few months before, his old parishioners and friends had sent him some beautiful and original pieces of sculptured silver work in commemoration of his finished fourscore years. The gift was carried to him on a lovely Sunday morning in August, with bright and sweet flowers from his old parish in Charlestown. This act seemed to round his life in its fulness, and the silver cup and plate now are lasting memorials of him in King's Chapel, Boston, where he was last called to be preacher, and where they are seen on the communion table at Christmas, Easter, and Whitsunday.[1]

Dr. Walker represented the ethical and philosophical elements in our early Christian life, and his preaching

---

[1] I cannot but associate him with the two other friends of early days, who bore also the name of Walker, and also a fourth of the name, Timothy Walker, of Cincinnati, to whom I am indebted for much kindness. Our family physician, William J. Walker, died first, and our schoolmaster, Cornelius Walker, lived until last year, the same tough personality to the last.

was the dominant influence in our town, and it had influence in the whole neighborhood. Many cool headed men thought him a safer guide than Dr. Channing, who was more of an enthusiast for ideas, and who brought new elements of reform and progress into the pulpit and literature of Massachusetts, not without serious alarm to the large class of weighty men who, like his class-mate Judge Story, had been liberals in religion and in some respects radicals, whilst they were stiff conservatives in society and politics. Dr. Channing was surely a great power in those days, and his influence is too large a subject to be dwelt upon in this hasty sketch. I will only say of him now, that his widest and most lasting work is seldom recognized — his persistent union of the idea of dignity of human nature with the positive faith in Christ as a divine person and the prevailing mediator. Strong individualist as he was, and so jealous of the interference of associations with the individual soul, as to be little of a churchman, he dwelt earnestly upon the reconciliation of the sects, and the reunion of Christendom under the reign of Christ. Vehement as he was against the Calvinistic dogma of the total wreck of human nature by the Fall, and earnest champion as he was for the existence and force of the moral sense in man, he never encouraged self-dependence apart from divine grace, and we find in his pages many intimations of convictions not unfriendly to the old Catholic view of man, as needing God's grace not merely to forgive his sins, but to meet his aspirations and to help his endeavors after that divine life which came from God to Eden, and was offered anew and fully in Christ. Before this century closes, William Ellery Channing, with all the limitations in his range of learning and his reach of thought, will be honored as one of the heralds of the Catholicity that is to be wrought out through the union of the priestly, the evangelical, and the liberal elements in the Church of the living God. He held to the end to his connection with Christ and the church; in his last discourse among the Berkshire hills, he prayed for the coming of the kingdom of the Son, and those of us who have received from his hands the cup of communion, will never forget how devout he was in its administration, and how full of love for the risen Lord.

The studies that made the most mark upon our set at the Cambridge Theological School were more in the ethical, literary, and philosophical than in the dogmatic and ecclesiastical line. I remember in a careful study for an essay on Sir James Mackintosh, how strong was the impression that Bishop Butler's sermons on Human Nature made upon me in vindication of the Moral Sense, and how much Coleridge's "Aids to Reflection" did to back up this impression, and also to throw light on the relation of the pure reason to the truths of religion, and the graces and virtues of Christianity. The poets, too, came in for their share of influence, and Goethe and

Wordsworth were read with much delight, as interpreters of the harmony of the universe, and of the need of living in the serenity and earnestness that become the great temple in which we are, and of opening into our religious life the freedom and beauty and grandeur of nature, and of the noblest art.

The theologian who did most to correct the subjective one-sidedness, and the ideal sentimentalism of our school life, was Olshausen, who was first introduced to me by my steadfast friend, James Freeman Clarke, at Louisville, Kentucky, and whom we studied many a morning and evening together, and commented upon and translated his learned and devout pages. Olshausen impressed me much by his habit of gathering up the meaning of Scripture texts under dominant principles, and even more by his philosophy of matter and spirit, body and soul, and the Incarnation and the Church, in which the material and the spiritual elements and forces were so combined and reconciled. He taught me to see as never before the realism of Christianity, and the way of shunning the dreamy subjectivity of transcendentalism, and of believing in the Incarnate Word, the Enduring Church, and the immortal life without sinking into materialism. I never can forget the benefit, and have had Olshausen's works always at hand, although later thinkers and scholars may have interfered with his former place in the library.

In the first term of parish life, for several years, De

Wette was a favorite author, and I studied him much and translated his two volumes on "Practical Ethics." His value was in the freshness and comprehensiveness of his critical learning, his recognition of the devout as well as the ethical side of religion, and perhaps not least of all in his distribution, according to the method of Fries, of the faculties of the mind into Wissen, Glauben, and Ahnung, knowing, believing, and aspiring, a division which gave room for the facts of science, the ideas of theology, and the mysteries of religion. Every guide was then a helper who relieved us from the prosaic moralizing and meagre theology of the time, and encouraged us to preach and to pray, as if there were a soul as well as understanding in man, a spirit as well as a letter in revelation, and God were with us now in the church as well as of old with his chosen prophets in his law. I was sorry not to go to Basle, to the grave of De Wette, for he was friend as well as teacher, and we had corresponded together. He was a gentle and brave spirit, and had suffered much for conscience sake. He lives now in his works, and his translation of the Bible is likely to be a lasting monument of his learning and truthfulness.

Then as the range of care and enterprise increased, there came more ambitious studies for public uses, and the preacher who had a large parish in a university town was moved to do what he could to instruct the young people in the personages and principles of church history with proper consultation of original sources. What a world was opened in the old fathers and the modern reformers! Of the old fathers, Augustine made the most mark upon me, and his flaming sense of the work of God's grace upon man, his sagacious recognition of the continuity of history and the essential unity of the race, his generous interpretation of nature in connection with the scriptures, and his broad vision of the new city of God that was changing the face of the world, and building the new Jerusalem upon the broad foundation of the Roman empire, all these made the saintly Bishop of Hippo a light and power with the novice at his books; and still the spell remains in these latter years, when I see from my window, here under the trees, the spire of the church that bears his name, and I sometimes give a lecture upon his life and his work. With such ancient studies, the new scholars and thinkers were heard, and to none of these do I owe more gratitude than to Frederick Maurice, especially to his " Kingdom of Christ " and his " Religions of the World," with their profound insight into the institutions and ideas of the historical church, and the adaptation of its truth and grace to all the needs of man. At the same time the arts of industry and education were not neglected, and the student, fond as he was of Keble and Williams, and of the restorers of ancient devotion, was no stranger to the workshops, and the schools and the university, little claim as he may have had to a leading place there.

In this great city of New York the scene afterwards changed, and men and affairs threatened to crowd out study, but the work went on, and if the stirring town was too aggressive, the quiet country was more soothing, and books and the pen had new charm when you could play the peripatetic, and stretch your legs at will at intervals of weariness with reading and writing. Acquaintance was still kept up with the current thought of Europe and America, and time was found for a great subject such as Dante, who began modern thought, or Schleiermacher, who has tried to keep it within Christ's grace, for Goethe, who saw the universe in its beauty, or Hartmann, who unveils its pain and death; and weeks and months were pressed for time and thought to study and write upon them with an approach to fidelity. Historical studies of home subjects came in for their share with lectures and addresses upon events and personages of New England and of New York. Learned and accomplished scholars were at hand to help all generous studies, and no man who has lived and worked with any earnestness in our city for the last twenty-five years, can fail to be grateful for the kind fellowship of society and liberal gift of information through word and books. Scholarship has been to me comprehensive, catholic indeed, in New York; and Liberal and Evangelical, Congregationalist, Presbyterian, Methodist, Episcopalian, and Roman Catholic, Jews and Christians, have been friends and brothers in this companionship of letters. It is a good thing to have regular and organized help in study, and I recall with never lessening satisfaction the results of such help in two conspicuous instances. Happy were the ten years or more that ended somewhere about 1850, when a score of New England clergymen who were not willing to abandon the gospel and church for the new light of rationalism, combined together in the Union Pastoral Association, and met once a month for conversation, deliberation, and worship. The men and their gifts were various, but the spirit was one. Edward B. Hall and Ephraim and Andrew P. Peabody, Frederick D. Huntington and J. I. T. Coolidge, Frederick H. Hedge, and George Putnam, S. K. Lothrop, T. B. Fox, and James W. Thompson were of the number, and their names indicate the comprehensiveness and the temper of the association. It was a great loss to have this companionship broken by death and distances, and great is the satisfaction in the virtual renewal of its privileges after twenty years, by new fellowship with a company of scholars who are humane, thoughtful, and progressive as were the old set, and with little difference except in more positive and historical church institutions and convictions.

But why urge so earnestly especial associations, when life itself in pastoral circles is constant association, and a man has always enough to study around him, and he ought always to find motive enough to think seriously, and to work bravely. When the vicissitudes and characters of parish life are taken out of the sphere of private gossip and personal caprice, and lifted into the sphere of Christian faith and church communion, great is the transformation; and they help on its better spirit alike by their sacrifice and their cheer. It is well to do what we can to bring about this result by elevating sociality into religious purposes, instead of letting religion down into personal frivolity. If church clothes and ways may be too stiff and stately, parlor clothes and ways may be too easy in some respects, and too costly and conventional also; and it is a grave question whether anything is gained by the new familiarity in religious affairs, which regards a picnic as the Pentecost, puts a tea-table in place of the Eucharist, and is eager to bring dances and plays as near as possible if not into the sanctuary. Much is done by encouraging the people to bring the education of their children within positive church influences under their pastor. The Sunday school should be the children's church, and with hymn and prayer, thoughtful instruction should be mingled, and they should be led to take part in public worship, and to feel the cheer and the power of the associations and influences that go with a wise church order, and open to the child's soul the heavenly graces that were owned in Baptism, and that introduced him to his place in the Kingdom of God. The evening Sunday service is full of opportunity for such instruction and influence, and no seasons of my pastoral life are more precious in remembrance than the years which redeemed the Sunday evening from empty seats and indifference, and cheered the gathered people with sweet music, and Scripture lessons and psalms, called them to join in responses, and encouraged the preacher to bring out things, new and old, from his studies, and to combine to the best of his ability the stores of culture, whether from history, literature, art or science with the truths of religion.

I cannot leave without mention one author to whose thoughts I have probably given more study the last twenty years or more, than to any other man's, and whom I can name more fitly now as he treats so much of matters greatly agitated in our time, especially the relation of religion to the church and the nation. I remember bringing Richard Rothe's three solid volumes of "Theological Ethics" into the country long years ago, and beginning the introductory essay of some two hundred pages with amazement, that a man of known sense could possibly be so obscure and dull. But he held me closely to him for some weeks, and I have read him more or less ever since. His book is regarded by many of the best scholars as the most thorough and valuable work ever written upon the subject, and as the most important contribution to theology in our time. He is apparently more prized in Germany than any other recent author who has positively Christian convictions, and everything that he left on paper when he died, in 1868, has been published, and even his fragmentary notes have been edited. I have here on my table the last of these publications, the first volume of his devotional evening instructions to theological students (1834–37), a book full of tenderness and wisdom. I have written out my studies of his mind in full elsewhere, and I will only say now how precious he has been as an interpreter of the source of virtue as well as duty in God and Christ, and with what insight and breadth he brings the whole range of life within the power of Christian faith and love, and especially how strongly he insists upon the state or the nation as divinely ordained, and as the coming sphere of Godly manhood. Germany in one respect has taken him at his word, and he who in his lifetime was regarded as a dreamer in his idea of having the church consummated, and perhaps absorbed in the nation, is now found to be the prophet of the present German empire, with its state church, and perhaps its state that may claim too imperiously to be the sufficient church. The recent development of affairs in Christendom has not led me to accept this view of the church and the nation, and surely in our America nothing could be worse for us, than undertaking to make over the church to the national government, or even to slight the institutions of the church and the clergy with the intention of putting the mind and conscience of the people wholly into politics. We need reform sadly, every thinking man knows, but our experience in leaving even so much of education within the control of politicians, warns us to beware of taking religion away from its spiritual foundations and functions, and making it over in any way to secular powers. The more independent and positive our American Church is, the better her influence over the nation, the stronger her moral power in civil reform. England is seeing this evidently, and her church is striving to win the people by spiritual methods, in view of the dangers that threaten her civic relations ; and as matters are now, the Church of England more and more seeks jurisdiction within her own authorities, and less and less depends upon court power. Her gain of strength the last forty years has been from her own spiritual life. It is tribute enough to Rothe's rendering of civic virtue to affirm with him the insufficiency of merely ceremonial service, and the danger of merely sacerdotal sway over religion. Patriot as he was, and loyal son of a father who served Frederick the Great, he loved his nation with a Christian heart, and he had a more living sense of Christ as the present Saviour, than any of the theological leaders of his time. We need his ethics of patriotism here in America, and we can have this without accepting his theory of the consummation of the state in the dissolution of the historical church, or of the making over of its functions to an ecclesiastical commission, or a committee of devotion. The heavenly powers, of course, enter into all fidelity, and inspire all virtue and sacrifice; but they have their own scriptures and ministry and shrines, and those who have watched the course of affairs in America, and tried to find and to give divine peace and motive, must confess that the church has its own hallowed sphere, and that there in a peculiar sense the tabernacle of God is with men. To me the historical church has been the best teacher, and in her various forms, from the Puritan pastor of my childhood to the studies and companionships of these sober years, the church has been teacher and comforter, with a liberty ever enlarging, and thought and purpose ever more inspiriting. Rothe had the superstitions of Rome so constantly before his eyes after his long residence there, that he saw no security against Romish bondage except in the state. Many men who have seen the Pope, and lived in Rome, are still glad to keep the two great words together, Christ and the Church.

VI. — THE OUTLOOK.

Those of us, who have reached threescore years have no great cause to be anxious as to what is to happen to us personally in this world, as our career is so far run, and the end is near. But for our children and grandchildren, for our country and our race, there are many perplexing questions which it is hard to settle, and which now cloud the prospect. These late years, that now pass in review, have been full of changes and disappointments to communities and families, and although a man who has lived all the while on the same hill-side in summer and in the same street in winter, and loved the same books and held essentially the same faith, and followed the same habits of pen and voice, has no reason to complain of a broken life; yet there have been great breaks in the life of us all who have learned that we are in the same boat with our neighbors, our nation, and our race. In fact the map of the world within that time has been changed, and the actual and prospective lines of civil and religious domination have been vastly altered. In our own country there is hardly a man in power who was heard of twenty years ago, and the men who are now up for the highest offices, with a single exception, were not conspicuous enough to be named then in the very generous cyclopædias and dictionaries of the time.

The local communities that I have personally known have signally changed. My native town, Charlestown, has become a part of Boston, and after preaching in St. John's Church there on the eve of the annexations in 1874, I heard the chimes of old Christ Church bells, that seemed to celebrate the union, and to recall the days when to me, a child, those bells were the only voice to speak of the mother church of our Puritan race. The village of Nashua is now a thriving city, centre of lines of railroad, and with a funded debt noted upon the price current honorably. The city of Providence has gone from 25,000 inhabitants to near 100,000, and with great loss of citizens by death, and of property by misfortune, her career is prosperous; and if we judge by the permanence of her present mayor in office, who was one of our Bible-class, and Sunday-school boys, her policy is settled and her basis sure. New York has nearly doubled her population and vastly magnified her territory, and in spite of the knavery that has robbed her, and of the dangers that threaten her trade and her order, the city was never so fair to the eye, and so hopeful in the essentials of prosperity, however checked in her imperial pride. There the tide of business rolls on, and although the particles constantly pass away, the stream flows on very much the same, and is likely to flow for ages.

It has been not easy for industrious and intelligent men always to earn a fair living in the great city, and wary thinkers and observers say that our children are to have a harder time than we have had. But sunshine as well as cloud has its surprises, and light breaks upon the darkness when night is deepest. If one asks anxiously what evil is coming, a brighter spirit may ask what good is near? It is vain to try, however, to hide the fact, that the present time is not especially fruitful in optimists, that there is a tone of sadness in the most vital literature and art of our time, that the cultivated classes are not particularly merry now, and that many careful thinkers see breakers ahead. Mr. W. R. Greg may not be one of the wisest of men, but he is surely one of the keenest observers, and the most candid of writers; and he treats not only of England, but of Europe and America, when he sees "Rocks Ahead" in the political supremacy of the lower classes, the decline of industry and the divorce of intelligence from religion. Professor Huxley is not especially cheering in what he lately said at Baltimore of our prospective two hundred millions of people in 1976, under the despotism of universal suffrage, and from Professor von Laveleye of Lüttich, who is a corresponding member of the Institute of France, we have a tract dated Nördlingen, 1876, which points out the pressing danger to civilized nations from three prominent assaults upon the religious idea which is so essential to morality and even to civilization, — the tendency of natural science to rest in materialism and to deny God and immortality; the incessant pursuit of wealth with the attendant habits of luxury; and thirdly the new socialism, which accepts the rising philosophy of material force, denies all spiritual realities, and threatens to set up its own rule of might. So calm and candid and profound a thinker as the younger Fichte, so called not from his youth, for he was born in 1797, but from contrast with his father, the great philosopher of that name, wrote in the last work of his that we have seen, the Letters to Dr. E. Zeller on the latest movement of German speculation, with the preface dated Spring, 1876, shortly before he died: "It is not so much the unbelief which is in the first instance to be complained of. This is only the symptom and working of a deeper evil; of the increasing decay of all ideal dispositions, of occupation and satisfaction with the sensuous, phenomenal, and perishable. In practical relations, this appears in a soul-corroding luxury, which, according to necessary laws, ends in Pessimism; in art an empirical realism which selfishly feels only after consequences; in science, in great discoveries and actual achievements of exact investigation, besides a collection of empirical material in fragmentary individual researches, and in dislike of all guiding speculative ideas, an overestimate of the value of such unconnected, peculiarly fruitless results, in short an empiricism without ideas, whose last result can be only a theoretical materialism, which followed consequently threatens to end naturally in moral nihilism. If this is unquestionably the characteristic of the present temper of the world and the age, then the future, left to itself, must expect only more advanced developments of it. And thus it is to be feared, that we are gradually approaching an abyss, which hides within itself conditions, which historically the Roman empire presented under the rule of the Cæsars. There, as now, great intellectual culture and many sided susceptibility towards the æsthetic beautified enjoyments of life were combined with frightful self-seeking and reckless cruelty. Over all swept a deep feeling of the worthlessness of all earthly existence, which looked to death by suicide as the ready resort, when pleasure is exhausted, and sorrow or want invade.."

This is a somewhat dark picture of our time, but there is much truth in its drawing and coloring, and the prospect before us is surely not all sunshine and roses. It is evident that ideal principles are at a discount now, and the age moves by the facts of nature and the science which these facts teach, and by the forces which this science can bring into the field. We are not to quarrel with this disposition, but rather try to carry it up into the higher sphere, and to acknowledge all the facts, to rise from them into the higher science of God and the soul, and to win the force that this high science bestows. We are disposed to quarrel with our age for not being practical and energetic enough. Our young people seem to me to be too nervous and fidgety, in danger of being distracted by over-excitement; they are too self-indulgent and exacting, with desires far in excess of their achievement; they are unsettled, and in peril of losing the loyal convictions that are the ground of all peace and power, whether in private or in public life.

As to the present shaking of the old faith and rise of materialism, it is not well to be timid, much less despairing. The new science undoubtedly makes many infidels and destroys many old traditions; but it is not necessarily atheistic or materialistic. If the theory of Evolution is so explained as to lose God in material atoms and agencies, it is perverted from its just bearings; and the Christian man who traces the work of God in the ages of

Creation, and in the æons of progress, may rejoice in the Incarnation and the Church as the crown of creation, and the complete manifestation of God. It cannot be denied, however, that there are two systems of nature that now are held in high quarters, that are disheartening and demoralizing. We may illustrate them by the atheism of Haeckel, and the Pantheism of Schopenhauer and Von Hartmann. Few serious thinkers will agree with the monstrous atheism of Haeckel, who ascribes all movement and organism, all thought, feeling and will, all life and personality, to atoms and mechanical forces. The present tendency among intellectual adventurers and speculative free thinkers, lies the other way, and the pantheistic movement that Spinoza headed two centuries ago, has borne fruits very different from what he seems to have anticipated in the pantheistic Pessimism of the present day which ascribes all conscious life to an unconscious and almighty power, and finds no personal Providence, no mercy before the throne of Sovereign Law. It may be as the younger Fichte before his death, recently wrote, that this school of thought has culminated, and is now declining, yet its power is still great, and it is making converts still.

These new fatalists profess indeed a code of mercy, and claim to be examples of genuine and self-sacrificing humanity, in virtually accepting the creed of Buddha, which declares that a sense of the inherent wretchedness

life, and of the blessedness of being out of it, should lead
men to pity and to help each other in the sympathy of
common misery. So it is that Pessimism preaches its doctrine of the Cross, and does not disdain to consecrate the
great sorrow of mankind by beautiful art, whilst it offers
not redemption from sin and death, but the redemption
which is death forever. It is said that Richard Wagner
holds the pessimist philosophy, and that he believes in
music as the prelude of the Nirvana, where pain and personality are lost in the unconscious all. If so the Passion Trilogy of Bayreuth, which emperors and princes
lately thronged to hear, resembles in a measure the Passion Play of Ober-Ammergau in the near mountains, with
the difference that the Passion Trilogy holds out in its
music of the future nothing of the Redeemer whom those
mountain peasants set forth upon the cross. But names
and theories must not blind us to the excellences of men,
and to the movements of humanity. Wagner's music may
be prophetic of a pathos of sacrifice and faith deeper than
his theory, and it may exalt the worship of the church
of the future more than he believes. Such notions cannot
satisfy the soul nor meet the facts of history, or the wants
of society. These system makers may say, for example,
that love between man and woman is the one sin, whether
without law or with law, and that to live and to have
children is treason against mankind, and that the world
is now on its last legs, and had better be left to die. The

world is old and shaky and childhood died with Greece, they say. They do not believe it when they come to the real test. Hartmann has lately married, and he writes of his charming wife and of his playful child, from his Berlin home in the midst of the gardens. That child is young as childhood ever was in Greece, and our boys and girls are as merry as the little ones who bowed down for father Abraham's blessing, or they who laughed and wept by turns when they heard old Homer's song. Life is and will be in spite of what we say, or write, or dream, and this two yearling girl who is running about the room, or gamboling among the flowers and chickens, and who the other evening cried out at the moon, and began to climb up the piazza pillar to get to it for a plaything, has a dominant force of blood and nerve and brain and soul, that will keep the world going better than the dry philosophers whom such as she make no scruple of pulling by the nose in her glee and her dash.

Life is a great fact and a great force, and so is God. Reason of him as we may, or deny or limit his being and attributes, and he is the same — not only within nature, but above it, not only immanent, as the new thinkers are so fond of saying, but transcendent, or above nature, even He whom the heaven of heavens cannot contain. Without Him the future is a blank, as the past is an enigma and the present a desert.

It may be true as Uhlhorn, Fichte and various other

writers have hinted, that the present age in many respects resembles the Rome of the Cæsars, but it does not follow that all is dark in our future on that account. The empire of the Cæsars was the external condition of the rise and progress of the universal Kingdom of Christ, and as a recent author has truly said, the Christian era began virtually with the accession of Augustus, nearly thirty years before our Lord's birth. If the luxury and superstition of the empire called for the Redeemer's coming, the Roman language, roads, and law, prepared the way of its triumph. Now that the twentieth century, since Octavius became Augustus Cæsar, has begun, and we find a new, more universal empire of civilization opening upon us with dangers so alarming, we may as well look for the favorable conditions of this civilization, and see in its new science and arts, its new forces and combinations, helps for the coming Kingdom of God. When has there been such a preparation for the rule of piety and humanity, for the opening of nature to man, and of man to God. To say nothing of the fact that the speech of the Anglo-German race is mastering the literature and business of the world, consider the startling fact that the nations of the globe have but one arithmetic, which is the language of trade, they sing and march by pretty much the same music, which is the language of feeling, and they carry the burdens of industry by the same engines, and send the tidings of correspondence by the same flashing wire. Who shall be the Augustus Cæsar of this new Universal Kingdom, and who shall be the high priest of this new fellowship of nations and men?

Our reply is prompt, sufficient, and decisive. The God of our fathers will be with us as with them. Let us favor all science, whether physical or social, all art, alike the industrial and the beautiful, all association, whether domestic, neighborly, national or cosmopolitan. Let us preach the principles of peace, and set forth its code of reconciliation between nations. But how can there be any unity, any faith, any progress, any blessing without the living God, who is above all, in all, and moving all to the Supreme Good?

The most familiar of truths is the grandest of powers, and the spring of all the best hope and progress. It was spoken at our Baptism, in guardian promise, and deepens in tenderness at every Communion; it is sung in the Gloria in Excelsis, with the pathos of its sufferer, and the jubilee of its victor; it runs through the Te Deum, which is the anthem of civilization as well as the hymn of worship, and no words that are heard among men mean more to our time than the clause, Likewise the Holy Ghost the Comforter. That Friend be with us when we meet and when we part.

WALDSTEIN, FAIRFIELD, Conn., *September* 16, 1876.